WATCHING ME,
WATCHING YOU

WATCHING ME, WATCHING YOU

A collection of 20 erotic stories

Edited by Gwennan Thomas

Published by Xcite Books Ltd – 2013
ISBN 9781908766175

Printed and bound in the UK

Cover design by Madamadari

Contents

As Seen Through Windows	Giselle Renarde	1
The Breaking Point	Veronica Wilde	10
Cheaters Never Prosper	Landon Dixon	20
Temptation Lives Next Door	Beverly Langland	30
Who's Watching Who?	J R Roberts	45
Deliberate Display	Abigail Thornton	56
The Convent Girls' Tale	Marlene Yong	71
Going Native	John McKeown	81
Laundry Day	Sommer Marsden	97
Private Performance	Lucy Felthouse	105
Showtime	Alex Jordaine	114
Escape at *Erotica*	Philippa Blaise	127
Coming Attractions	Landon Dixon	142
Watch and Learn	Chloe Richmond	150
Skimpy	Scarlett Blue	166
Your Ultimate Fantasy	Elizabeth Coldwell	175
Between Friends	Roxy Martin	184
The Watcher	Catelyn Cash	195
Cheating Made Easy	Lynn Lake	211
Come Underground	Demelza Hart	219

As Seen Through Windows
by Giselle Renarde

Every morning when I wake up, I open the curtains over my bed and then I let out a big sigh and fall back into my pillows. That's my morning routine. Doesn't matter what the weather's like. Could be raining, sunny, sleeting, snowing. I sigh every morning because I don't want to get up.

There are a lot of days when I call in sick even though I'm not physically ill. I don't do anything fun on those days off. I just stay in bed, under a few cosy layers of blankets. Sometimes I sit up and watch the day go by. I live in a condo complex, and when I look out my bedroom window, I see a lot of other bedroom windows. Living room windows too, but the bedrooms are more interesting.

There's a courtyard between my building and the next, so if I look straight down I see the tops of a few young trees. I wonder if I'll live here long enough to see them grow all the way up to my floor and obscure my view of the building across the way. On the one hand, it would be nice to look outside and see leaves, hear birds, all that. On the other hand, I'd never see Dirk and Shola ever again.

Dirk and Shola probably aren't their real names. "Dirk" just seems appropriate for the big black man over there because he looks like he's got a good sense of humour, and Dirk is a funny name. I call the woman Shola because her long waves of auburn hair remind me of a woman I used to work with whose name was also Shola. I have no idea what their real names are. Those are just the ones I bestowed upon them one day while I was watching them fuck.

1

And now I've revealed way too much about myself. Yes, I'm the kind of girl who enjoys spying. It's not like I'll go out of my way to do it, but if I happen to glance out the window and the shadows across our buildings fall so there's no glare, and if I happen to spot through those glareless windows a couple going at it? Well, I'm not going to look away. But, really, who would?

I don't think Dirk and Shola live together. From what I've observed, the condo is hers and he only comes for the odd visit, always during the day. Shola never closes the blinds (in fact, I don't think she has any blinds) so I often watch her in the evenings. At night, when our condo units are all illuminated from within, it's much easier to see what people are up to. I sit in the dark sometimes, just watching her. It's not that she's doing anything particularly interesting, but it sort of feels like having company. Like having a friend.

In a sense, I spend my evenings with Shola. I very rarely go out, and neither does she. If I had to guess, I'd say she works from home, something involving her computer. She doesn't get out of bed until mid-morning, or later, but once she's up she's on that laptop morning, noon, and night. She gets her bowl of cereal, sits down on the couch, and balances her laptop on her knees while she eats. I've even seen her take that thing into the bathroom. She must be a really hard worker. Although, I suspect she spends some time on YouTube, because I often see her laughing the way I do when I'm watching crazy cat clips.

I also think she spends a bit of time on porn sites, because … well, first of all, she never really gets dressed. Shola usually wears something slinky around the house, like a silk negligee, or even something more adventurous like a corset. Maybe it helps her concentrate to be so bound up. She has one corset-type outfit that's a lovely shade of purple, with lace up the front and matching panties. Usually, she'll wear stockings too, since the corset has garters hanging off the bottom. It never takes her long to get "dressed", but she always ends up looking very well put together.

The reason I think she sometimes watches porn is that I'll often see her set down her laptop on the coffee table. She'll stand up and slide off her panties, then sit back down and straddle the computer, in a sense, just open her legs to it. The first few times I saw her do this, I wished I had a better view. That's why I bought myself a good pair of binoculars.

She starts slow, rubbing her naked mound in smooth, sweeping circles. If I'm in the right mood, I'll even join in. Shola is a beautiful woman, and watching her touch herself always sparks a forgotten arousal in me. I watch her work her clit with her fingertips, round and round. Her pussy is so wet it glistens. Mine isn't quite there, but I work at it, holding the binoculars with one hand, flicking my clit with the other.

I don't get off – I haven't had an orgasm since I was in my twenties – but that's not really the point. I love watching Shola dance her fingers around her pussy, slapping her clit every so often and gasping in response. She has a drawer full of toys. Sometimes she'll turn on one of her vibrators, press it to her clit, and come pretty much right away. Her face contorts beautifully as she comes. I almost think I can hear her across the courtyard, even though both our windows are closed and she's rather far away.

Other times, she'll place a dildo on the couch and straddle it. She works her clit while she lowers herself down on the thing. She takes her time because the fake cock is massive. Shola must be incredibly wet to take on a dildo that size in one smooth motion. I'd love to touch her pussy one day. I bet it would feel soft and welcoming, and so moist her juice would drip all the way down my arm. Something tells me she'd be tight too, but that wouldn't stop me wanting to shove my whole fist inside of her. She's beautiful, and so is her cunt.

3

I sigh as I watch her ride that big dildo. She works her clit while she's bouncing, and I watch her pussy devour the thing. It's purple, just like her corset. She rides it like a cock, like a man. She rides it the same way she rides Dirk, when he's around.

But I've noticed that Shola always folds her laptop down when Dirk is on his way up. If I'm home watching, like I am today, and I see her answer the phone, I can tell right away if it's him ringing up from down in the lobby. He doesn't have a key of his own, apparently – another sure sign that the two don't live together. I know it's him because I see the way she looks around. She always glances at her computer first, and she usually closes it before she does anything else. After that, she tidies dishes, mail, whatever's lying around. That's about all she gets around to before he knocks on her door.

Shola stands behind her door while she opens it. I would assume that's because she doesn't want any neighbours who happen to be passing by in the hallway to see her so scantily clad. Every time I see her do that, I feel a little guilty in the pit of my stomach. I'm a neighbour and I'm watching her live and eat and work and get off – on her own and with Dirk. Would Shola be embarrassed if she knew? She probably would be, and I feel bad about it, but not bad enough to stop watching.

When Shola closes the door, Dirk looks her up and down. I see his lips moving, and I imagine he's saying, 'Mmm-mmm, you look fine!' That's what I would say if I were him.

Shola smiles and pulls him into the bedroom. He kicks off his shoes en route. He's dressed in a security uniform, as always, and it suddenly occurs to me that he might be the guard for Shola's building. That makes perfect sense! It's just after noon. He probably comes up on his lunch hour for a bit of afternoon delight, then goes back to work after. I wonder if he's married. I don't see a ring on his finger, but

4

you never know. Maybe after work he heads home to his wife and kids. Maybe Shola is just his bit on the side. That would explain why he never stays the night.

I wonder how they met. I wonder how this thing started between them. One of life's great mysteries, I suppose.

She pushes him down on the bed and he lets her. She unbuttons his shirt, then unzips his pants. She does all the work, getting him undressed. I've seen Dirk naked many, many times, but I always get antsy at this stage. I want Shola to move faster, show me what's underneath those familiar layers of clothing.

His skin is dark, like polished wood. She licks his chest and I see him groan. I feel it in me. I wonder if she'll ride him today. Usually, that's what she does. I think Dirk likes it when someone else is in charge. If they were performing solely for my viewing pleasure, I'd rather see him take her from behind, pound that firm cock into her juicy cunt over and over, then pull out and spray thick ropes of come all up her back. That would be my preference.

But I'm not calling the shots. They are.

Dirk says something, and Shola laughs, nods, rifles through her underwear drawer. She holds up two silk scarves, and he bounces his feet against the mattress. She looks around like she's not sure, and then sheepishly digs something out of her closet. When she gets near enough to the window, I can see that it's a length of rope. Dirk grins from ear to ear, nodding, making some joke, I imagine, like, 'Oh you just happen to have one of those, huh?'

First, Shola secures his feet to the bedframe. She pulls tight and he jerks back, like he's surprised that she knows what she's doing. I can see his mind reeling.

Next, Shola uses the silk scarves to tie Dirk's wrists to the headboard. When he's totally strung up, he looks like an X on her bed. She gazes at him inquisitively, one hand on her hip, the other supporting her chin in mid-air. Shola's mind is reeling too. She's wondering what she should do with him.

Dirk says something, and the tension between them is broken. Shola climbs into bed and sets herself between his spread feet. His cock sticks straight up in the air, but she doesn't grab for it. Instead, she licks him. She starts at his ankle, and he watches her work her way up past his knee. She bites his thigh and he grins. Then she looks up at him and they share a moment, and I watch as it all plays out.

He must think she's about to suck his cock. That's what I would be thinking if I were him. But Shola starts over on his other ankle, licking a smooth trail up to his thigh. When she gets close to his dick, she stops. She bypasses his erection and licks his belly, working her way up to his nipples. I watch her flicking them with her velvety, pink tongue, one and then the other. Then she sucks and he smiles.

After his nipples, she veers toward his neck and nibbles there, working her way up to his full lips. Just as she's about to kiss him, though, she pulls away and smirks. They converse back and forth, both chuckling, and then Shola straddles Dirk's face by manoeuvring her calves underneath his shoulders.

Shola's thigh is blocking my view of her mound and his mouth, but it's crystal clear what's happening. She's hovering over him. He's licking her clit. Long, slow strokes, I bet. That's the one thing I miss about partnered sex: the sensation of someone else's tongue on my pussy. There's nothing else in the world that can replicate that sensation. I know they make little sex toys and vibrator attachments that look like tongues, but how could that possibly feel the same as warm, wet flesh on flesh?

I bet Dirk enjoys eating pussy. I bet he loves the taste of Shola's cunt. If I had to guess, I'd say she tastes musky and sweet and tangy and a little sour. Imagine if I could sneak into her apartment right now. You know what I'd do? First off, I'd put on one of her corsets and a pair of her panties. They'd be too small on me, of course, but that's half the appeal. I'd feel the elastic of her thong digging into my belly and my thighs, hugging my pussy and rubbing against my asshole. Her corset would suck in my gut and bring my boobs jutting forward. I'd barely be able to breathe, but that just might bring me closer to orgasm. If I could only use half my lung capacity, I would come or I'd pass out trying.

If Shola were riding Dirk's face like she is right now, I would climb in behind her. I'd straddle Dirk's big body, but I'd press my front against Shola's back. I'd feel the sizzle of her skin where my boobs were bare. I'd rub up against her until they burst out the front of the corset, and then my nipples would harden against her back. I don't think I'd "do" anything, like fuck Dirk or demand satisfaction. I think I'd just reach around Shola's body and play with her tits while Dirk licked her pussy. We'd bring her to orgasm together.

If Dirk wasn't around and I was alone with Shola, that would be a different story. I would love to feel her tongue on my clit. There's something about her that makes me think she'd be great at eating pussy. I would sit on her couch and open my legs. She'd kneel between them and hold my thighs apart. The sight of that pretty face diving at my mound would probably reawaken my capacity for orgasm, and the sensation of her warm tongue would surely put me over the edge. I can't imagine being with her and not coming.

But it doesn't bother me to see Shola with Dirk. After all, we're only close in fantasyland. In real life, she wouldn't know me from a hole in the ground. Anyway, I like watching her receive pleasure, whether it's from herself, from porn, or from good old Dirk. He seems to do a pretty good job of getting her off, anyway. I wish I could see his tongue as he licks her, but her reaction says it all. Her eyes roll in her head, and she leans back so far her long hair dances against Dirk's erection. She turns her head like she's trying to reach it. She sticks out her tongue, but she can't quite get there, can't quite lick him.

When Shola pulls herself to standing, then awkwardly steps away from Dirk, I catch sight of his face and tremors run through me. His chin and cheeks are glistening with Shola's pussy juice. I can't tell you how I envy him. He licks his lips and I lick mine, hoping to taste my favourite girl. All I taste is cherry Chapstick, but I know what Dirk's got on his tongue. He's got Shola.

She turns full around with her legs spread on either side of his wide chest. Bowing down on top of him, she grabs his cock with both hands and shoves her pussy in his face. They're sixty-nining with her on top. I bet Dirk would just love to take that great ass of Shola's in his hands and squeeze, but she's secured him too firmly to the bedposts. He isn't going anywhere.

Pumping his big shaft in her two hands, Shola licks Dirk's cockhead. I can feel his reaction, even across the courtyard. I almost can't imagine what it would be like to have a dick, but I try. Whenever I'm watching Shola devour Dirk's erections, I always think how it would feel to drive it down someone's throat, or lie back like Dirk and let Shola go to town on me. The warmth of her mouth must make him crazy.

Dirk's moving more now than he was before. His feet and his hands are rattling the bed. I bet he's grunting and slurping as he works Shola's clit. I bet he's holding back as well. He probably wants to come already, after all the build-up.

Shola pulls away from his mouth again. She crawls down the bed without looking back, and collapses on his dick. I gaze from the junction of their bodies to the expression on Shola's face. Her eyes are clenched shut. I bet it hurts. He's so big.

She can't really move in that position, so she turns around until she's straddling him but facing him too. When their gazes meet, they both smile. They say something and laugh. It's adorable. Then Shola sets her palms down on his chest and starts riding him slowly. I bet she's brushing her clit against his pelvis. Her pussy's probably pulpy and throbbing after feeling the wrath of Dirk's tongue.

I wish she would take off her corset now. I want to see her breasts swinging while she fucks him, but it's not up to me. Would Dirk like to see her tits, I wonder? Not that he'd be able to touch them. His hands are still bound over his head.

Shola works hard and fast. I watch her bum jiggle as she rides him. She's amazing, this woman. The pleasure she's giving Dirk is right there on his face. He doesn't hide a thing.

I can only imagine how tight her pussy must be, and how it might feel when she hugs his cock with it. She picks up speed and Dirk throws his head side to side. He's coming. I can see it not only in his face, but in the way his body writhes and hops. He's coming, and so is she. She stops moving and straightens up, rubbing her clit with her whole hand, up and down, frenzied motions. They're coming together. You always hear that people don't do that in real life, but Shola and Dirk do. All the time.

Once she's untied him, they lie together on the bed and talk. I wish I could hear what they're saying. Maybe I should learn to read lips. Of maybe, if I knew, I wouldn't like them so much any more. Who knows? Maybe they're horrible people.

But I don't think so. I watch them so often that they've nestled in close to my heart. I wouldn't want to ruin the affection we share by actually meeting them. Better to stay by my window, watching. That way, they'll always be my friends.

The Breaking Point
by Veronica Wilde

'We've got a job this Friday night, Savana,' said Martin. 'Small dinner party, a group of co-workers. There's only 11 of them so it'll just be you on the tables.'

Martin was my boss. He owned a catering business with his brother and I'd been waitressing all summer for them at their events.

I nodded, because money was money, even though a dinner party of co-workers sounded boring. 'Sounds good. What kind of co-workers?'

He named a well-known software company. Not that that guaranteed good tips, but it was a start. Then he said what really mattered to me. 'Sounds like all men, so nothing too fussy.'

All men. I smiled. That was exactly the kind of catering job I liked.

Catering was just my summer job, before I went back to college for my third year. So far, it had been dull. Last summer I'd had a clerical job on the 37th floor of a Boston insurance office, but this summer I was on the Maine shoreline, where there weren't a lot of offices of any kind. So catering it was. The tips were good, but it lacked one benefit of my old office job – the opportunity to indulge my secret love of flashing.

Flashing was something I'd discovered at 18, the summer after I graduated, when a neighbour accidentally caught me sunbathing topless. Since then, the wicked thrill of enjoying his stunned gaze on my nipples had escalated to letting men "accidentally" see my panties on the subway, or while bending over in a store. It gave me a sordid thrill, something to masturbate over later.

My favourite flashing prey were businessmen, the kind you just knew were ruthless, aggressive jerks on the job, but fell silent with awe when they saw a college girl's panties. Last summer's office job had delivered up the perfect specimen, a gruff, fiftyish vice-president who barked at the support staff when he acknowledged them at all. Everyone hated him but I fantasised about him ordering me to strip, or bossing me around in all kinds of deliciously degrading ways. My pet fantasy involved him pulling me over his knee to spank me for some kind of office infraction. I dreamed of him taking down my panties and smacking my bare, quivering ass, then ordering me to spread my legs wide and show him my pussy. As the summer went on, my skirts got shorter and shorter and I would bend over filing cabinets in front of him, or crawl under desks to retrieve a pen. Each time I'd spread my legs just enough, while he stared at my crotch until I was wet and throbbing. But unfortunately the summer ended without him laying even one inappropriate finger on me.

So be it. This summer my job was catering, and though the money was good, the opportunities for flashing were hit or miss. All of the wait staff were instructed to dress in black, but I wore different outfits depending on the occasion; black pants and black button-down shirt for more formal occasions, black miniskirt and black T-shirt for casual events. The skirt had been strategically selected, because it was a tight knit and could be tugged down to a respectable length, or edged high up my thighs. It was no accident that I got great tips when I wore it. And though Martin and Stan, the brothers who ran the catering business, never said a word, it was obvious they capitalised on what I was working too. Though they had a large staff of part-time help, it was me who got most of the smaller, informal assignments.

Given the all-male crowd that Friday night, I wore the miniskirt. By that point in the summer, I was fairly tan, which brought out my green eyes, and I left my long, honey-brown hair loose that night. Dressing at home, I was sufficiently satisfied that I looked fresh, wholesome and innocently sexy. A dinner party of businessmen: this would be my kind of night. I could definitely bring the skirt up a little, bend over to retrieve some dropped napkins. It wouldn't go as far as my fantasies did – it never did – but the tips should be sweet.

The dinner party was hosted just off the beach, at a cottage that looked classic and weather-beaten on the outside but was remodelled to look like a luxurious magazine spread inside. The host wasn't around when I met Martin, Stan and their bartender, Topher, at five o'clock. Topher had already set up the bar on the back deck, where the men would be eating. Lanterns hung in trees to create a golden ambience, rocking in the ocean breeze. I wandered through the living room to scan the family photos: fortyish blonde wife, two preppy-looking sons, a daughter in a field hockey uniform. And a salt-and-pepper husband, his face almost hard with confidence. The kind of middle-aged executive who thinks his skill in the boardroom entitles him to all kinds of dirty indulgences with girls. I swallowed hard, looking at it.

'Savana!' Martin barked. 'Set the damn tables already.'

Martin wasn't really a jerk. He was just brusque by nature, domineering with the servers and obsequious with the clients. Stan, his brother, never raised his voice but had an ominous, predatory gaze that made many of the female servers uneasy. I could never decide if I wanted him to discipline me or not; I dreamed at times of flashing him, of teasing his cock until he put me in my place – but I sensed that he could turn the tables on me in ways I couldn't foresee.

'Doing it now.'

I set the two tables on the deck while chatting with Topher, the bartender. He was a nice enough guy, who I never even thought about flashing. He was so enthralled just to ogle my legs or the shape of my small boobs, or ogle any woman, really, that it seemed pointless.

The men arrived at dusk. The host entered first, more handsome than in his photos, with a broad-shouldered, bearish build. His co-workers ranged from their late twenties to their fifties, not entirely the group of middle-aged guys I fantasised about, but close. I was waiting with a professional smile, greeting them all with a friendly but neutral expression. I never made knowing eye contact or gave out a devilish grin. Not me. I was the innocent 20-year-old college student until the end. Exposing myself wouldn't have been as much fun otherwise. Still, I didn't miss the glances, from shy admiration to outright leers from some. Yep, tonight would be fun. And profitable too.

The host ignored me. That hurt. Maybe he liked voluptuous women, or those his own age; I was definitely the lean and leggy type – coltish was the word I'd heard about me, and I knew that didn't appeal to all men. Finally, when I was serving the stuffed artichokes, I saw his eyes linger on my waist. Specifically, he was looking at the waist of my skirt, which was of course hiked unusually high to show maximum thigh. He smiled knowingly. An ominous feeling passed over me. I tried to shake it off.

The music was drowned out by their talk. Yes, these guys worked together but they clearly had that bond I'd seen in other highly successful people – people who travel more than they stay home, people who know foreign countries better than their own neighbourhood, and never stop talking about work because it consumes all of their time. And of course, I was well aware of some of the seedier ways businessmen bonded together. As the wine and Scotch flowed, their eyes lingered on my legs more and more, and I flashed my panties several times – picking up a dropped fork, then standing on a chair to adjust a lantern.

After I bent over to retrieve a napkin, my legs spread just a little, I straightened up to find a blond man in his thirties going deep red as he stared at my panty-clad cunt.

I smirked and turned back to the other table, my elbow knocking off a bottle of wine. It smashed on the deck.

All chatter stopped. Just the song from the stereo played on, some classic rock ballad that sounded inane compared to dread mounting in me. I'd never broken anything this summer, not even a glass. Now an entire bottle of wine lay pooling on the deck. Babbling apologies, I knelt and mopped it up with a towel as best I could.

'Savana.' My boss Martin had appeared on the deck and his face was dark with fury.

'I'm sorry.' I felt near tears, clumsy and stupid.

Martin turned to the host. 'I know that was from your cellar. I hope it wasn't too expensive.'

'About 600 dollars,' the host said flatly.

He had to be kidding. Why have such expensive wine on the table at a casual get-together? With trembling hands, I stopped mopping and looked up. The host's grey eyes met mine without anger, but also without mercy.

'Yes, it was a rare one,' he continued. 'Saved for this occasion, in fact.'

Martin appeared to be at a loss for words. 'I-I'm so sorry. I can take it out of her paycheque …'

There was a slight pause as everyone likely did the obvious estimates of my meagre wages and how much I would have to work to repay that 600 dollars.

The host's eyes never left me. 'Come here.'

I got to my feet, the broken glass still a mess on the wooden deck, and approached him on shaky legs. Topher was watching from the bar and Stan had come out of the kitchen to watch as well. That made it worse.

The host assessed me from his chair. 'Look at you,' he

14

said. 'Just a girl, still. A clumsy, callow, inexperienced girl who likes to show herself off.'

Not really how I wanted any man to see me, but if it got me out of paying for his ridiculous wine, I'd go with it.

'Maybe it's not fair,' he said, 'that I expect you to pay for it like a responsible adult. Maybe instead I should punish you like the silly, immature girl you are.'

I thought – I hoped – he meant send me home. Nothing else seemed possible.

He looked at Martin. 'Do you have any objection to me spanking her?'

My face went a hot red. This had to be a joke.

Martin looked stunned. 'I … Savana?'

The host looked at me. That same sardonic smile crept across his lips as when he'd looked at my skirt earlier, and I realised he knew exactly what I was about. He'd seen right into the heart of my dirtiest fantasies, and that meant – the realisation hit me with a thrill – that he knew how to deliver them too.

'I …' It came out as a whisper. My throat closed with a burning shame and yet a delirious excitement flooded my pussy at the same time. All I could do was nod.

'Excellent.' He gestured to me to come closer.

Oh my God. He was serious. He was really going to do this. My stomach fluttered. But, I reasoned, he wouldn't actually make it hurt. It would be more of a gesture than anything; a little performance to show off to his co-workers and embarrass me for ruining his wine.

I stood between his legs, as directed. Without blinking, he tugged my short skirt up around my waist and showed my panties to the room. They were pink silk, chosen for flashing purposes to contrast with both my tan thighs and the black skirt. And now they were on clear display to everyone here. I tried desperately to remind myself that normally I loved teasing men with glimpses of my underwear. But being showcased like this made me feel like livestock being assessed on the auction block.

'That's my kind of ass,' someone commented. 'Tight and perky.'

I glared at him but he didn't notice. All of the men were looking at me from the waist down.

The host slipped a finger inside my panties and tickled my asshole. I jumped. Just do it already, I begged him silently. Standing here like this with my skirt pushed up and my panties on display was unbearable. Martin, Topher and Stan were watching with unabashed curiosity and lust and I honestly didn't know how I could ever face them again.

The host's large hand ran up the inside of my thighs, parting them. I jumped again, disgusted at the erotic current jolting my clit. Being spanked in public was bad enough. Showing how much it turned me on would be a humiliation from which I would never recover.

His hand stopped just short of cupping my pussy. My every nerve screamed out silent commands to touch my clit, play with me, anything to assuage this tension collecting inside me.

Instead, the host took my hips and pulled me effortlessly over his lap. Just like that, I was sprawled over his knees, my ass in the air, and feeling more undignified than I had ever felt in my life. All of the businessmen had collected around us now, making no bones about their enthusiasm for witnessing my debasement. I refused to let myself cry.

'Let's see her pussy,' one of the men urged.

My head jerked up to protest. Yet the host grasped my panties and with one tug, they were down to my knees. He nudged my legs apart until my bare bottom and my newly waxed slit were on full show for everyone there. My face turned scarlet with heat as Martin, Stan and Topher moved directly to get a good look at it. Oh God. A small warm gush soaked me. I prayed they didn't notice.

Without warning, the host's hand landed on my right cheek. A murmur went through the men and he spanked me again, this time on the bottom of my left cheek. It was harder than I expected and that, combined with the deviant thrill of the night air on my pussy, made me jump and quiver as his massive hand came down again and again. I was determined to grit my teeth and take it but soon I was squirming and struggling despite myself, losing all dignity as he spread my legs even wider to the delighted hollers of the men.

With a dirty chuckle, one of them reached forward to pull off my shirt. 'Hey!' I protested. This hadn't been part of the deal. Everyone laughed as my bra came off next, my small tits dangling for the entire party to see as he groped them with open delight. Tears of shame and frustration filled my eyes as I realised just how hopeless it was to fight my own twisted desire for this.

The host spanked the insides of each thigh before returning to my ass. The heat of the sting seemed to connect right to my clit and before I knew it, I was wiggling hard on his lap, succumbing to the thrill of being stripped, fondled and spanked in public just like my dirtiest dream. Again and again his hand came down as I shamelessly rubbed my clit against his hard leg. The men laughed at me, saying it was obvious how much I wanted it and that I'd probably smashed the wine on purpose.

What happened next was something foreign to even my fantasies: the host slipped his hand between my legs and spanked my cunt, his hand covering my entire pelvis from my clit to the bottom of my lips. Oh God. No one had spanked my pussy before, I'd never even imagined it, and though he did it lightly compared to the spanking on my bottom, it was still a shock to feel the rhythmic slapping on my clit. But I apparently was over the knee of a master spanker, because he knew exactly what to do. With his left hand, he smacked my cheeks, making them bounce in a disgraceful rhythm, while his right hand pushed against my pussy over and over in a delicious friction until I was writhing helplessly on his lap.

His fingers began to work over my clit, tickling me with expert agility. A long groan of bliss escaped me as he played with me, stroking and caressing my pussy with a skilled tenderness that was the polar opposite of the smacks on my bottom. The sheer sordid thrill of being degraded like this, with the added humiliation of the men knowing how much I loved it, ran through me like wildfire. I ached to be fucked, I was desperate for it. I spread my thighs as wide as I could, wordlessly begging to be entered.

The host's fingers pushed inside me, probing, rubbing and thrusting into my hottest depths. I almost wept with gratitude as my mind swam with fantasies of every man here lining up to use my pussy, one dick after another taking turns inside me. In my wanton delirium, I imagined even Stan fucking my mouth and slapping my tits, while Martin pulled my hair and pounded into my cunt.

'Oh God,' I gasped. My long hair hung in my face and my body felt like wet fire. Around me, phone cameras were clicking and the knowledge that I would be one of those naked girls men jerked off to online, a stripped and spanked object of punishment, exploded inside me in a violent, drenching orgasm. I came all over the host's pants, fluid streaming down my legs. It kept coming and coming, all of the men hooting as they crowded around for a better look at my convulsing, ejaculating pussy. The spanking stopped but I was so far gone and devoid of all dignity that I fingered myself before their delighted eyes, extending my orgasm on and on.

Finally I was done. I could barely think or breathe. Someone helped me stand up, as if aware that my wet legs were shaking too hard to rely on. I could barely focus enough to find my clothes but someone else handed them to me and I stumbled inside the house and found the bathroom. There I put a cool washcloth on my burning-hot cheeks, and caught my breath and tried to reconcile everything I had just done and learned about myself.

Martin, Stan and Topher still hired me for events but never mentioned the spanking. Martin was embarrassed to meet my eyes, Topher seemed scared of me and, oddly, Stan now seemed to view with a grudging respect. Hey, it was just a summer job. But it had to be one of them who texted me a picture from a strange phone number: a photo of a naked girl sprawled over a businessman's lap, a long tumble of hair concealing her face and her upturned ass a bright strawberry-pink. I couldn't help admiring her bravery and abandon, or thinking of all the other adventures that awaited her, and no matter how I often stared at it, I could scarcely believe it was me.

Cheaters Never Prosper
by Landon Dixon

I was chewing the rubber at Tony's Diner, gnawing on one of his vulcanised steaks, when a dame pushed through the doors of the grease joint and took a gander around, made a bee line for me in the last booth down.

'I only got dough for one plate of heartburn,' I told her, as she folded herself down on the bench across from yours truly.

She looked down on her luck, like a lot of guys and dolls courtesy of the Great D gripping the nation. A redhead with flighty blue eyes and a thin, nervous face, slim figure ragged by a faded green dress. She clutched a battered black purse on the table, her fingers dancing over the worn leather. I forked a chunk of grade C beef into my kisser and chewed, daring her to put the bite on me.

'I-I don't want any food, Mr Janson,' she quailed, voice thin and reedy.

I grunted, offered, 'Uh-huh. Looks like you could use some meat on your bones.' I sawed a chunk of steak free and set it out on an outstretched fork before it fossilized.

She shook her head, her eyes flaring, knuckles burning whiter on her purse. 'Your secretary told me you were having lunch here. My name is Mabel Hughes. I need you to find out if my husband is cheating on me, Mr Janson!'

The last part came out in a gush, blowing warm and wet over me and my meat. I took a swig of straight black coffee, washing down the last of the shoe leather. 'What makes you think the gob's cheating on you?'

'I-I just feel that something's wrong. Arthur's been acting strange lately, coldly towards me, unfeeling. Almost as if ...' Tears sprang into her jaded orbs, glittering like zirconias. 'As if he doesn't care about me, or our marriage, any more!'

Tony waddled over with the tab. The guy had a lot of nerve, to go along with a whole lot of gut. 'You having the pie, Henry?' He leered at the dame. 'Coconut cream – fresh and moist.'

'The only thing fresh and moist around this dump is your mouth, Tony,' I countered. I picked up the bill, wiped my nose on it. 'One bowel movement is all my doctor allows a day, anyway.'

Tony's greasy face clenched like a monkey's fist, but his oily eyes didn't leave Mabel's cleavage for a moment.

I dug into my pocket, flipped two-bits and a thumbnail of lint onto the table, along with a cent tip. Then me and Mabel made tracks for the door, hit the street, headed for my office.

It was a sunny day, hot, not a breeze to speak of or bask in coming off Lake Michigan. I let Mabel lead the way, slipping in behind her. The sun lit up her thin dress like a cooch show, giving me a pleasant view of her surprisingly shapely body. Trim waist, taut buttocks, long, slender legs and sculpted ankles. My outlook brightened. The gumshoe racket was as grim as any other capitalist enterprise circa 1932.

Doris, my secretary, dusted herself off and took her leave for lunch as soon as we set feet inside my two-room office on Front Street. I ushered Mabel into the inner sanctum, pointed out a chair to her, flopped down in my own faded leather one behind the battered metal desk.

'I-I'm afraid I can't pay you ... right now, Mr Janson.' My prospect tanked right in front of me, eschewing the wobbly wooden client chair.

She bit her lip, bounced her eyes off the floor. I slumped further down in my chair, perforce to sliding right out and showing the dame the door. But then she suddenly brushed her dress off her shoulders with a couple of bold strokes. The garment sagged to the floor along with my jaw. Mabel had forgotten to slip on any underwear today – she was as naked as a newspaper baron's greed, right there in front of me.

I gaped, eyes riding up and down her alabaster-coloured and textured physique like tourists in the Board of Trade Building. Her breasts were high and taut, cupcake-sized with prominent cherry tips. The ginger patch of fur between her legs proved she was no dye job. Her nude body trembled only a trifle.

'Will you consider this a down payment, Mr Janson?'

I rehinged my jaw, resocketed my eyes. 'H-Henry,' I gulped. 'Call me Henry.'

She cruised around the desk, breasts bobbing, stomach and thigh muscles rippling, pussy glistening. Money was what I needed, everyone did. But sex was what I wanted, with everyone I could get my hands on.

I jumped to my feet and grabbed the glowing white and red quail in my arms, mashed my masculine mouth-flaps up against her soft, scarlet-hued lips. She tossed her arms around my rugged form, and we melted together, kissing passionately. For a woman worried about marriage infidelity, she had a wacky way of expressing her concern.

But I was a man of action, not philosophy. You offer me a tasty treat on a silver platter and this ginzo's gonna take it, not stop chewing on it till he's spent the last of his hunger. I ran my hands down Mabel's curved back, over and onto her mounded butt cheeks.

She moaned in my mouth, gave me her tongue to taste and entwine, as I squeezed her buttocks, plied the hot, smooth, humped flesh. The room temperature soared another hundred degrees. My clothes had to come off. It was the fashion of the day.

Jacket, tie, shirt, pants, and underwear joined Mabel's

22

dress on the floorboards. She ran her fingers through my chest hair, feeling my throbbing desire against her belly, seven inches and swelling. I grasped her breasts, coveted the pert, perky pair, fully tuned her jutting nipples into our mutual lust.

'You-you understand I wouldn't do this ... unless it was for the good of my marriage?'

Her eyes were glassy, her voice thick and husky. Her logic had more holes than Hoover's recovery plan.

But I wasn't there to debate, or judge. My cockhead was doing all the thinking for me right then. I bent my dome down and pushed her tits up, swallowed a rigid, rubbery nipple and sucked like I was leech-lipped.

Mabel moaned and tilted her head back, her body and breasts shuddering in my mitts, her crimson-coated fingernails biting into my shoulders. I vacced one nipple then the other, bouncing my head over and inhaling and tugging. My cock was a length of molten steel pulsating between us, mushroomed hood poking at the crinkly fur of her soft, wet spot.

I mouthed and mauled her nipples and breasts until the one pair shone, the other pair reddened with feeling. Then I dropped to my knees on the hardwood, hands tracing the slightly starved hourglass of Mabel's figure all the way down. I'm known as one of the dirtiest dicks in the business. There isn't any length I won't go to for my clients. I went pussy-length for this one, with my tongue.

'Oh! Yes!' Mabel cried, as I licked wet and wide all though her downy copper fur and along her puffy pink lips.

She tasted ten times better than anything Tony could serve up, steaming, hot and juicy. I gripped her buttocks and flat-out painted her pussy, tongue-stroking over and over like a tomcat grooming his mate before digging my licker right into her slit, deep, squirming it around inside her pink tunnel.

Her buttocks quivered between my fingers, breasts

23

jumping overhead. She was as ripe and tangy as a Florida orange. I was about to pay some lip service to the swollen pink nub of her clit, when she suddenly yanked me to my feet by the hair, sprawled herself out on my desktop.

She lifted her legs, gripped her tits, gazing crazily up at me. I went for payment in full, grasping my iron erection and poking the helmeted tip into her pussy, plunging metalled shaft home.

We both spasmed and groaned, my cock buried in Mabel's velvety heat and wetness.

'Fuck me, Henry! Fuck me like my husband's fucking some hussy!'

I wouldn't have used quite those words. But then I'm not a pulp scribe, I'm a real-life dick. So I used my manly skills, grasping Mabel's thighs to my chest and pumping my cock back and forth in her pussy.

I rocked her to and fro, rattling the furniture and the frail. She moaned, the desk creaking. Her tits shuddered in her hands, butt cheeks rippling against my thighs, body bouncing to the pussy-pounding rhythm of my prick. The wet smacking of heated flesh against flesh echoed in the stuffy confines, faster and faster.

I thumped, humped, grunted, groaned, my cock churning a fire in the hole. Then I bucked and blasted, blazing with joy. Mabel shuddered wildly on the end of my shooting rod, glaring up at me with eyes gone crazy as the Bonus Army.

The dame informed me that she'd told her hubby with the suspected cheating heart that she was going out of town to visit her parents in Joliet. She gave me a picture of the lug, his home address. I tired the curb two houses down from the yellow home on the sycamore-lined street just after five that afternoon, settled down in my car seat for some surveillance.

At 6.12, Arthur arrived home from work. He drove a green, two-door Ford fresh off the assembly line, sported a pinstriped chocolate-brown suit and a tan fedora. His black moustache was waxed, his black hair pomaded in style under the fashionable lid, his nails were neatly clipped and there was a shine on his shoes any buffer would be proud of. He looked, all in all, plenty prosperous, compared to threadbare Mabel. I dashboarded the binoculars when he let himself into the house – subject confirmed.

Object spotted, when a doll clipped down the sidewalk on a set of high heels, headed for the Hughes's hutch. She was tall, titted, long-legged, wearing a light blue silk scarf over her glossy black locks, a dark blue dress that she filled out fine front and back, pale blue hose and dark blue shoes.

She was a rhapsody in blue, making me want to burst out singing her praises. But she had her mind on other man-matters, taking a sharp right onto the flagstone path of the Hughes's house, walking up to the door and entering. Brazen and blatant as Mae West at a church social.

I rubbed my chin, my dick. There was only one way to find out for sure. They don't call us peepers for nothing. I shelved the binocs and scooped up the Speed Graphic off the seat next to me, then set sail in pursuit of the dirty truth, ready to picture it. It was another bright, scorching summer day. Unlike the lady in blue, I tried to limit my conspicuousness, by hustling across the street and the front lawn, in back of the house. I shouldered the wall, gripping my camera, inching along.

The first window was the bathroom – nothing to see and click there. A window down below looked into the basement – nothing going on underground.

I sprouted sweat, the camera slipping in my hands. The backyard was a neatly trimmed patch of grass walled in by a whitewashed board fence. I was hidden from most of the neighbours. I sidled under the next window at half my normal height, instantly heard grunting and groaning spilling out over the sill. Bingo-bango!

I spun around, crouching, peeked over the ledge and in through the lace curtains of the open window. Arthur was on top of the no-longer-blue woman, banging her like a Barnum & Bailey parade drum.

'Proof-positive,' I exhaled, shunting the camera up over the windowsill and focusing in on the lust-birds.

Arthur's well-cut suit and the woman's well-tailored dress were distant memories on the red-carpeted floor of the well-appointed bedroom. The man's pale, heaped buttocks clutched in fourth gear as he drove dong-long into the laid-out woman. He was grasping her partially flattened breasts at the sides, smearing her lipstick and make-up with his tongue. She had her lithe, ivory legs wrapped around his wasp-waist, her long, strong arms around his broad shoulders, bouncing in rhythm to the guy's urgent thrusting, meeting his frantic licker with a lush, pink, swirling mouth-organ of her own.

I gave the sexual performance an A – for adultery.

'Yes, Arthur! Make love to me, Arthur!'

'Oh, Harriet! I love you, Harriet!'

Dialogue, to go along with the lewd action, the squeaking steel springs sound effects.

I got ready to shoot something other than my load.

Then a hand clamped down on my shoulder.

I just about launched out of my shoes and into the sky on an Icarus trajectory.

I jerked my head around and stared into Mabel Hughes's blazing high beams.

'You caught him cheating, didn't you!?'

Her Plain Jane face was contorted with anger. 'Uh, see for yourself.'

She pushed me aside with the strength of a woman scorned, and screwed, looked into the bedroom at the sex scene thundering on unabated. Then she swung around and hissed 'Damn him!' tore my pants open and ripped my cock out. 'Fuck me, Henry! Cheat with me! While we watch them cheat!'

Her see-through green dress came off just as easily the

second time around, plunging down like the stock market circa October 24, 1929. Mabel was brilliantly bare in front of me all over again. She turned back to the window, stuck the gleaming white moons of her butt out at me.

I stared at her ass, as she stared into the open bedroom window. The hot sounds of sex gusted out from inside the house. My cock quickly filled the heated distance between my loins and Mabel's butt, out there in the open air. I probed her ginger bush with my boiled cap, hit her dripping pink tunnel with engorged member, shafting her pussy to the balls.

The bed creaked faster, the groaning coming more urgent inside. We didn't have any time to lose; I didn't have any shame to sacrifice. I gripped Mabel's hips tight as she was gripping the windowsill and slammed back and forth inside her, almost rocking her right into the home.

Our breath came in hissing, teeth-clenched gasps, so as not to disturb the frenzy on the other side of the wall, which we were both watching and emulating. Arthur thrust wildly into Harriet, their naked, entwined bodies bouncing higher and higher on the dancing bed.

I wrenched my hands off Mabel's hips and shot them in around her arched body, grabbed onto her flapping tits. I crushed the succulent mounds in my sweaty mitts, clutching the dame close to me, cocking her pussy to beat the band. She shuddered with each and every shunt of my dick, her overheated body bouncing against mine.

Perspiration dewed the both of us, all over. I bit into her slender neck, inhaling the scent of her hair and body, churning her cunt. She gripped my hands on her tits, pulled on her own hard, pointing nipples, glaring straight ahead at the torrid bedroom scene that had vengefully inspired the torrid backyard scene.

'Oh, God, yes, Arthur! Fuck me! Fuck me!' Harriet screamed.

'Oh, God, yes, Henry! Fuck me! Fuck me!' Mabel

rasped.

We two adulterous lechers went at it hammer and tongs. Arthur beat me to nirvana by a ball whisker.

The guy bellowed, blasted, jerking on top of Harriet, jumping around in her arms and legs as he let loose in her pussy. She just about raised the roof with her echoing shriek of ecstasy, getting orgasm as good as she was getting his orgasm.

It was too much for this X-rated private eye. I torqued Mabel's silken tunnel at full ramming speed, then erupted inside her in a mind and body-blazing burst, jolted and jolted hard and repeatedly by blistering joy. The woman receiving my sperm salute in great gushing gobs didn't hold back, either. She spasmed against my shivering torso, up on her toes, coming and coming and coming.

Then confronting. 'You cheated on me, Arthur!' she raged through the window. 'You cheated on me!'

Arthur leapt off Harriet like he'd taken a cattle prod up the ass. He stormed over to the window and yelled at the naked woman in my arms, 'We're divorced, Mabel! Get that through your head! I'm a remarried man!'

My cock shrivelled inside my crazed client.

'Why do you cheat on me, Arthur!?' she persisted hysterically, grasping at the man's hands, at the straws of what once was. 'Forcing me to get even! Why can't we be together – just the two of us!?'

Arthur shoved Mabel's claws back through the window and slammed the wood-bordered pane down. 'Leave my wife and me alone!' was his closing statement on the whole wacky matter.

I took a step back. My cock fell out of Mabel like the bottom out of the Oklahoma real estate market. I tucked and buttoned, scooped up my camera and scooted away from that home sweat home back to my parked jalopy. I jarred screws loose rocketing away from Mabel and her delusions of marriage.

I'm a hawkshaw, not a psychiatrist. I handle cases, not head cases. There were more of us dicks in the phone book. My hunch was Mabel would be making the rounds. I pitied and envied my colleagues.

Temptation Lives Next Door
by Beverly Langland

Alison Thornton hated the idea that anyone would label her a pervert. Yet, Alison was a voyeur. Ever since she had first moved into the neighbourhood and spotted the young beauty who lived next door she had suffered from the same compulsion – the overwhelming urge to take just one more look out of the window.

Alison was a twitcher, a birdwatcher of sorts, and the particular bird who currently had her enthralled was a young woman named Lucy. Despite Alison's reservations, her arousal when spying on the girl was genuine, and on more than one occasion, she'd given in to her imagination and found herself masturbating. Girls like Lucy were off limits to a woman like Alison, and all the more exciting for remaining (just) out of reach. OK, so Lucy was over 18, but ultimately Alison was still violating her trust.

Lucy had become an obsession. As she watched the girl spread out on the sun lounger, supposedly in the seclusion of her own back garden, Alison couldn't resist slipping her hand inside the waistband of her knickers. Sometimes she just liked to stand watching with her hand nestled against her sex – poised for action, feeling her clitoris tingling beneath her fingertips. She considered this a test of resolve, a promise of things to come. Most days she could – and would – tease herself for hours without giving in to the urge to move her fingers. Other times, the digits would seemingly curl inwards of their own volition and then, of course, the onward journey would be inevitable. Alison had always been a prolific masturbator even at the height of her affairs. She was, she supposed, highly sexed.

Now, Lucy was off to university and when she left, Alison would be bereft. Only that morning they had chatted, the younger woman full of excitement about finishing college. As she listened, Alison was thinking of other things – nasty, dirty things, thoughts she was certain would make the girl blush. In Alison's mind, whatever Lucy's age, she would always remain an innocent, an angel. Considering the many boyfriends she'd seen visiting next door, complete innocence seemed unlikely, but Alison didn't like to let reality mar her vision of perfection.

Lucy's head was tilted slightly to one side, her blonde hair cascading over one shoulder like a golden river heading for the valley of her cleavage. The freckles that lightly dusted the tops of her breasts were not visible from this distance, though when the two were talking, Alison often found herself counting them when she should have been looking at the girl's face. The breasts themselves were rather small and sat high on Lucy's chest, above the kind of washboard-flat stomach that is only achievable by the young and dedicated. To complement this, she had legs long enough to put a catwalk model to shame.

Lucy's eyes were closed, her face turned towards the sun as she lay enjoying its warmth. The distraction in next door's garden meant it would likely be one of those days where Alison wouldn't get anything done. She knew she should get back to work, knuckle down, but the temptation to sneak just one more peek would be too great. She would always find some excuse to get up from her desk and then she'd wander back to the window. Now, as she peered around the curtains, she saw Lucy had positioned the sun lounger to offer her a perfect view. The girl's tiny bikini offered little protection from the midday sun – nor from her neighbour's prying eyes. She had one leg raised with her thighs parted slightly. Alison stood watching in silence as Lucy lifted her right hand and brought her fingers to rest on her bikini briefs. There was a small movement, innocent surely, but Alison couldn't help imagining that beneath the costume Lucy's clitoris had stirred.

As usual, impure thoughts filled Alison's head but this time, perhaps, they were justified. She stood transfixed as she watched the girl lazily snake a hand inside the waistband of her briefs. Her raging heart silenced as she willed Lucy to slip it in further – her dream scenario had come true, her vigilance finally reaping rewards. Lucy seemingly did Alison's bidding, pausing only to sit up and quickly check the coast was clear before relaxing back onto the lounger to resume her exploration. Alison sought her own throbbing clitoris, pinching the nubbin between two fingers in an effort to quell her passion, but all she achieved was further arousal. Enthralled, she moved her fingers in unison with the girl's, eyes fixed, imagining the soft feel of Lucy's wet flesh.

Unfortunately, the fantasy was all too brief. Alison heard a voice call from her neighbour's open doorway and Lucy withdrew her hand and sat bolt upright. A young man came into the garden and the two set to talking. After the euphoria of moments earlier, Alison's heart felt suddenly leaden. Was this the boyfriend? Was this the person over whom Lucy had been fantasising? Alison could not watch any longer. She hated imagining Lucy with anyone, let alone such a brash-looking boy. It was time for a shower, Alison decided. Time to purge herself once again, to finish what she had started during that brief moment when she and Lucy had connected in the most primitive of ways.

Somewhat relieved, Alison got out of the shower and started towelling herself, then an unexpected knock on the door sent her scurrying to answer it. It was probably the postie – a dark-haired woman whom Alison had been (optimistically) chatting up. She opened the door wearing only her short robe. Young Lucy stood in the porch in all her glory. Alison couldn't quite suppress her surprise. The girl looked at her with those green eyes and she blushed. She felt as if she had been caught shoplifting – or worse.

'Lucy!'

'May I come in, Ali?'

'Yes, yes, of course.'

This was the first time Alison had been alone with Lucy in quite a while. The studio was a mess, but she was more concerned about her state of undress. She couldn't stop those wicked thoughts creeping back into her head one at a time until it was running riot with them. Her whole body started tingling, her nipples in particular tightening to taut, hard bullets beneath the terrycloth. Lucy had slipped a T-shirt and short wraparound skirt on over her bikini. On her dainty feet she wore pink flip-flops, with her toenails painted to match. She strode straight into Alison's domain.

In just a few short years and before Alison's eyes, Lucy had grown into a confident and forthright young woman – perhaps a little too demanding, another detail Alison conveniently left out of her fantasies.

Lucy came straight to the point of her visit. 'Ali, I'm feeling randy, and since I'm leaving tomorrow, I thought it time we stopped playing games and got down to it.'

Alison quickly checked the empty hallway then closed the door. 'What games?'

'Don't pretend you don't know what I'm talking about. You watching me tease you. You want to jump my bones. I'm curious. So …'

Poor Alison was stunned into silence. Her sordid little world had been laid bare in one statement, leaving her exposed – she was actually shaking with fright. She didn't move. She couldn't do anything. Lucy stepped close, reminding her just how tall she had grown. Even in her flat-soled flip-flops, she was almost a head taller.

Lucy placed her hands on each side of the older woman's cheeks, forcing her to look directly into those green eyes. 'That was an invitation, silly. Anyone else would have been in my knickers by now.'

She didn't move away and Alison could feel that lithe body pressed against her own. Just the smell of the girl sent shivers down her spine. She had just been given an open invitation, but could she cross that line?

An agonising few moments of hesitation followed but, in the end, Alison could not resist Lucy's soft, sweet mouth. She stood on her tiptoes until their lips were almost touching, waiting to see if the girl would back away. She didn't. They kissed. Not a French kiss, but enough of a kiss for the two of them to angle their heads. It was short-lived, yet loaded with passion. The girl's lips were heavenly, everything Alison had imagined.

They kissed again. Lucy was inexperienced at tongue-play, a little awkward even, but she was participating, kissing back. They broke apart, breathless. What now? The older woman stood trancelike as the girl slowly undid the ties of her robe and pulled the loose ends apart, fully exposing her breasts. They swayed, with tight knots for nipples. Alison loved the way Lucy seemed mesmerized by them – and, to be fair, she did have good breasts for a woman of her age. Lucy traced a line around a nipple with her fingernail. 'Ali, I've never been with a woman ...'

Oh God, Lucy's innocence was turning Alison's pussy to mush. 'Don't worry, I'll show you how.'

Her words sounded corny. They *were* corny. The whole situation was like something out of a bad porn movie. This was crazy. Or at least, Alison was acting crazy. She should send Lucy home to her mother – or back to the boyfriend or to another girl so she could experiment with someone her own age. Once again, though, the temptation proved too great. Alison could not abandon this opportunity. She wanted nothing more than to draw the girl to her breast, to have Lucy suckle while she held her angel in her arms. But Lucy stepped away, leaving her vulnerable, embarrassed, desperate to cover herself back up. Was the girl toying with her? Had she come to play some sort of cruel joke?

'What do you want, Lucy?' asked Alison.

'Something to remember you by. A memento.'

'Of course, sweetheart. Anything! What kind of a something were you thinking of?'

'Well –' Lucy's beautiful green eyes held the older woman's gaze, making Alison's heart skip a beat '– I'd like … no, I *want* to watch you masturbate.'

'Pardon?' Surely Alison couldn't have heard her right? Instinctively, she looked around, uncertain of what she expected to find. The police? A hidden camera? She had spent so long sneaking around that she couldn't shrug off the awful feeling of wrongdoing. 'Say again, honey?'

'Oh, you're so funny, Ms Thornton! You should see your face!' the girl giggled.

Alison didn't need to look in the mirror. She felt her cheeks burn hot, flushed red from embarrassment, from guilt. A sense of dread, of horror filled her. What did Lucy really know about her? Had she seen her at the window – watching day after day? Lucy's gaze drifted from Alison's face to her breasts, and the woman realised Lucy was sizing her up. Alison took in a deep breath as if her heart had stopped and she had only just realised it. She didn't know what to do or say.

In the end, Lucy broke the awkward silence. 'You will do it, won't you, Alison?' Alison forced herself to look at the young woman. To her recollection, that was the first time Lucy had used her first name in full, rather than calling her "Ali", and she'd made it sound so sensuous. She wanted to hear Lucy mouth the syllables again and again and again. The dread built in her once again, but this time for a different reason. Alison knew she would do anything for this girl, even if that meant … She shook her head. The idea was outrageous, preposterous! 'Why would you ask such a thing of me?'

'Why? Because you're always watching me and I

thought it only fair. I know what a voyeur is, but what does it feel like to watch? I have the hots for you, Ali. When I was touching myself earlier, I was imagining you standing at the window playing with yourself. You were masturbating while you watched me?'

There seemed no point in lying. Lucy appeared to have her neighbour's *modus operandi* figured out – and this was Alison's fantasy come true, after all. 'Yes.'

'That's so fucking cool! No one has ever had the hots for me before!'

'I don't for one moment believe that.'

'Well, no one I like, anyway. I like you, Alison. Enough to walk into your nasty lesbian lair all alone.'

'Is that how people think of me, as a nasty lesbian?'

'What do you think? You're a predator, Alison. You prey on young women.'

'Please, I am *not* a predator! What I do is harmless. Unforgivable, but harmless.'

'That's a shame. I was hoping the nasty lesbian would eat me. You do want to eat me, don't you, Alison?'

Lucy's green eyes were dancing again. She was obviously enjoying teasing her prying neighbour, leaving Alison feeling utterly helpless. Lucy used her perfect smile with devastating precision, knowing the effect it had on people. Alison had played this scene out many times in her head, only in her version she had done the seducing. In reality, Lucy had the upper hand – a simple case of supply and demand, and what Lucy was seemingly offering Alison was priceless. The words came painfully slowly from Alison's mouth. 'Yes, sweetheart. I'd like to eat you very much.'

'So, let's play! You show me yours, and I'll …' Lucy was stepping out of her bikini bottoms, letting her skirt fall back from those smooth, long legs to reveal a glimpse of inner thigh. It might have been only a game to her, but for Alison, it was the pinnacle of her life! Lucy tossed the warm briefs to the older woman. 'Sniff these if it'll help.'

Christ, the girl was relentless. Hadn't she embarrassed Alison enough for one day? Yet, Alison didn't care about the humiliation, deliberate or otherwise. The red-faced woman was too excited to care about little things like shame, too aroused to think about consequences. She felt as if she was in heaven and she had her angel with her. An angel who had just removed her bikini bra and sat in an armchair, awaiting her next move. Alison couldn't take her eyes from Lucy's pert breasts, the rose-brushed nipples standing proud. She had to resist the urge to run over to the chair, to fall to her knees and take those firm mounds in her hands, to taste of the forbidden fruit. She knew Lucy wouldn't give herself so easily, not until Alison had performed for her entertainment. And what Lucy wanted, Lucy usually got, and with interest.

Alison sat on the edge of the sofa bed, an air of expectation hanging in the small room. She had no idea how to proceed in front of this girl. She was aroused, but her mind was a swirl of emotion. Then she remembered Lucy's briefs. She held them to her nose and breathed in deeply, letting the girl's musk fill her senses. The image of the young woman with her hand inside these same briefs came to mind. Alison had been so turned on watching, and she was turned on now remembering. She lifted her feet onto the bed and parted her legs, the towelling falling away revealing her wet, horny, sex. Exposing herself to Lucy sent a shiver down Alison's spine. Even in her wildest fantasy, she hadn't felt this good – and as yet, she hadn't even touched the object of her affection.

Knowing Lucy's eyes were on her caused the tingle in Alison's belly to grow. She shifted her weight, opening her legs wider, allowing the cool air to engulf her pussy. The natural red of her hair sat in tight curls, her labia already glistening with the evidence of her excitement. Alison did nothing for a moment, hoping that she could perhaps turn the tables and tease Lucy, but that idea failed from the outset. Lucy would always have the upper hand, and anyway, Alison revelled in the notion of being in the girl's thrall. Alison touched herself, like she had done countless times before, rubbing her fingers over her sex until the tips of them were slick with honey – until they started to glide and almost take a life of their own.

Lucy's eyes initially grew wide while she watched, her knowing smile broadening. Alison tried to smile in return but suspected her effort looked more like a grimace, for her fingers seemed set to fast-forward. She had wanted to play out the scene slowly, but these events, like the rest of her sleazy little life, seemed out of her control. The slow circling of her clitoris she had intended quickly grew in pace until Alison found herself trapped in a spiral of desire that threatened to suck her under. Lucy was idly swinging her knee outwards, revealing and hiding her crotch. The promise of what lay between that deep valley drove Alison on. Once again, she put Lucy's briefs to her face, closing her eyes, immersing herself completely in the fragrance. Lust overcome her as the scent once again filled her head. The circling of her fingers became rough strokes, getting shorter and shorter …

When Alison opened her eyes again, she saw Lucy rubbing her clitoris. Her legs were spread wide and the blonde hair Alison had expected to see wasn't there. The girl had shaved. Her pussy was completely smooth and all the more enticing for her efforts. She looked so innocent, unused, radiant in every way – so perfect. Almost dreamy, at least through Alison's lust-fogged eyes. Yet, the sight of her lewdly touching herself was more than the older woman could take and a thunderous climax overtook her. The agony and bliss seemed to last for minutes and every time Alison managed to reopen her eyes to gaze at Lucy playing with herself, she hit another peak.

Finally, Alison's spasms started to subside. Her whole

body tingled with the afterglow of her orgasm but now, looking at Lucy eyeing her hungrily, she realised that she hadn't finished her supplication. Lucy's eyes were smoking with desire – adult desire – and Alison could wait no longer. She slid to the floor and padded across the empty space between them on all fours. She paused at Lucy's feet to kiss her delicate toes. She wanted to devour her completely from the bottom up but as always, Alison's impatience won. Anyway, she had a greater goal in mind, a prize she relished more than any other, and that prize was ultimately within her grasp at last. Alison kissed her way up Lucy's calves, laying siege to the underside of her knees for a moment, then slowly – agonisingly slowly – along the girl's soft inner thighs.

Lucy lay back in the armchair and accepted her worshipper's kisses as if she were due them by right. In Alison's eyes she was a goddess – one who had willingly mounted the pedestal placed before her. Doubtless, there would be other worshippers in years to come, but Alison took great pleasure in knowing she was the first – well, the first woman at least. Lucy's exposed pussy was too great a temptation. She was making slow, lazy circles on the girl's inner thighs, inching closer to her sex, but its odour was intoxicating. Alison was drunk on the heady fragrance. She could not wait. She had to taste her angel.

Lucy parted her legs further, allowing Alison to place a hand against her bared pussy – it felt so warm and wet. Alison licked her fingers, tasting. She wanted more of the nectar so she spread Lucy's sex until the girl's clitoris emerged, hard and round like a precious pearl. She lowered her mouth to the nubbin, the tip of her tongue reaching out to touch the juicy pink flesh for the first time. She didn't apply pressure, so as not to enter the moist folds, but simply tasted the honey of which she had so often dreamed. Lucy tensed slightly, an involuntary action, and her ragged breathing, that had seemingly filled the studio, stilled for the moment.

After the rushed pace of what had gone before, Alison wanted to slow things down, to savour every moment – but Lucy's erect clitoris was right in front of her eyes, glistening as bright as a beacon, drawing her closer. She sucked it into her mouth and felt the girl's hips respond to the stimulation, moving upwards, pressing her sex against Alison's lips. Lucy was half-sitting, half-lying back, squirming in the chair, moaning and asking Alison to put her tongue in her pussy. Small, kittenish sounds started coming from the girl as Alison set to work in earnest, using all the skills she had gleaned over the years.

Lucy was watching her carefully. Alison could feel her curious eyes. Alison paused to smile, and then returned to working on pleasuring her angel. She parted Lucy's labia and delved deeper. Lucy was soaking, flooding her mouth with honey, and she drew in as much of it as she could gather. Alison was in heaven. Lucy's juices were pure nectar, and the girl was more than happy to oblige in letting her taste them, looking as if she too had joined Alison on another plane. So Alison probed deeper, curling her tongue and fucking her princess, yet she never neglected that beautiful pearl. She kept going back to Lucy's twitching clitoris, working on the swelling protrusion, letting the girl know she hadn't forgotten its importance. After each visit to it, Lucy grew more excited and as her moans increased, Alison worked faster and with more diligence until Lucy started to grind and gyrate.

The girl's hands reached out, clutching for Alison's head, fingers wrapping in her thick hair, pulling and pressing the lapping woman's tongue deeper into her beautiful young cunt. Her eyes started to roll, then her eyelids closed, and Alison sensed she was drifting towards bliss. The older woman could have ended Lucy's misery but she was relentless – she wanted her angel's first time to be perfect, and she had her own selfish reason for that. She was

40

enjoying herself so much she didn't want their lovemaking to end. Her pussy still burned from earlier, and she had been fingering herself slowly, to keep her own passion alive. Yet, her own bodily needs were of little concern to her. Really, there was only one pussy on her mind – the one her tongue was buried in.

That practised tongue worked tirelessly, increasing in momentum until Lucy grew agitated, moving uneasily in the chair, her hips beginning the jig of climax. There would be no stopping the girl now, so Alison clasped her mouth over Lucy's clitoris and sucked the hard flesh between her teeth, clasping tight on to the nubbin, nibbling and stretching the flesh mercilessly. Lucy lost control, bumping against Alison's face, grinding hard as she came. Her body stiffened and a warm, delicious gush of nectar flowed into Alison's mouth. The more- experienced woman kept her lips clamped in position until Lucy relaxed and Alison heard her breathe easy.

Lucy looked down and responded to the pleasure on Alison's face with a silly grin of her own, causing Alison's heart to flutter and almost break through her chest. Lucy had that effect on her and she realised the girl would always have her enslaved with that smile.

Alison placed soft kisses on the girl's tender lips, flushed red and swollen but still perfect. She had gone down on many women, but Lucy's youthful exuberance made her feel alive, as if this was her first time too. She looked up at her younger lover, eyes bright like a puppy waiting for praise, waiting for validation. She was aware that Lucy's love juices were smeared over her chin and cheeks and that she probably looked an ugly mess. But Alison didn't care how she looked. Her lips tingled still. Her whole body seemed infused with Lucy's scent. She wanted to bathe in the fragrance for ever more.

Alison also wanted to confess her love for Lucy but didn't wish to scare her away. The teenager had her whole life in front of her – and Alison suspected that old baggage would not be wanted on that voyage. So instead, she professed her love with a kiss.

Lucy didn't resist as Alison feared she might, but accepted her gift. She licked her lips pointedly, tasting herself. 'What do you taste like, Alison?' she asked.

'Much like you, I suppose. Would you like to find out?'

'I'm not a dirty lesbian!' Alison's heart sank, but Lucy cheered her with a beaming smile. 'But I am a dirty girl, or believe I could be. Do you have one of those strap-on dildos? I thought perhaps you could … you know.'

'Why don't you unroll the sofa bed while I get ready?'

Alison was in the bathroom for only a few minutes, yet when she came back, Lucy was already lying on the bed, waiting. Wearing the strap-on, Alison lay on the bed next to her and, lovesick, got butterflies just thinking about what they intended to do. She leaned forward to kiss her angel on the mouth, but kept it light and brief, so keen was she to move down to Lucy's breasts.

The girl's nipples grew instantly hard against her tongue. Lucy moaned as Alison sucked on them, her hands roaming across her younger lover's warm belly, edging lower, searching … but Lucy was keen to proceed without further foreplay. She pulled Alison on top of her and in between her spread legs.

Somehow, defiling her angel with a plastic phallus felt wrong to Alison. The false cock, not overly large, still looked intrusive nestled against Lucy's shaven pussy. She grew decidedly nervous, watching, delaying as the girl lay looking into her eyes. Lucy obviously noticed Alison's concern. 'Don't worry, I'm not a virgin.'

Alison reached for the hard plastic shaft and guided its bulbous tip to the entrance of Lucy's vagina. The girl was still wet from her licking, her labia bloated a little, slightly red and parted. Alison had no trouble feeding her the first inch or so of the toy, but hesitated before sliding it in further, enjoying her brief moment of power. Her guilt and the sense that she was taking advantage were fading fast too. Lucy was a woman who knew her own mind. Alison was only doing what Lucy desired.

She pressed her hips forward, sliding the false cock deeper, gazing at the girl's face, watching as her eyes opened wider and wider. Surprise? Wonder? Delight? For the first time in Alison's life she wished the cock was real, wished she could feel the tightness of Lucy's vaginal muscles gripping her warm flesh. Sadly, such pleasures were not meant to be. Instead, she had to rely on Lucy's expressive eyes. 'What does that feel like, honey?'

'Hard! So very hard. Is there more?' Alison pushed the dildo in deeper, again watching Lucy's eyes. The feedback from the strap-on was not sensitive, but Alison knew she had nudged something deep inside the girl. Lucy gasped. This time there was a definite look of wonder in her eyes.

Alison felt a sudden flash of guilt – no matter how much Lucy wanted this she still felt slightly uneasy about defiling such perfection. Now the girl was rubbing tiny, quick circles around her clitoris, working on her nipples as she neared orgasm. Her eyes opened wide for an instant, and her mouth stretched in a silent scream. She drew in a deep breath … 'Fuck!'

A simple exclamation that highlighted everything in Alison's head. She was thrilled to have made her angel come so hard, but she was still wound up too. Her nipples ached and she felt like she'd cry if she didn't soon get her own release. So she kept pounding into the girl, her ardour carrying her ever onwards. She was so close, so close …

When Alison's orgasm came, the rush of emotion was a blessed relief – a jolt so great its sheer force stopped her in her tracks. She was pressing down on the dildo, jerking frantically, unaware of anything else but the sheer ecstasy of those few seconds. She opened her eyes and realised Lucy was coming again, raising her hips and grinding against the toy. Alison forced herself to continue, using short, savage thrusts until the girl cried out for her to stop.

Alison rolled over next to Lucy, both women breathing hard. They lay in silence, until Lucy sat up, bright eyed. 'That was so intense! Thank you, Alison.'

'There's no need to thank me, sweetheart. Don't you realise how happy you've made me?'

'I've never thought anyone could come that hard.'

'You did all right yourself for a beginner. I hope you're not too sore.'

'I don't care if I am.'

Lucy was already up from the sofa bed and looking for her clothes. By the time Alison turned to face her, she was fully dressed in her bikini, T-shirt and skirt, and combing the tangles out of her long hair with her fingers.

'Sorry,' she said, 'no time to hang around. I must get home before … well, I don't want to be late.' She strode over to Alison who hadn't yet fully recovered and was now feeling silly with the false cock sticking up from her crotch. Lucy kissed her once on the lips, smiled, then affected a mock-serious expression. 'Alison, who will you spy on once I've gone?'

Alison blushed, turning a deeper red. She did not like to think of herself as a pervert. Yet there was no point denying the truth – not with Lucy. Alison was a voyeur. She was now a defiler of innocent young women too. Yet, she was in heaven. 'I'll think of something,' she said.

'I have a webcam on my laptop. I can set it up in my new digs so you can keep an eye on me, if you like.' The girl gave Alison a wicked wink.

'Oh Lucy! You must think I'm a terrible person.'

'Yes, quite despicable! Thank you again, Ali. You've certainly given me something to remember. Bye!'

Who's Watching Who?
by J R Roberts

I love my day off during the week. Tuesday, the day I don't set my alarm clock to startle me into forced wakefulness. Pure heaven to wake up naturally as the May sunshine starts to send its warming rays through the pretty white voile curtain hanging at my bedroom window, chasing away the cool of the night. The twitter of cheeky sparrows and the coos and burbles of courting pigeons, mixed with the muted hum of distant traffic filters in, the gentle music of the morning that I am so familiar with. The crystal suspended at the window spins on its invisible thread sending rainbow sparkles around the room.

I live on the top floor of a three-storey apartment block, so no one can see in. These lovely warm spring mornings are to be cherished – we get so few with our unpredictable English weather. I push back the thin duvet with its pale lemon cover, kick it right off the bottom of the bed and stretch out on the white cotton sheet. The warm breeze creeping through the open window ruffles the curtain and caresses my body. I always sleep naked.

Should I get up and make a cup of tea or just lounge for a bit longer? So many difficult decisions to make on a girl's day off! I roll on to my tummy and doze a bit longer.

Crash! I'm startled awake. There is the frantic beating of wings as a flock of panicked pigeons takes flight from the roof. What the hell was that? The soothing song of the morning is replaced by the harsh sound of men's voices mingling with bangs, crashes, metallic clangs and a van door slamming. Oh no, it's the builders starting work. The old warehouse opposite my block is being converted into luxury apartments. My neighbours and I opposed the planning application, but we didn't stand a chance against a rich developer with connections.

They've already gutted the old building and started the rebuild. The plans say it will be three storeys, so the top floor will be on an eye level with me – damn, I guess I'll need some proper curtains soon. The shell of the ground floor has been completed and they're working on the first floor, so for now they're still below my level. But each day the building reaches upwards, threatening my privacy.

I feel a little exposed, stretched out naked on the bed with a crew of builders just below me. As I think of this, a wicked little smile settles on my face – what will happen when they're working on the top floor? There'll be nothing between them and a clear view into my bedroom except a flimsy voile curtain sprinkled with gold stars fluttering in the breeze, allowing them glimpses of my naked body on the bed. Will they look, or be gentlemen and keep their eyes on their work? A few weeks ago, I saw them nudge each other as a leggy young woman teetered along in high heels on the street below. A wolf-whistle, shrill and crude, cut through the other city sounds to follow her up the road. She ignored it, hurrying on without a backward glance, and I heard them chuckle to each other.

I stand up and watch them from behind the voile. As long as my apartment is not lit from inside, it should hide me. There are five regular builders and one in particular has caught my eye, dark-haired, tall and slim. They all wear white hard hats with a logo on the front, fluorescent vests that usually end up being tied around their waists when their T-shirts come off in the warm weather, jeans or shorts, and builders' boots. I am treated to views of muscled, tanned chests and backs, strong arms with bulging biceps and the flash of boxer shorts above their waistbands. As we are experiencing an early mini heatwave and the days are getting hotter they glisten with sweat, stopping for cold soft drinks and holding the icy cans to their foreheads to cool off. Hmm ... I can't complain about the view.

Nothing to rush up for today so I think I'll go and get that cup of tea.

I pull on a pink vest-top and a pair of white knickers and, as I walk past the full-length mirror in my bedroom, I stop to view my appearance. Pretty good figure. Small but pert breasts crowned by ruby nipples – visible through the soft jersey of the vest. A flat tummy and a nice, rounded bum that looks great in jeans. Hips a little narrow, maybe a bit boyish. Legs slim, which gives them the appearance of being longer, especially when I slip on a pair of killer heels and stand on tiptoe for the full effect. My unruly mane of chestnut hair frames my face and falls in a wavy cascade down my back. I refuse to straighten it, which is the current fashion – I like to be different in subtle ways, to stand out from the crowd. All in all, not a bad package, I think, and I wink at myself in the mirror as I pad off into the kitchen.

Tea made and a plate of toast in my hand, I wander back to the lounge. In here, the windows are floor to ceiling, giving me a panoramic view of the city – for now anyway, until the monster building opposite creeps up and blocks the view from my ivory tower. The main window is split in half, the top part opening a limited amount. I set my tea and toast down and pull aside the same thin curtain as I have in the bedroom and push the window open to its limit. The breeze wafts in, flipping the edges of the curtain, and I settle cross-legged on the carpet to enjoy my breakfast and watch the building work below.

Sitting close to the window, I scan the scene below for my favourite builder. I capture him with my gaze and study him from my private vantage point. He's tall, certainly over six feet, and though he isn't the most handsome, he's definitely the sexiest – slim hips and a neat little bum encased in his blue denim jeans. His shoulders are broad and as his damp T-shirt sticks to his back in the heat, I see the muscles tighten and flex under the material. It's going to be scorching today so I think that shirt will soon be off.

I've been single for a while, after the messy breakdown of a long relationship, but just lately I've found myself thinking it would be nice to be part of a couple again. Nights out and quiet nights in, in front of the TV with a DVD and a beer, cuddled up on the sofa. And I really miss sex. One-night stands just aren't my thing. Fantasies, my fingers and a trusty vibe are my bedroom companions for now but more and more I'm longing for a male body in my bed, warm and comforting, hard and urgent …

My mind begins to wander as I watch "my" builder.

Today they are erecting scaffolding. Skilfully, they hand materials to each other as they expertly construct a metal skeleton around the rising blockwork of the building, so soon to invade my airspace. Maybe this will be my last Tuesday with total privacy above the city. I wonder what my new facing neighbour will be like – probably, with my luck, a lecherous old peeping Tom!

My builder is high up on the scaffolding frame just below me; I can see the muscles in his strong brown arms tense and bulge as he lifts and balances poles and planks as they are added to the bones of the growing structure.

The men call to each other occasionally, a laugh can be heard, muffled conversations.

Then someone shouts, 'Adam!'

My builder answers, 'Yo?'

'Want a Coke?'

'Yeah, mate.'

A builder lower down throws him a can, which he catches with one hand.

So my builder is Adam.

The alien building sounds and the workmen's shouts die away as they take their break, and the pigeons start to settle and coo again.

It is as if Adam is re-enacting that famous Diet Coke advert just for me! He takes off his white hard hat and wipes his sweaty brow with his forearm, then rubs his hand through his damp, dark hair, making it spiky and scruffy. He balances his hat on the end of a pole and peels off his sweaty T-shirt, wiping it down the centre of his chest before tucking a corner into the top of his jeans, revealing the waistband of his boxers. Then he leans back against a horizontal pole of the scaffolding to relax and opens his can of drink – he's close enough that I hear the hiss.

His body is wet with sweat and very brown from hours spent working in the sun, making his skin shine. He's muscled in a wiry way, not an inch of fat on him – maybe a little too skinny, in fact. From what I can see he has little body hair apart from that oh-so-sexy line which stretches down his stomach and disappears into the top of his underwear. His jeans are low on his hips, as men wear them, displaying a flat, firm stomach and the taut muscles that run up each side from his groin to his pelvis. And as he relaxes back, taking long swigs of cold cola and watching the world below move slowly by, I watch him.

My fingers gently stroke the front of my knickers as I fantasise about him.

Naked and aroused, he must look amazing. I imagine kneeling in front of him, unzipping his jeans, easing him out. His penis lying hot and heavy in my hand, twitching as if it has a mind of its own, as blood rushes to engorge it. And as I grasp it firmly, flesh and blood become as hard as bone. My eyes close as I imagine him like this, hips thrust forward, swollen cock inches from my face. Sitting on the floor of my apartment, living the moment in my mind, I lean forward, flicking my tongue out to taste the salty pearl-drop of fluid leaking from him …

I open my eyes to see him looking straight up at the window and I jerk back and snatch my hand away from my crotch like a naughty child caught with her finger in the honeypot. Did he sense that he was being watched? He can't see through the curtain, can he? No, no lights are on in the apartment so he can't.

Suddenly I want to be naked, just as I'm imagining him naked. I feel daring as I stand up in front of the window, hidden only by the mesh curtain, and pull my vest top off over my head. Slowly, my knickers come down and I flick them across the room with my foot. A strip, just for him. His gaze has turned away and he's about to go back to work. But I'm off to fantasyland and he's coming with me.

My breasts feel smooth and warm as I think of him stroking them, nipples beginning to stiffen under my touch. I'm getting aroused and he's leading me back to my bed.

I take a last look at him through the bedroom window – he's replaced his hat and has gone back to work on the scaffolding. Once I'm lying on the bed I'm too low to see him, but in my mind he is right here with me.

As I lie flat on my back, my hands do the caressing but in my mind it is Adam. He uses feather-light touches to tease and arouse me even more. Fingers circling sensitive nipples and gentle tugs feel like soft lips and a flicking tongue. A track of fingers walking down my body, over my ribs and the soft flesh of my belly, feels like a trail of kisses. My hips instinctively rise as I picture him moving around to kneel on the floor and my legs slowly open to give those insistent lips full access to my waiting body.

My eyes are closed and I'm away with my fantasy. Lost to the world, in my secret erotic world where only the man I choose comes with me.

'Adam,' I whisper.

The tip of a wet, probing finger becomes a warm, slick tongue, stroking is licking, and my free hand mimes entwining itself in his short, dark hair as I pull him in to me. My hips rise and fall as this tall, slim, sexy builder lavishes pleasure on me. Moans escape me and my temperature rises

50

as a breeze ruffles the curtain through the open window, sent to cool my hot body.

My movements and caresses become more urgent as I ask my invisible lover, 'Make me come.'

I relax and slow things down, quietening the rhythm of my body. Then I build the tension again, twice over until I'm desperate for the orgasm that waits impatiently in my body for me to release it. I'm alone on my bed, a wanton woman intent on her own pleasure, using the image of a man she's never met to satisfy her needs. I think of him, lean and hard, and I'm ready to push for my climax.

'Adam … oh, Adam.'

I cry out for him as firm pressure from wet fingers gives me the friction I need, and the hot flush preceding orgasm creeps over me. I hover on the brink, desperate to slip over it into ecstasy, and the sudden thought of him climbing onto the bed, pushing my legs wide and thrusting his hard, hot penis into me sends me spinning over the edge. Moans and cries come flooding from me as my body jerks and I writhe with my climax, coaxing every sensation from myself, riding it for as long as I can stay astride it. Beautiful, absolutely beautiful!

I stroke myself gently as my entire body continues to tingle, and I slowly sink back to reality. I smile to myself and a long, contented sigh leaves me.

Lying spread-eagled on the bed, absent-mindedly stroking my tingling crotch with one hand and tickling my breast with the other, I turn my head towards the window and open my eyes. It takes me a moment to focus and realise what I see.

The voile curtain has flicked up in the breeze and snagged on the window catch. Half of the window is exposed and through the gap, I can see a tall, slim, dark builder on a newly erected level of scaffolding watching me. I freeze in horror and expect him to look away but he doesn't, and I'm sure a smile plays around one corner of his mouth as he raises an eyebrow. In a very undignified way, I scramble off the bed, snatch the curtain down and stand with my back pressed against the wall beside the window, hot this time with embarrassment, my heart thumping, not daring to move, holding my breath. How long has he been there? How much has he seen? Enough. Will he tell the others? How am I ever going to walk out of the front entrance of my apartment block knowing he might recognise me?

I began to smile, then giggle. Oh well, it's too late now, isn't it? What a naughty girl I've been.

I sprint out of the bedroom and into the bathroom, my cheeks still burning.

All day, horny as hell, Adam had nursed a semi. He'd seen the pretty, chestnut-haired woman before, coming and going from the apartment block opposite the building site. Today, Lady Luck had been on his side as he'd caught sight of her on her bed, through a gap in the curtains. His mind lingered on images of her with her legs spread wide, one hand between them teasing herself, fingers dipping inside. The other hand was stroking her breast, tweaking the nipple as she arched her back. Her long, silky hair spread over the pillow and covered part of her face as she moved her head from side to side, chin tilted up, lips parted, and he could imagine the soft, animal moans that escaped her, the words she might utter as she touched herself in just the right way. He wished he knew how to touch her in just that way, wished it was him she was crying out for, that he was the one forcing those sexual sounds from her with his fingers and mouth.

His working day finished, alone on his bed at last, in the small, stuffy room of the bedsit he was renting while he worked in this city, he could do what he had so badly needed to do since the morning's chance viewing.

He grasped his hard penis through the sheet, wrapping

52

the fabric around it as he imagined it buried in her hair. He hadn't had good sex for a long time and he desperately wanted to make love to this beautiful woman. "Mrs Palmer" had been his only sexual companion for some time. It would be awkward now if she recognised him, but he had to find a way to meet this sexy lady.

It felt so good now to encourage his cock to its full potential after keeping it cruelly in check all day. He unwrapped it from the sheet and toyed with it, slowly squeezing and pulling. Oh yeah, it felt good to have a throbbing hard-on. His balls tightened and tingled. However slow and gentle he intended to be if he ever got this lovely woman to bed, in his fantasy now she was his for the taking.

Again, he pictured her on the bed naked, soaking wet from her own caresses and waiting for him. He'd stand at the end of the bed and watch her, hips tilted forward, feet apart and his huge, hard cock in his hand, pushing his foreskin up and back, the smooth head emerging and swelling in his firm grip. He imagined her pleading brown eyes veiled with lust and the way her firm breasts rose and fell with her quickened breathing – a female in full heat waiting for the hottest male to claim her.

He knelt up on the bed with a need to act out his penetration of her, and slowed his strokes. In his mind, he was kneeling between her taut, satiny thighs and she pushed her pelvis up urgently to meet him. He reached underneath her to grasp her buttocks and lift her higher, slipping a couple of pillows beneath them to keep them raised. As she lay in this ready position, he could feel himself rubbing the wet tip of his cock over the slick, perfect pink lips of her pussy, enjoying the scene before him while teasing her.

He groaned as he skimmed a finger over his bulging cockhead, the skin stretched to the limit, his own juice oozing from the end, and imagined blending it with hers.

Propped in that position she wouldn't be able to reach him so all the play would be in his hands. He would press a

53

thumb into the puffy flesh on each side of her succulent labia, the whole area swollen with arousal, and watch her deep pink petals open like a flower to reveal the silken flesh inside, inviting him to come in. And in his mind, he did. Still holding her open with his thumbs, his palms and fingers splaying her legs wide, he pushed in hard.

He could imagine how her tight tunnel walls would engulf him, how she'd squirm to accommodate him, unable to move away. He was big and he knew it. He gripped her hips now, to hold her still and thrust again. This time he imagined the feeling of his balls hitting her bum and the head of his cock butting up against the top of her vagina, no further to go, totally immersed inside her.

This was the superb feeling that always pushed Adam to the edge – indeed, in his early days of lovemaking it had, many times, to his embarrassment, sent him over it far too quickly. A wiser and more experienced lover now, he still craved this feeling but was able to control it, toy with it, push it to the limit and pull it back until he and she were ready. Some women couldn't take it but he so hoped she would. Now when he wanked he liked to bump the head of his cock against the palm of his free hand.

He masturbated in his favourite way, with both hands, kneeling on the bed. In the hot, stuffy little room, sweat ran down his back and the centre of his chest, every muscle in his body tensing as he fought for release, wrestling the beast in his hands into submission. The heat and tension built until his orgasm hit him with its full, explosive force. He wanted to roar out loud but had to stifle it to a strangled moan for fear of being heard. Hot come hit the palm of his free hand and he pulled and pulled until the contractions subsided, coaxing out every drop of fluid.

He collapsed back onto the bed and the sheet felt cool against his damp skin. His breathing settled and a sense of peace spread over him. He didn't knock one out very often but tonight he was rampant. Christ, he felt that after a rest, he could imagine her in another position and do it all over again. But it was late and the very physical job of erecting scaffolding meant tiredness was taking its toll, the calm after sex making him drift off...

Adam found himself looking forward to work tomorrow.

Deliberate Display
by Abigail Thornton

I noticed them immediately as they made such an odd couple – at six foot, Ruth towered over her husband and there was something thrillingly Amazonian about her wide shoulders and gym-toned muscles. I couldn't help but imagine Ruth dominating the bedroom; holding her husband down while she ...

Those unbidden thoughts proved to be close to the truth; there were numerous complaints and, as the holiday rep, it was my duty to deal with them. Most of the routine complaints I dealt with day to day in my work related to levels of noise but these were very specific: allegations of "improper business" being conducted in one of the rooms. I had been pleasantly surprised by the details of what had been observed, but not at all by the perpetrators – the newlyweds, Ruth and Callum.

They'd been painfully demanding since they'd arrived and I'd upgraded them to one of the posh suites at the top of the hotel, both to shut them up and keep them out of the way. But they were still overlooked by hundreds of other rooms from the neighbouring hotels. And, this being Benidorm, most of those rooms were full as people grasped one last lingering taste of summer. The season was drawing to a close and I was feeling jaded; run down by the demands of the 18-30 crowd looking for a bit of sun, sea, sand and sex. As a way of getting away from it all, and my relationship break-up in particular, it had been a wonderful experience, but I was more than ready to get back to my friends and family. However, by giving in to Ruth's initial demands, I'd set myself-up for a stream of calls, and, since I wanted an easy final week, I'd been inclined to say yes to her every request, rather than enforce company policy.

The complaints had gathered in the form of phone messages and bits of paper tacked to my desk. I don't care, I thought to myself. Let them have their fun, they're newlyweds – what do you expect? But then I'd been shown the photos, taken as "evidence" by the husband of a couple staying directly opposite the room in question. I dutifully copied them on to my laptop, then gasped at both the clarity and the content as I clicked on the thumbnails.

There were nearly 200 in total – enthusiastic "proof" of the whole sex session. Something struck me as odd about the lovemaking in the pictures: not only were the curtains open and the lights on, the couple were positioned awkwardly across the bed, facing the window. It seemed unnatural – not that I'm an expert. Were they doing it in purpose? Did they want to be seen, to be watched? Was Ruth's final spunky smile directed at her own reflection in the window ... or at the audience beyond? Had it been a deliberate display? Intrigued, that was what I set out to investigate as I caught the lift.

'There have been, er, complaints ...' It was difficult to have a polite conversation with a man who had an erection moving under his towel. It was bobbing, throbbing – not that I was looking.

'Complaints? What kind? About the noise?'

'No – not about the noise.'

'Who is it, darling?' Ruth's distinctive voice sounded from somewhere deep inside the suite.

'It's Julie,' Callum said.

'Julie who?'

'Julie Thompson,' he called back, having read my name badge. I felt a flutter of annoyance. There had been no mistaking the fact that Callum's eyes had wandered from my badge to the subtle cleavage afforded by my regulation blouse. He was a newly married man and shouldn't have been doing that. I had an urge to fasten another button but knew that it would be too obvious and would only draw further unwanted attention.

There was the sound of soft footsteps. Ruth arrived, wrapping an arm around her husband's waist. They were indeed a very odd couple, mismatched somehow: Callum was Irish, five-foot-seven, and liked to talk about the incomprehensible things he did with computers. Ruth, over six feet tall and with silky hair cascading over her broad shoulders, came across as being totally up herself. Yes, she was beautiful, but it's hard to like someone who sees themselves as being "superior". I wasn't surprised to discover that she still didn't know who I was despite having made daily demands of me for nearly two weeks.

Ruth was wearing her husband's creased shirt, no doubt having picked it up from where it had been thrown at the start of this latest round of lovemaking – even the maids had been complaining. Her hair was lighter than when she'd arrived, and most of the silkiness had gone. I couldn't help but feel a thrill of satisfaction that she was failing to prevent the sun and salt water from turning it into something approximating straw – like they had done to mine. Annoyingly, the lack of hair control had increased Ruth's beauty – she seemed softer now, more real ... more attractive, more alluring; a vulnerability exposed. Her sun-kissed skin was vibrant and energised, perfectly highlighted by the stark whiteness of her husband's shirt. Ruth had done up only two buttons, the lower one being mismatched – the result of which was half the shirt was being tugged up and I could clearly see the "V" of her pubic area, although it wasn't hosting a single pube.

Officially, all I had to do was say something subtle, perhaps ask if they wouldn't mind closing their curtains before they went back to bed. But I wanted to know why they were doing it. Before I managed to find the right words, Ruth gave me a dazzling smile and swept her arm around my shoulder – dragging the shirt up towards her navel – before offering me a swig of champagne from the bottle dangling from her fingers.

'Ahh, Julie! Come on in. Come and help us celebrate our marriage.' I was too numb to resist the faux friendship as Ruth happily wrestled me into the room, with her husband closing the door behind us. She was holding on to me, steering me into the lounge. Another trail of clothes, as described by the maids, told the tale of what had been happening in the time leading up to my arrival. Shoes scattered by the door; trousers scrunched by the bin; a red dress tossed over the television; a pile of underwear by the couch and a purple tube of lubricant standing erect on the table. My mind skipped back to the sordid pictures. Not content with "normal" sex, Callum and Ruth had been indulging in more "unconventional" sexual practices – and looked set to repeat them tonight.

'I want to be able to sit on my balcony without seeing that anal slut,' had been one of the more specific complaints which had been carefully filed "for urgent attention" on my desk. I wondered whether the people who'd made it were watching now as I engaged with a man hiding his erection under a towel and a woman unconcerned that her pussy was on show. I looked down – I couldn't help it – and they looked down in unison so that all three of us were staring at Ruth's exposed crotch.

'You like my wife's pussy?' Callum asked, tugging at his shirt to fully expose his wife's groin. Ruth's legs parted slightly and I caught a glimpse of glistening labia before I dragged my eyes away. My head was swimming.

'Perhaps you'd like to see my husband's cock?' Ruth asked, adding a sultry look to the husky tone in her voice. My body was frozen in place by overridden thought processes. I did want to see Callum's cock in the flesh. My level of arousal leaped as Ruth tugged at the knotted towel and did a slow reveal to leave Callum naked with his erection pointing in my general direction. He stood there shamelessly and I felt the heat rising as my body responded. Who *did* that? Particularly newlyweds in a goldfish-bowl of an apartment with the curtains open and the lights on.

Moments later, their nudity was complete as Ruth twanged the remaining buttons and dropped the shirt on the floor. She wore no jewellery – she had the kind of body where any kind of adornment would detract rather than enhance its effect.

They were so brazen and my breath caught as Ruth's hand moved down and gripped her husband's cock. They were both watching me, eager for my reaction as she began stroking it, pulling the skin back and forth, revealing more and more of the angry purple of Callum's glans.

As the initial shock began to fade, I was overwhelmed by feelings of guilt. I felt like a pervert, intruding into the consummation of a marriage. But intertwined with the guilt was a terrible excitement. It was the first time I had seen two people naked together and my official duties were forgotten as the hunger between my legs became irresistible. As I watched Ruth caress her husband, my mind was filling with a fantasy where I stepped across the gap and grabbed a handful of cock with one hand, then brought the other up between her legs and slid a finger along her moist slit before hooking it up inside her pussy.

My own pussy was quivering with excitement, the nerves firing in anticipation of being stimulated. But for now I just watched – there was a weight of inhibition pressing in on me. Part of me was still their holiday rep, watching as they touched each other inappropriately.

It felt like I was in a daydream as Ruth started wanking Callum's cock. He let out a few noises of appreciation as her hand worked up and down his shaft. I longed to do the same, to wrap my hand around it and feel the skin moving back and forth over the hard core within.

A ghost of a smile appeared on Ruth's lips. They knew – we all knew – that the fact I was still there spoke of my acceptance.

'Why don't you come over and have a feel?' The words came from Ruth's lips but I suspected that she was voicing Callum's desires. As though in a trance, I stepped forward and took his cock in my hand. So hot, so hard, so eager. Natural instincts took over and my hand started stroking by itself; lightly at first, feeling the length of it, the girth and the fiery heat. This cock belonged to Ruth – I was wanking a "married" cock for the first time. It was against my beliefs to do this. Married men were strictly out of bounds. But that rule didn't take account of a willing spouse watching me, encouraging me to do it.

I wanted to feel it inside me. The thought was so dirty. I closed my eyes as I imagined it probing between my fleshy labia, searching for my opening, and, having found it, squeezing inside me. I groaned as I pictured the scene in more detail and felt my pussy clenching around the phantom intruder. I hungered for him – desperate to push him back onto the sofa, mount him and feed his cock into my twitching hole. I needed to feel him inside me.

Lips on mine snapped me out of my little reverie. My eyes flew open and saw Ruth's face pressing against mine. My hand found her hip and then dropped down on to her bare bum. As she pulled in closer, I allowed my hand to move around her waist and then trail between her buttocks. My whole body was thudding with excitement as my fingertip explored the moist roughness of Ruth's arsehole. She sighed and wriggled against me, enjoying what I was doing to her. I liked girls' bums but I'd never felt a bumhole which had been stretched open by a cock before. At least, not that I knew of. But as I stood there being kissed by Ruth, I knew that the cock in my right hand had been inside the

61

bumhole I was exploring with my left middle finger.

I don't know what I'd been expecting – I thought there'd be a tell, something physical which would flash like a beacon to advertise what she'd been doing; that she'd been having anal sex. But it just felt normal. Tight, even. I pressed my finger into Ruth's anus, expecting my slender digit to penetrate her easily. Instead, her sphincter resisted and she pushed in against me even harder as she tried to escape.

'Easy, tiger!' she said, gripping my wrist and guiding my hand away from her arse. I flushed as I suddenly realised what I was doing – Ruth had no idea that I knew about her anal antics and I imagined what my response would be if someone tried to stick something up my bum without using any lubrication. The colour deepened as my embarrassment grew.

'Oh honey, you look so hot,' Ruth said, pushing my hair back behind my shoulder before tracing her fingertip down the edge of my blouse. 'Perhaps we should …'

I knew what she was going to do but watched in mute horror as she yanked at the buttons. I released her husband's cock as she threw my blouse onto the floor behind me. I had to fight the urge to pick it up and fold it neatly over the back of the sofa.

I fully expected her to undo my bra but what she did next was so much sexier – she pulled the cup away, very tenderly, took a brief peek at the exposed breast, the erect nipple, and smiled at Callum. We were sharing a secret from her husband, and it was delicious.

That little display let me know that Ruth was in charge of proceedings, the alpha – as I had suspected – but actually seeing it happen excited me more than the feel of her husband's throbbing erection in my hand. Ruth yanked on my zip and moments later my skirt went loose and dropped to the floor. Both Callum and Ruth pressed in against me and the feeling of so much skin on mine – soft, smooth femininity and hard, hairy masculinity – combined to make my body erupt with desire. I was desperate to get fully naked with them. Ruth kissed me again and this time I kissed her back, opening my mouth against hers as I brought my hand up between her legs. They parted and I felt the heat and then soft wetness.

'Oh … God, yes,' she whispered, as my fingers found the bump of her clitoral hood. I didn't explore further. I circled my fingertip gently around and around, a ceaseless motion that spread her juices from within her slit up onto her shaved mound. Her body was rocking back and forth, her eyes closed, her mouth moving with unspoken words. She was concentrating, concentrating on the sensations I was giving her. My own pussy was crying out for attention but it would have to wait. It felt good to deny myself.

I gently increased the speed of my fingers and felt the tension rise in Ruth's body. I just hoped that I could take her to that perfect peak of pleasure. I didn't want to tease her: I wanted to make her orgasm; I wanted to make that ridiculously hot body quiver with ecstasy; give Ruth an intense moment of sexual release.

I rubbed harder, feeling the soft flesh of her labia stretching. She sighed and her fingers dug into my hips.

'Fuck her,' she groaned, simultaneously sliding her hands down, dragging my knickers with them. I felt the air circulate between my legs as the skimpy material dropped down my thighs. There was no hesitation as Callum pulled away and moved in behind me. He'd been anticipating the command and I wondered how many times they'd done this before; how many times they had fucked a girl together. The idea sent sexual thrills deep into my core. I wanted it, wanted to share myself with them; wanted Ruth's husband to fuck me.

I parted my legs and stuck my bum out, presenting myself to Callum. He undid my bra, exposing my tits to his wife. She pushed in closer, crouching slightly to squash her soft boobs against mine. The blunt heat of Callum's cock moved between my legs, searching for my opening.

'You're about to become the first woman I've let my husband fuck.' She emphasised "husband" and the word made me gasp just before Callum's cock, now condom-clad, found the mouth of my vagina and pushed.

It surged into me, the force of his thrust lifting both of my feet off the ground. He caught my weight and held me up. The power of the man was shocking and he held me aloft as he thrust into me; fierce, primal thrusts which quickly satisfied my need.

Callum supported me with my legs bent at the knee and spread wide, first in front of Ruth and then the window. It was a wanton display which I found embarrassingly pornographic. Then I realised what he was doing – the open curtains, the lights – he was showing me to the audience. Like a trophy.

I was horrified. I knew that people could see and that there were most likely eyes and possibly cameras watching, watching the cock driving into me over and over. But I was also excited. Relief came only as Ruth's naked body stepped in front of me. My legs wrapped around her waist and pulled her in against me to hide my most intimate flesh.

'Ahh, every inch of you is beautiful,' Ruth sighed approvingly as her hands ran over my body. I couldn't help but imagine that the cock thrusting so urgently into my pussy was somehow hers. My body melted with the power of the fantasy.

'Oh Ruth!' I sighed, tightening the grip of my thighs, relishing the soft warmth of her body, enjoying the proximity of her pussy to mine. There was an elemental power radiating through every touch, every caress. The hot, hairy authority suspending me, holding me aloft, pressing into me from behind; the vision of female loveliness trapped between my legs. Ruth's hand dropped down and did wonderful things to my clit. Her thumb started to draw forth urges and sensations that I hadn't known I was capable of; husband and wife, working together to pleasure me … in full view of everyone.

Perhaps it was the shock of having an audience which kept my orgasm at bay for so long – for I have never known such perfect stimulation. It was like Ruth was inside my head, reading my need to go faster or harder, before backing off and starting the cycle over again. She had total control over me, which was both alarming and very, very exciting.

'I'm going to make you come,' Ruth said at last, looking me in the eye. The way she said it, like a statement in a court of law, made the pressure drop in my belly as my adrenaline surged. The knowledge that she was going to relieve my aching need and give me ultimate pleasure in itself made me shudder.

Hot tension rose to fever pitch as the rigid length of Callum's cock buried itself inside my pussy while his wife intensified the perfect stimulation of my swollen clit. I resisted for as long as I dared, but in the end I dropped my weight onto Ruth's fingers, simultaneously impaling myself more deeply on her husband's cock.

Callum breathed heavily in my ear and groaned with his own release. Despite the condom I actually felt a hot burst inside my vagina and the need to orgasm became overwhelming. Muscles tightened into agonising knots before releasing in a glorious symphony of utter relief.

I'm normally very controlled, even at the height of orgasm, but as though playing to my audience, I let go with a torrent of filthy exclamations and uncontrolled moans. It was the most complete release of my life … and yet I wanted more.

Callum's deflating cock was still moving inside me, although the reduction in size and my wetness meant my pussy was making outrageous slurping noises – slurping noises which attracted Ruth's mouth. She licked and sucked at the juices long after the heat of my orgasm had dispersed and stopped only as Callum let out a shaky breath and dropped me softly back onto my feet before tumbling theatrically onto the couch.

'My turn,' Ruth sighed, 'and since my husband doesn't look up to the job ...' Callum grinned as she turned and knelt over the sofa, giving me a perfect view of her powerful back, bum and legs. I had an urge to explore all of it, from her shoulder blades, down the fluted hollow of her spine and over the intriguing landscape of her bum.

Every part of her was smooth and sexy as my lips worked their way down. I knew what I wanted to do and hoped that she'd let me.

Arriving at Ruth's bum, I kissed my way across her flesh slowly and sensuously. I could see my target at the interface of her bum cheeks: her beautiful arsehole. I marvelled at it – a vertical crease surrounded by a fan of inviting crinkles. How had she taken a cock in that tiny non-hole? Despite my recent orgasm, a tingle of sexual heat was building. My body shivered with extreme excitement as I kissed and licked my way into Ruth's anal cleft and lapped at the source of my obsession.

'Ooh fuck!' Ruth gasped, as I hardened my tongue into a nub and ground it into her bumhole and brought my thumb up between her legs. I started rubbing her clitoris just as she had rubbed mine. Ruth's knees came apart, which had the effect of opening up her bum crack; she was encouraging me deeper, inviting me into the most taboo region of her body. I obliged.

The gap was sufficient to accommodate my chin and I was able to push forward, pressing my lips and tongue against Ruth's anus. I could feel her body responding, the muscles tightening already. My thumb rubbed the bottom of her wet slit, circling her clitoris over and over. Ruth's hips rolled from side to side, and I heard gasps and groans escaping from the cushions.

The rhythm of her hips became more violent and I was

forced to retreat but the distance did nothing to quench my anal desire. Ruth's bumhole was shiny with my saliva and it gave me an idea – I licked my fingers and speared her with two of them, my index finger forcing its way into her arse, while my middle one simultaneously slipped into her pussy. The twin penetration looked stunning and the dance of Ruth's hips became even more desperate. Then it stopped. Her hand gripped my wrist while her bum pushed back hard against my fingers, forcing a much deeper penetration. A second later I felt her muscles constricting, clenching as she orgasmed frantically.

Ruth disappeared into the bathroom, leaving me with her husband and his erection. I was horny and eager to fuck him again. Without waiting for Ruth's permission, I moved up over him and guided his cock back into my pussy. It felt so good, slower this time, more relaxed – some of the sexual fires having burned themselves out.

Not for long. Ruth came back and smiled, nastily. 'Naughty, naughty,' she said. 'Did I give you permission to fuck my husband again?' I shook my head. 'No, that's right – I didn't.' And she spanked me. Not playfully; she did it again and again with hard stinging slaps. I didn't know what to do, so I just crouched there and took it, until my bottom was glowing and the tears were running down my cheeks.

It hurt like hell but I enjoyed the punishment and felt a pang of regret when it stopped. 'That's enough,' Ruth said sharply, her hand caressing my fiery buttocks. Cold gel coiled over my skin and she worked it in, providing delicious relief. Then her fingers drifted down between my buttocks. I knew what was going to happen and was thrilled.

That was how I orgasmed for the second time – with Ruth's fingers deep in my burning bum while I ground my pussy on Callum's cock.

As I was recovering, I felt Ruth's breath tickling against my ear like a lover's tongue. 'I want to see my husband's cock in your bum,' she whispered, so softly that there was no way he could have heard.

I had thought that I couldn't take any more but those words struck a chord with me. Suddenly, I was starting afresh, unbearably turned on. I didn't reply but eased myself off Callum's cock, slid forward an inch and dropped, feeling Ruth's guiding hand between my punished buttocks. It was very slippery down there and my arse simply stretched open as I applied gentle pressure and weight.

I squealed as Callum gripped me around the hips, pulling down with his hands as he thrust upwards, perhaps not realising that his cock was now in my arse. Only as he sank fully into my bottom did a dirty thought occur to me. I pulled myself off Callum's cock and positioned him so that as I mounted him in reverse-cowgirl, I could see my full frontal reflection in the window, knowing that I was also giving the best possible view to my audience, whether they be real or imaginary. I wondered whether there was a long-lensed camera pointing at the action between my legs. I hoped so.

Making sure to spread my legs as wide as possible, I sank back down on Callum's shaft, feeding it back into my hungry arse. The view from the reflection was fantastic, like watching myself in a live porno on a huge television. Reaching down, I stretched my pussy lips open as my arse sucked longingly on Callum's meat.

I imagined guys bringing themselves off while watching me through the window – energetically wanking as they fantasised about fucking me. I'd never felt so dirty, so wanton. 'Fuck me ... fuck me hard,' I heard myself beg, and the pounding steadily increased until my whole body was incandescent with pain and pleasure.

Ruth was forgotten as I played with my clit, watching the reflection of myself being arse-fucked. My entire body started to tremble again and I came for the third time in an agonising explosion of ecstasy. I was spent and pulled Callum's slippery cock free, skinned off the condom and wanked him until I was treated to the view and feel of his hot spunk spurting up my body. Considering what he'd been doing over the last few days I was impressed by the quantity of spunk that sprayed from his jerking cock. I was pleased with the visual effect as it started dribbling down the curve of my belly. Another dirty thought popped into my head as I rubbed the juices into my glistening skin. I looked out of the window, addressing my audience, before licking and sucking my fingers clean.

As I stood up, Ruth joined me. 'Time to end the show,' she said, with a smile. I didn't even react to the admission that she knew all about the onlookers. 'Grab a curtain.'

I took one of the heavy curtains and dragged it across, meeting Ruth in the middle. I wasn't surprised that our display finished with a little flourish. Ruth kissed me; or rather we kissed, for I was a more than willing participant. The material met in the middle and we were done.

'You knew,' I said, 'they were watching.'

'They didn't have to watch, but I was really hoping someone might.'

'Someone did – I've seen the photos.'

'Photos?' Ruth's eyes sparkled. 'You've seen them? Are they good?' The words tumbled out of her.

'They're –' I paused, trying to think of the best way to describe them '– wonderful.'

'There were three of them at it last night. Disgusting – that's what it was.' It was the morning after and I had been trying to find a way to sit comfortably on my throbbing bum when the same complaining couple had barged into my little office. I was desperately tired – but you have to take the consequences if you choose to stay up all night drinking champagne and shagging. I envied Ruth and Callum tucked up in bed, no doubt recharging for another round of debauchery. Not for the first time, I thought about using the master key to slip back into their suite – but duty called.

The woman paused, waiting for me to speak.

'I'm sorry?'

'I said, what are you going to do about it?'

I muttered something about "ongoing investigations" and "doing everything we can". She wasn't happy but there was nothing further to say. I could hear her raging to the receptionist outside even as the husband lingered.

'That was quite the show you put on last night,' he said, meaningfully. 'I'm surprised to find you sitting down,' he added, cracking a smile.

'I hoped you'd be watching. Did you take any –' My pounding heart had already washed away my tiredness.

'Photos?' he interrupted, waggling a disc at me. 'She's not seen them,' he said, inclining his head to the lobby, 'but I thought you'd want a copy.'

'That's very thoughtful of you,' I replied, taking the proffered disc with a smile.

'Well, thank you for arranging yourself so … so indecently. I've attached my card, if you ever feel like posing professionally.' I thought he was joking until I saw the photographic studio's details on the card.

'I'll think about it,' I said, smirking at the idea of getting naked again. I slipped the disc and the card into my pocket, making sure that the notepaper with Mr and Mrs Callum Martin's home contact details was still in there too. It felt good to have one or two offers worth following up on for when I finally got home.

The Convent Girls' Tale
by Marlene Yong

That afternoon, I met Vanessa in the restaurant of an expensive hotel in St John's Wood. When she arrived, I noticed male heads turning – as always. I won't say that Vanessa is the most beautiful woman I've ever known, but she's certainly the most voluptuous and sexually magnetic. Beside her I, Dympna, look positively dowdy – which was why I only agreed to meet her in a discreet eatery, and then only once a month.

We go back a long way, Vanessa and myself. To a convent a few miles from Dublin, in fact. As two skinny but not unattractive teenagers, we both caught the eye of our fair share of boys, though things were all pretty innocent back then. But as we reached adulthood, she left me miles behind. I developed my own skills, though. I wasn't bad-looking but I needed something to equalise the odds. And I discovered I had an extremely rewarding if unexpected talent. I could deliver one hell of a blowjob.

My tongue had always been exceptionally long and agile and I playfully experimented and practised in front of a mirror, twisting it into a variety of shapes, extending its length, even manipulating it to make wide circles in the air with the tip. When this began, it was just fun. I little realised how useful this aptitude would prove to be.

Our sexual adventures began at 18 when, after bedtime, we'd slip out into the convent garden and through a wicket gate in the wall, which the nuns believed was completely jammed shut and therefore safe. A couple of lads would

71

meet us outside and we'd separate into pairs and drift into the shelter of some trees behind a low wall.

I kissed and necked with Brian a few times but one night he opened his mouth wide, forcing my lips apart. Next moment, I felt his tongue jab in between them. I was shocked but decided to play along and see what it was like. I slithered my own in and around his mouth, licking his palate and rotating my tongue round his. He pulled away looking at me strangely. '*Jaysus*, Dympna, where'd you learn to kiss like that?' he gasped.

After that there was no stopping me. I suppose I was naïve; I was also infatuated. In my innocence, I let him lick my breasts and caress my hole with his fingers. I also grasped his thing while he jerked his arse backwards and forwards as if he was trying to make something happen. Nothing ever did and it was only when Vanessa told me afterwards that some kind of creamy juice was supposed to shoot out of the thing that I got some idea of what he'd been expecting.

Soon I was agreeing to whatever he asked me to do, except allowing him to stick his thing into me. And that was only because I'd had so many warnings from the nuns and the priest who came to the convent to hear confession.

I was, as I've said, still rather innocent then. But Brian kept complaining that me using my hand was not "sexy" enough. One day he said that surely I could use my marvellous tongue as he didn't want me to get up the creek. At first I didn't understand what he wanted me to do. When I finally caught on, I shouted, 'You dirty scut!' and ran back into the convent and refused to see him for weeks. Eventually I relented, though. And soon we were back to kissing and groping.

Then one night – it must have been a few days before my period, a time when I used to get all hot and feel funny, wanting something but I couldn't tell what – he pushed me onto the low wall so that I was lying on my back with my skirt up and my knickers round about my ankles. I was about to protest that he mustn't put his thing in me, but he bent down and began licking at my crack. Christ! I nearly screamed at the very pleasure of it.

He went on doing this for a while until I thought I was going to explode. 'Will you do it for me too, Dympna?' he urged. 'I've had a wash. I'm entirely clean.' And he shoved his prick into my mouth before I could change my mind. I was so excited by then that I set my tongue to work automatically. It wasn't planned; it wasn't even a conscious action. It just seemed ... the thing to do.

It didn't take long either. Within a minute my mouth filled with a salty cream and Brian's body was shaking all over. 'God, Dympna,' he moaned. 'I've never come off like that before.'

That was my first time. Over the next few years, especially after Vanessa and myself had come to England and found digs, I had plenty of time to develop my skills. Although I didn't attract such dishy men as Vanessa, once I'd gone down on a guy he'd stick with me until I had to shake him off. One of them explained it to me. 'Dympna, you give better head than any woman I've ever fucked. It's the blowjob of a lifetime. A blowjob no man would ever forget.'

After a few weeks in London, Vanessa and myself went our separate ways. I knew I could never keep up with her. She was glamorous and sexy: stunning to look at when she dolled herself up. And she only screwed men with lots of readies who'd take her to places I could only dream of. I heard that when she strolled down the beach at Cannes or Juan Les Pins, men's heads turned, eyes glazed and dozens of lustful studs fantasised about those stupendous boobs threatening to tumble out of her tiny halter top, her long legs that went up to velvet thighs, her rich auburn hair highlighting the curve of her neck. But above all it were those eyes – dark, brooding, inviting, teasing – that hypnotized every guy who came into contact with her.

Next to her I would have faded into the background.

Vanessa eventually married a man called Ed Marson, who'd made a packet in hedge funds and acquired a magnificent house in Amersham. It's a massive Victorian barn of a place which Ed had gutted, then refurbished. They have an enormous lounge with a stone fireplace, a picture window overlooking the lawn and a huge, ornate mirror that covers most of the wall at the opposite end. A king-sized settee squatted facing the mirror.

Ed was in partnership with a Phil something-or-other and, during the occasional meetings I had with Vanessa, she rabbited on about how she fancied this Phil fella rotten. Phil, she told me, was six-three, a good-looking guy, rugged, with dark brown hair.

So that afternoon at a secluded corner table in the hotel restaurant, I sensed what she was about to tell me. Ultra-chic, as usual, she sauntered over and parked herself opposite me. Her eyes glittered and she spoke with repressed excitement. 'Dympna,' she began. 'Remember what I was saying last time we met? About fancying Phil, Ed's partner?'

I nodded eagerly. I knew what was coming. Vanessa loved relating her sexual encounters in explicit detail and in the raunchiest language. Sometimes I suspected she even wrote out and rehearsed a titillating script before recounting her adventures. She left little to the imagination: even just hearing her exploits made my breasts and groin tingle. We are all voyeurs – except for a few exhibitionists.

'Well ...' she went on. 'Last Tuesday I decided to do something about Phil. So I called into the office.'

She poured a cup of coffee from the pot a waiter had just brought and gulped some down. 'Phil knew who I was, of course,' she continued. 'I pretended an interest in an investment he'd once suggested and invited him to come over to the house that evening to discuss it with Ed and myself. Even sitting facing him across his desk, I felt myself getting hot and horny. He really is a hunk, Dympna. Tall with a Roman nose, dark brown eyes and sooo masculine.'

For a second an enigmatic, almost sly, expression crinkled Vanessa's eyes, then vanished.

'I spent the rest of the day imagining what his body would feel like pressed against mine. Before he arrived I dressed ... um ... suitably.' Vanessa gazed into the distance in happy recollection. She loved reminiscing about her salacious preparations for a seduction.

'I wore a skirt so short Phil would glimpse my pubes pressed up against my tights – skin-coloured and no knickers, of course. I also left the top buttons on my blouse undone. Beneath it a push-up half-bra. I tell you, Dympna, just dressing up like that was enough to make me throb all over.

'By the time Phil arrived, I was churning inside. Thinking about what was going to happen got me all hot and bothered, but ... well, he is Ed's partner after all.'

I said nothing, allowing her to continue.

'Once I saw him standing on the doorstep, though, it was too late. There was no going back. I sat him on the settee while I mixed drinks and told him that Ed had been delayed and wouldn't be home for hours. I went on to drop hints about "problems" between myself and Ed, implying that he wasn't seeing to my needs as often as I wanted, didn't rise to the occasion when required, always kept to the same routine, and so on. I could see Phil was getting horny but he wasn't nibbling.

'So I sat down close to him on the settee and asked him about the investment he'd mentioned weeks before. I wasn't really listening to what he said. The scent of his aftershave was sending little sparks through my cunt and made me all sweaty and wet. I deliberately allowed my skirt to slide up, giving him a bird's eye view of my crotch each time I crossed and uncrossed my legs.

'I could tell Phil was still hesitant about fucking me – I am his partner's wife, after all – so I rested my hand on his leg and slid it up and down his thigh. Each time the backs of my fingers grazed his thing, I felt it jump up – it was like a puppy after a bone! I was so randy my nipples were positively smouldering and I had to struggle to control my breathing.'

Before continuing, Vanessa topped up the coffee in her cup and emptied half of it down her throat. In my mind's eye, I could see every detail of the scene she was describing, Masked by the restaurant table, I had located the "V" of my mons through my skirt and was pressing my fingers hard against the mound, relishing the sensations that radiated through my vaginal channel.

'At last,' Vanessa went on, 'Phil seemed to work up the courage and placed his hand on my leg. He gradually copied my movements until his knuckles were kneading my pubes. God, I was so moist. It was … it was like the first time a lad touches you down there. Then, all of a sudden, he turned and looked right at me with those deep, piercing eyes. I swear, Dympna, by then my knickers were soaking! My hands were shaking as I scrabbled for his cock through his trousers. I-I tore his zip down and grabbed his cock. His hard cock.'

In the excitement of her recollection, Vanessa slopped coffee over the rim of her cup. I could see sweat on her forehead. She licked her lips. Telling me about her experience was titillating her. It was doing the same to me too, particularly as I knew that Vanessa was holding something back. A familiar languor crept over me. I realised that I was rubbing my thighs together and my own panties were rapidly growing moist.

A question occurred to me. 'Weren't you worried that Ed would return at any moment?' Even though I knew the answer, I was taken by surprise when Vanessa shrugged the suggestion off with a sharp 'No!'

'Phil,' she went on, 'tried to get his fingers into me by

tearing open the crotch of my tights. But somehow he couldn't manage it. Eventually, he grabbed the waistband and ripped them down. Christ, was I wide! If he'd tried, he could have practically got his hand in. I believe I could actually feel my clit swell and harden. I wanted him. Oh, Dympna, you can't imagine how much I longed to have him inside me at that moment.'

Vanessa paused to savour the memory then carried on. 'Anyways, I lifted one foot onto the settee and spread my legs as wide as possible. I looked at that big mirror on the wall, saw the reflection of my pussy in it. The lips were curled back and the inside looked so pink ... so glossy.'

Unexpectedly, she fell silent, but I knew she was concealing something from me and was considering whether to tell me or not. And that knowledge added a powerful frisson to the fluttering in my own quim produced by my busy fingers beneath the table top. 'Go on,' I urged as I spread myself surreptitiously. 'You can't just leave me in the air. Finish your story.'

'Well ...' Vanessa resumed, 'by now I hardly cared what I was doing. I levered Phil's prick and balls out through the gap in his underpants. Then I stood up, turned my back to him, lifted the hem of my skirt and bent forward. This brought my arse level with his face. The muscles in my pussy were clenching and unclenching. Jesus, I could even feel the blood pulsing in my labia. I shouted, "Lick me. Hard!"

'That was all the encouragement he needed, I can tell you! The settee is low enough that he only had to lean forward a couple of inches to run his tongue up and down my pussy lips. Seconds later I was wetter than ever, from his spittle and my own ... well, *secretions*.' She paused, recalling and relishing the moment.

'Dympna, I nearly went ballistic! My legs shook, out of control; my tits swelled to bursting; my throat constricted. I was in paradise. Or something close to it anyway.

'I lowered myself onto his erection – my legs were trembling – and lay back against him like a lap dancer. I caught another view of ourselves in the mirror. By arching my back, I could just make out his prick slithering in and out of my cunt, wet and glistening. I'd never felt so wanton in my life before. I wanted to do everything. And anything.

'I made sure I caught Phil's eye in the mirror, then unbuttoned my blouse to expose my half-bra. I held his gaze as I lifted out my boobs and licked my nipples. They tingled – no, more than that. It felt painful but delicious all at once. Like little arrows were shooting through them.

'I felt his cock jerking and twitching inside me, knew he was about to come. Suddenly, a wild impulse came over me, Dympna. I did something so outrageous that it shocks me now just to think of it. I pulled myself off him, spun round and threw myself on my knees directly in front of his hard-on. There was something I'd always wanted to try.

'I slid one hand beneath his balls and fingered my clit with the other. "*Bukkake* me," I begged him, utterly shameless now. "What?" he panted. Seeing he didn't understand I repeated it, slower this time. "*Bu-kka-ke.*" He looked confused. "Come on my face!" I yelled and tilted my head back. In that moment, he had such a shameless, lustful look on his face, I could have eaten him up.

'His sperm rained down, splashing my cheeks, hair, eyes and my mouth – I felt most whorish of all when it splashed on my lips and tongue. I was trembling as I brought my hands up and smeared his spunk over my neck, ears, breasts. That's when I started to come. I came so hard. You've no idea how powerful, how sexy, it felt, Dympna. You'd never believe it but minutes later, I was still coming, juices pouring from me.'

Vanessa paused in her narrative. Her cheeks glowed red with arousal at the memory and her pleasure in recounting it.

Below the surface of the table I too was spending. Her account on its own would not have brought me to an orgasm in a restaurant, but knowing what I did, what she was hiding, drove me over the top. I had to grit my teeth to conceal evidence of the ripples running through my cunt at that moment. Fortunately, Vanessa, engrossed in her own reverie, noticed nothing.

'And then …?' I asked once I'd slowed my breathing back down again.

'That was it! I told Phil I didn't want Ed to come home and find us like that and I coaxed him out of the house. He asked if we might repeat our … er … encounter … and I said I'd think about it. Maybe I will.' Her eyes went misty for a moment, then she giggled. 'Oh, Dympna, I wish you'd been there! You'd have loved it.'

She peered at the Rolex on her wrist. 'Anyway, must fly. Ed's expecting me. You pick up the tab, would you, love? It's on me next time, I promise.'

Moments later, she was on the other side of the hotel restaurant's revolving glass door, waving goodbye.

She wished I'd been there? I chuckled and sipped the last of my coffee, now lukewarm.

As I said, we are all voyeurs. Ed certainly is. And he'd delighted in every contortion of Vanessa's body as she'd seduced Phil. He'd had a perfect view of every inch of their flesh through the expensive two-way mirror he'd installed in a tiny room adjoining the lounge. He'd gawked, just as he'd done on countless other occasions when Vanessa – a born exhibitionist – had brought her one-night stands back to their home. And he'd watched, of course, with her knowledge and connivance.

But, as he'd ogled Vanessa's gymnastics with Phil, he'd climaxed as he'd never climaxed before. His body had shaken with pleasure as his balls emptied in an orgasm which seemed to go on for ever.

How do I know all this?

I know, because the reason Ed was ejecting such copious jets of sperm was because, at that moment, he was also receiving the blowjob of a lifetime – a blowjob he would never forget!

Going Native
by John McKeown

The couple fell onto the bed tearing at each other's evening dress like the wild animals they were.

The male bit at the female's pearl-strung neck hanging back over the edge of the bed, pulling her shiny black skirt up to her waist at the same time. Her fishnet stocking-clad thighs spread wide. She leaned up, a lipstick-smeared grin on her face as the male tugged at the zip of his trousers. And tugged some more, to no effect. The female pushed his hands away and, giggling, pulled down the zip, reached a hand in and drew out his long, thick, stiff penis.

The audience leaned forward, rapt. Gasps of fascinated repulsion escaping a few of them.

A few laughingly shielded their eyes, others leaned further forward with exaggerated inquisitive irony as the image swung into close-up to show the male pushing his penis past the gauze-thin panties he held aside with one finger, and into the glistening moistness of the female's vagina. She clasped him tightly with her thighs, one stocking bearing a hole revealing an oval of white flesh which, despite the furious pumping action he concentrated on the female, the male's fingers found and tore open. This seemed to redouble the fury with which he rammed himself between her splayed-open legs.

Hera looked at the light from the holo-image playing across the faces of the audience surrounding it. An outraged superiority, a disgust, on some of them, rib-digging hilarity on others, but no echo anywhere of the hot arousal, the envy,

81

the hunger for such direct, brutally joyous physicality anywhere among them.

The female's wild pleadings for more from the red-faced, rampaging male, filled the theatre, and Hera turned away in disgust. Those humans might well be inferior to themselves in many ways, but she still felt like an interloper, an intruder. Animals should be allowed their privacy too!

The female gasped in orgasm, half-hanging off the bed, as the male pumped the last of his semen deep inside her. Then he collapsed onto her.

The image changed then. There was an older male with grey hair on his chest and two blonde females. One female was sucking at his erect penis while he sucked the breasts of the other and played with her vagina and buttocks. Then it changed again and there was a whole group of the humans in various states of undress, locked together in various intricate ways.

The gasps and groans of disbelief from the audience became more uninhibited. Some even left the theatre. Eventually, the image widened, panning out to show the whole of the huge hotel, transparent to their gaze, awrithe with copulating bodies. Hera could take no more and left it to her co-tour guide to take audience questions and requests for closer views of any particular scene.

She drifted dejectedly to the nearest viewing deck and looked out at the majestic blue-green, cloud-whipped planet they'd soon be leaving for the next leg of their safari among the primitive races. Primitive they may be, she thought, but they're alive in a way our frigid civilization has forgotten.

Still almost reeling with her own daring, Hera dropped the few feet from the pod into a dark alley in the centre of the city. She programmed it to return to the same location in 48 Earth hours. But would 48 hours be long enough? Or far too long? She had no idea how she was going to react when she found what she was after, or indeed, if she was able to react at all. Like every other member of her race she'd had her hormone neutralization treatment when a young girl, and though she was genetically and anatomically almost the same as a human woman there was no guarantee that her body would be amenable to intercourse. As she'd heard so many humans say, was she really able to be "turned on" by a man, or, as her curiosity knew few limits, a woman?

But that's what she had jumped ship to find out.

When she left the alley the full force of the night city hit her. Traffic roared, full of humans – *people*, she had to start regarding them as people – hanging out of the windows. A wild medley of neon signs and advertisements assaulted her attention above shops and bars choked with people, mostly black men and women, shaking with loud music. And it was all real, inescapably real, not something that was being watched on a holo image from hundreds of miles out in space.

She began to walk down the street as naturally as possible, but already she could feel astonished eyes, and soon voices, trained upon her. As she walked on, amid a rising cacophony of whistling and baying, she felt hands reaching out to touch and grab. But what were they shouting? She adjusted the tiny translator in her ear.

'Whooo! Man, that is one stun-*tastic* chick!'

'Heyay! She may be white but that is one *badonkadonk* black butt – fo' shizzle!'

'Black, white – fuck the colour, man, I wanna piece of it. Who's in?'

'Me first, bro!'

'Yo' dick won't last a second in her, *jabroni*! We'll leave you the leftovers.'

A gang of black youths was following her. Without slowing her pace or looking round, she turned a corner of the main thoroughfare on to a quieter street. Suddenly they had her surrounded, grinning in a pack, but not daring as yet to get closer.

'Hey, don't you know you rollin' yo' ass in our 'hood? You gotta pay the toll, bitch.'

'I'm sorry, I don't understand. Do you mean some kind of pecuniary remuneration?'

'You bein' funny, bitch?'

'Perhaps, unintentionally, yes. I'm a stranger in town.'

'This ain't gettin' us nowhere, asshats – here!' The biggest of them made a grab for Hera.

Instantly he was dangling three feet off the pavement, with Hera's hand closed around his throat. They fell silent, mouths fell open, most of them backed off down the street, then ran as Hera shook their friend like a rag doll before putting him down.

'I'm sorry, but that's no way to treat a lady.'

As soon as his feet were on concrete he ran off in a rain of incomprehensible expletives. Two youths remained. Very promising material.

'I'm sorry, I don't want to hurt anyone. I'm new in town and I want someone to … to show me the ropes – I mean, I want to have some fun, a lot of fun. Understand?'

'Ropes? Yeah, we understand. Stick with us, er …'

'Hera.'

'Hera today, here tomorrow. Let's go!'

They bought "booze" and picked up a beautiful "chick" in a bar. Hera checked them into a room in a "serious" hotel, quieting the deskman's alarm with a thousand-dollar bill. She'd had the foresight to print off a roll of currency on board before leaving.

Hera had no idea what to do next, but the boys were happy, swigging the bottle of brandy and tossing crushed beer cans into the wastebasket from the bed. The girl eventually dimmed the lights and started dancing slowly and seductively, stripping off her tight clothes as the boys, one on either side of Hera, watched and applauded. The girl had a beautiful body and as she gyrated, fully naked, in

84

increasingly provocative attitudes, Hera began to appreciate the boys' appreciation of her. And then she could see their appreciation, as the "flies" of their pants rose and the unmistakable outlines of their large penises became apparent.

Xavier took his T-shirt off, unfastened the top button of his jeans, and began caressing his groin. Hera could feel her heart beating at an unprecedented, alarming rate. As she watched him watching the girl, his fingers slipping down to his swelling, she started having difficulty catching her breath. She would surely choke!

'Is this what it's like? This fear? It's terrible!'

Tyler turned to her suddenly and gave her a kiss on the cheek. 'No stress, babe, enjoy the show. Drink.'

She took the bottle and nearly did choke on the fiery liquid, but it seemed to ease her.

Tyler took his shirt off too, and Hera felt it would be polite to show some of her flesh also. She pulled her zip down over her breasts. The one in the middle now lay fully exposed, while those on either side were half-visible. The girl screamed. The boys' heads came together above Hera's treble buxomness.

'Looks like we hit gravy tonight, Ty.'

'Hera, would you mind if I just … It's the firs' time I have … ever … ever …'

Xavier's fingers gently pulled the zip the rest of the way down to her thighs, the ultra-soft, superfine material falling aside like cast-off snakeskin.

'A feast for the eyes, and the tongue – if that's cool, Hera?'

'Of course.'

Her breath was coming thick and fast now, her breasts heaving, and she could feel all restraint melting under the alcohol and the hot appreciation of the two young men. But she felt herself almost burst into flame when Xavier's velvet-soft lips closed around the stiffened nipple of the middle breast and began kissing and sucking, while Tyler took the right breast and sucked greedily at its equally hard nipple.

'Room for one more! Get your ass over here, Wanda!'

Wanda, full of trepidation, but fascinated, came over and sat next to Xavier.

'This's some kinda crazy movie, right?'

'Right. And you're up for an Oscar. Now give the lady some pleasure.'

Wanda straddled Hera with an obedient sigh and soon was avidly sucking and biting at the nipple of the vacated middle breast.

Hera closed her eyes. It was as though life was being blown into her from the mouths of these three humans. Her breasts were living things! Churning with life! She squeezed them as the three mouths sucked, devoured. She felt fingers stroking her flesh, which responded with uncontainable tremors, stroking her down to her belly, pushing her suit down her legs to her ankles and stripping it off. She lay completely naked with other creatures for the first time in her life. The fear was still there, but it was overwhelmed by a pleasure that kept steadily mounting.

She felt something tickling the lips of her vagina. She shuddered at this unknown sensation, but the tickling became more intense, and something was parting the lips, entering. She felt her whole body tightly clamping against the intrusion, but then soothing voices conspired to relax her, and she sucked eagerly at the brandy bottle held to her mouth. But she still shuddered as Wanda's tongue licked and probed and pushed ever inward, evoking an increasing sluice of moisture as its flickering movements continued. Hera was startled by a deep groan, a voice she didn't recognise. And then she realised – it was herself! Another, deeper, escaped her, and momentarily she felt like a bystander, a watcher of her own situation. But as the tongue gave way to something far larger harder and thicker, this brief objectivity was swept away in a tidal wave of sweet, gargantuan pleasure tinged with pain as Xavier's penis slid in, opening an unfamiliar depth of space inside her and slowly filling it with itself in one assured, gliding movement.

Hera knelt on all fours on the ruffled hotel bed. Wanda lay beneath, sucking at her triple breasts. Both were shaking as Xavier's muscular body penetrated Hera from behind. Lying flat on the bed, with his head between Xavier's legs, Tyler was assiduously licking Wanda's vagina, exposed to his dexterous tongue between splayed thighs. The contrast between the dark skin of the three humans and Hera's lunar whiteness was startling.

Captain Pythis, watching, though unmoved by the performance, was not blind to the crude aesthetics of the threesome. Callidora, his second-in-command sat next to him, the performance in the holo-image bathing her inscrutable profile.

'I can't believe you let her go, Captain.'

'And why? I'm still in control. I could see it coming anyway. Occasionally, perhaps because of some flaw in the tour company's vetting procedure, someone overly susceptible like Hera gets through.'

'But I don't see how she can do all this, with these ... these *animals*. Even if her desexing programming was inadequate, how could she stoop so low?'

Despite her apparent disgust, Callidora couldn't tear her eyes from the scene before her.

The black girl was holding her arms tight as, flat on the bed, Hera let out a continual groaning interspersed with pleadings as the black man, matted to her buttocks and back, drove himself into her.

Pythis laughed.

'My dear, a penis is a penis, wherever it appears. We have the cursed things too.'

He visualized the shrunken piece of flaccidity flush between his legs. Did it really bear any relation to the huge "pork sword", as he'd heard the humans refer to it, that the other black man toyed with, as he watched his friend's frenzied performance?

'Besides, too much exposure to this stuff –' he gave a dismissive brush at the holo-image '– seems able to overcome any amount of desexing. The sight of human animals and other primitive races "fucking" seems to have a kind of raw power that can stir up long-dormant desires.'

'So why are we endangering ourselves now, Captain?'

'We're in no danger. And besides, I have to check the quality of Hera's performance. I do hope there's more to come.'

'What do you mean, Captain?'

'I mean, Lieutenant, that there's a market for this stuff back home, believe it or not.'

Callidora looked curiously at Pythis before turning back to the screen, to see Hera and her "lover" bouncing off the bed in startlingly perfect unison – the black man cursing, Hera's arms clasping him frantically to her.

'*Sex With Aliens* is one of the company's extra lines – comic-pornography under the guise of "education". It's quite profitable. I'll cut you in for a share, if you like – a Lieutenant's salary isn't much better than a Captain's.'

Callidora, though familiar with Pythis's cynicism, was a little scandalised.

'Unfortunately, though, much of the stuff we sell sooner or later finds its way into the hands of the Radicals who use it to try and get their misguided followers breeding again. They plan to breed an army to overthrow the Authority, can you believe that?'

'But aren't you and the company helping them by selling this stuff?'

'As our sportive humans say, my dear, "A buck is a buck." But don't worry, our holo-tapes are designed to dissolve after just a few viewings. Though, worryingly, the Radicals' scientists are working on a way to override the fail-safe mechanism.'

Hera's groans and gasps, increasing in intensity, filled Pythis's quarters. She was bent double, her posture maximising the last deep thrusts of the black man's penis. Her face – pressed into the sheets, flushed red, the eyes tightly shut – was contorted in what looked to Callidora to be a kind of blissful agony. It finally became insupportable. The male, gripping her firmly around the waist, unleashed his hitherto valiantly withheld semen. Hera, bucking with the force of its release, gave a cry halfway between a curse and gratitude, flailing within his arms in orgasm.

Hours later, after debating with herself on a park bench, Hera returned to the ship. She asked Pythis to assign her different duties and accepted the docking of pay and the more serious bad conduct mark which would stain her otherwise pristine service record. She didn't care much. The old Hera would have cared, the new one – for she was new, transformed from the inside out – was indifferent. She knew there were more important things now. Such as feeling fully alive and fulfilled.

At 80 years of age, Hera was halfway through her life, but the first half had been lived as an automaton, and she was determined the rest of it would not be so wasted. But her brooding on how she could effect her emotional and sexual liberation was interrupted by the news that Callidora brought. Hera was to undergo immediate and full-scale hormonal neutralisation accompanied by cerebral synaptic realignment.

Fortunately for Hera, Pythis trusted Callidora to oversee her treatment. For Callidora, the Captain's holo-porn bootlegging activities, coupled with his treatment of Hera, were the last nail in the coffin of her allegiance to her place in their society's frigid status quo.

'We have to do our bit in the overthrow of the Authority,' she told Hera, both of them floating outside the vast hull of the ship in their vacuum-suits, looking up at the beautiful cloud-swathed planet.

'I can understand that, at one time, our population had to be rigidly controlled in order to preserve our world's resources and ecosystems. But population has been falling now for decades, and even if it rose again, we have the colonies to take the overflow. There's no need for the Authority to continue sterilisation. Who are these bastard old men, these damned gerontocrats, to tell us what we can and can't do with our bodies!'

'But where do we start?' Hera, recognising the North American landmass above her, was hungering for her human friends.

'Here and now.'

'What? Mutiny?'

'No. We have to get Pythis on our side. And then head home and make contact with the Radicals.'

That night, Callidora slid into Pythis's quarters and injected dream nano-serum into his arm. She'd spent the last few hours uploading selections from the Captain's holo-porn banks into the serum which, as she pulled down his sleeve, and crept back to Hera's quarters, would already be taking effect.

'Sweet dreams, Pythis – and sticky ones.'

Something swam across Pythis's unconsciousness. It swam back and stopped. It was female, with flowing, hair-fine filaments waving in the deep current on its head. A large, full-lipped orifice was mouthing some kind of greeting, its urgency accentuated with beckoning hands and lascivious flickerings of its long, curvaceous body, ending in the broad fan of a tail studded with luminosity. It was a fine specimen of the Mergirls of the ocean planet Nepente.

The nipples of her large, oscillating breasts glowed with luminosity too, and below her navel, hung with a necklace of scintillating points of light, her vagina was visible, glowing a hot pink through the semi-opacity of her piscine flesh; for it was mating season.

Her huge eyes shone and the lips almost split the face with a smile of recognition as she sped away, hotly pursued by her chosen mate. The Merman's erect member a third of the length of his long body, curved upwards in a horn shape toward a pointed head which, as the water rushed over it in his pursuit, forced a stream of tiny, glistening bubbles of semen away from its spear-tip.

But would he catch her before the rush of his progress forced his ejaculation? Pythis's consciousness followed. There she was, just ahead, the fan of her tail driving her rapidly upwards.

The Merman followed her up through the lightening water until she broke the surface. A bright golden sun was pouring out of a bright green sky, flooding with iridescence a spit of sand. The Mergirl plopped out of the water and lay down upon it, her vagina beating bright red like a heart, its every shell-like convolution palpitating with expectancy.

The Merman burst through the surface and landed on his back next to the girl. It was an ungainly arrival, but the girl laughed in appreciation and immediately the Merman had broken through the thin hymenal covering of fine scales that shielded the entrance to the girl's vulva and the whole horn was thrust unceremoniously inside. Pythis, close enough to touch, could see it penetrate through the soft, whorling configuration of her vagina, which ingested it in tight rhythmic swallows. Their bodies locked, their tails flapping, they rolled blindly in the rhythm of coitus, back and forth across the wet sand, until they hit the water again, rolling in and rolling out, churning the waves of the shallows into foam.

The thrashing of tails became the swaying of a vast field

of a kind of crimson-coloured plant. Suddenly, a great wave of shadow swept across them, accompanied by the beating of wings, and Pythis's vision was crowded by a host of excited naked arms and long legs borne up by sweeping, diaphanous wings, in whose beatings long strands of multicoloured hair swished, entangled. The stalks were now rigid, the crimson tubular skin drawn back on bulbous empurpled heads glistening in the sunlight. On these the winged females began to settle, after much jostling and argumentation and aerial fussiness. Some of the penile stamens of the sentient plants were too big, some too small for the numberless vulvas whose outfolded lips gleamed with moisture – a moisture manually encouraged by the fingers of the Aerials – which often dripped over a stamen, redoubling it in size and bringing it almost to the point of bursting, before the choosy Aerial flitted blithely on in search of a more commodious fit.

When the Aerials found what they were looking for – guided, seemingly, not just by the stamens' dimensions, but by smell, colour, and other, indefinable factors – they drew up their long, slim, pink or white or brown legs. Then, their vulva lips drawn back to their full extent – pressed back manually in some cases – they sank down upon the chosen head, dextrously controlling its precipitate eagerness with deft and subtle flutters of their wings and limbs. Pierced through, they swayed back and forth as they rode. Sometimes they were unseated, accidentally or by intent, and teasingly remounted the frantically bulging stamens whose network of engirdling arteries visibly throbbed with the surge of fluid.

Soon the air echoed with the resounding orgasmic cries of the Aerials as, one after another, they broke like bubbles under the explosive release of the stamen heads buried deep within their delicate bodies. Satisfied, the Aerials raised themselves off the stamens and fluttered off, leaving them to wilt, though here and there one still stood proudly erect, the parted eye in its head acting as an ear, listening for a fresh wave of wing beats. And on they came, the stamens stood firm again, and Pythis's vision was crowded with arms, scrabbling fingers and toes, and sparkling, dripping juices.

The images changed. A huge, shaggy-haired, leonine tribesman was chasing a supple-limbed, catlike female through a dense jungle. He burst into a clearing. She was nowhere to be seen. Suddenly, she dropped upon his back, her prehensile tail wrapping tightly around him, its tip probing beneath his loose loincloth to draw out his already stiff penis. She swung around, her tail coiling round the shaft. Dropping before him, she pulled it toward her mouth … The image changed again … and again …

Now a dark-skinned female humanoid knelt before a dark-skinned male, pulling his huge penis back and forth. With hand on hip, he pushed it in her mouth, swabbing it within, drawing it out, the female licking and playing her full lips rapidly up and down the thickly engorged shaft. The female turned round to face Pythis, and he could see the phallus angled between her backthrust buttocks and driven into her vagina, with a force which pushed her toward him. A smile broke across her face. Pythis jumped as if hit with electricity. Her fingers had touched him!

'Hold on, Tyler, our guest's awake. Wanna join in the action, Cap?'

Pythis's perception resolved itself. He was tied up on the hotel bed where he'd watched Hera's antics with the earthlings. He looked down at his nakedness. He was there. This was no dream.

The black female had untied him and, keeping a handgun trained upon his head, was grinding her hips against his genital area as he lay back on the bed. Another naked female, this one white, sucked at the black girl's breasts, while the black girl fondled hers in return. Pythis could hear the two black males playing cards in an adjoining room. There was no immediate prospect of escape. Though he felt peculiarly reluctant to make a determined effort.

He was feeling something grow stronger and more pronounced with each lithe grind of the black girl's hips, something he only recalled dimly feeling many years before, when he was a youngster. He tried to drum up real anger against Hera and Callidora for what they'd done. For he knew he'd been injected with nano-serum loaded with the finest holo-images from his bank of alien pornography and handed over to these sex-crazed apes.

The two mutineers were doubtless watching right now, and doubtless recording the proceedings to use against him. Still, he couldn't work up the fury he should be feeling. He could still see the plethora of strange matings from the serum shifting before his eyes, and in the middle of them, the black girl, massaging him with her hips. He could feel a strip of warm moistness. He could feel heat building in his groin, a dead part of his body twitching into life, his heart began picking up speed, the girl, grinning, began to move faster, the white girl began caressing his huge chest, and kissing his mouth, her two white breasts pressing their points into his rapidly sensitizing skin …

Hera couldn't help the surge of envy almost choking her as she watched Wanda's hips grinding into the Captain and the suckings of her breasts by the naked white girl. Her three nipples were tingling and eddies of cellular electricity were swirling round her clitoris, concentrating themselves there. She craved to be touched. How would Callidora react if she took her hand? Suddenly, the holo-image flickered and collapsed.

'What's happened?'

'I think he's on to us,' said Callidora. Found a way to disable the signal. He's a resourceful man, Hera.'

'What do we do?'

'I don't know. Wait … but … what's wrong, Hera? Why are you looking at me like that?'

Hera reached out and gently caressed Callidora's face.

'I'm sorry, I can't help myself. I'm alive and I can't stop it.'

'What's it like, this "alive" feeling?'

'I don't have the words to describe it. I can only show you, Callidora.'

'So, show me.'

Hera kissed Callidora. Her lips were so soft! The skin of her long neck was soft too, and firm, and growing warm. She lay back in the chair and let Hera pull down her zip, her lips escorting its slow progress down over her great compressed mound of firm breasts, releasing them.

The light flashing on Callidora's wrist console alerted her to the fact that Pythis's personal pod had been activated and had left the ship, doubtless to pick him up. But it didn't seem to matter. She lay back and savoured the delicious sensation of Hera's tongue lapping at her moist vaginal lips, her tongue-tip flicking her clitoris, flooding her with waves of vibrant pleasure. Callidora was learning fast, or relearning something innate and ineradicable. Again, her fingers sought Hera's vagina – or "pussy" as Hera preferred to call it – and caressed the moist, unbelievable softness. This elicited groans from her friend and redoubled the urgency with which her tongue licked Callidora's pussy. Callidora lost all sense of time as waves of pleasure bore her and Hera away …

Suddenly, she was startled awake. She patted Hera, who woke too and almost leaped out of the bed. Pythis was standing over them, flanked by two burly, grinning security men.

'I'll deal with this. Back to your stations.'

The men withdrew with lingering backward looks.

'Have you two any idea what I can do to you for what you've done?'

Hera shook her head childishly. Callidora looked round for something to hit him with. Better to go out with a fight.

Pythis pulled the sheet away from their love-stained nakedness. He smiled.

'I'm not a hundred per cent sure myself but I'm going to give it a damn good try.' With that, he undid his belt strip and pulled out a great missile of a penis.

'With your permission, ladies.'

They were both too stunned to say anything as Pythis stripped off and climbed between them.

'We've got a lot to learn. The whole planetful of us. But I've hired some help.' Pythis activated the door lock. Xavier, Tyler, Wanda and the white girl walked in.

'Hera! Babe! The Cap here made us an interstellar offer we just couldn't refuse.'

This is just too good to be happening, Hera thought, watching the humans strip and join them in the bed.

But it must be happening. How, otherwise, was she to account for the overwhelming feeling that someone, somewhere, was watching?

Laundry Day
by Sommer Marsden

The cell phone vibrated in my pocket and I ducked into the copy room, a huge stack of papers clutched to my chest, to peek.

You know what today is. That was the entire message and my stomach felt like it was floating and falling simultaneously as I read it.

Just to draw out the excitement I typed nothing more than *???*. Then I hit send and wandered back down the hall, feeling slightly stunned with anticipation.

I'd known all day what today was, but I hadn't let myself think about it until Clark's text had come across to vibrate and titillate.

The phone went off in my skirt pocket again and this time the motion of it went straight to my already wet pussy. I read it stealthily, shielding my shaking hand with the giant stack of papers I plunked down on my desk.

Don't be coy. Just 7 hours to go. Are you ready?

A small rush of fluid graced the crotch of my panties and I tried my best to keep my hands steady as I answered. *Of course I am. XOXO*

'What're you up to tonight?'

I damn near dropped the phone when I started, giving a little cry. Madeline eyed me suspiciously. 'Sorry,' I said to my cubicle mate.

'You need to cut back on the caffeine, Jade,' she said. She rolled her eyes, but smiled at me.

'Sorry. I was … lost in thought.'

'So, what *are* you doing tonight? Wednesday night, not exactly the hot night of the week.' She dumped some debris from a desk drawer into her waste can. 'I have a date with the end of a good book and a bottle of Riesling.'

'I have …' My tongue was sticking to the roof of my mouth I was so jacked up. My God, why had Clark sent that message? All I had in my mind now were tumbling images of naked bodies and kissing and fucking. 'Chores.'

'Oh, chores!' she sang out. 'Wow. You are a wild one, Jade. What kind of chores?'

'Just … laundry,' I said, my voice semi-hysterical. I sounded so bizarre even to myself that I had to laugh. But the laugh was high and wild and borderline crazy woman.

Madeline levelled a finger at me as her phone rang. 'Seriously, girl, cut the caffeine.'

Then she took her call and I pressed my thighs together tighter to keep them from shaking.

'Are you ready?' Clark asked, pushing me to the wall and kissing me deeply before I could answer.

My whole body reacted to him pinning me there. My whole being fell into that kiss. I parted my lips and let his tongue sweep over mine aggressively as he pushed his already hard cock to the front of me. It was a hot, hard line down the front of my soft silk skirt. Pressing the sodden split of my sex and making my clit thump in time with my pulse.

'I am. You know I am.'

'Chores tonight, love,' he laughed and started to unbutton my raincoat. The day has been grey and somewhat rainy.

'I'm worried. What if it rains too hard for us to see?'

'It won't,' Clark said, spinning me as he peeled my coat off to hang it on the coat tree by the door. 'I promise.' He kissed me once more, pausing to pinch my nipples through my crisp white blouse. My body sang with the bite of pain that was followed by a pleasure chaser. 'The lights in that room are insanely bright.'

I nodded and pushed my breasts into his hands, letting him kiss me once more. We were ravenous for each other come Wednesday nights. Sex was not an issue for us, we had it often and it was good, but Wednesday held a mystical quality. As if something otherworldly happened on Wednesday.

'I know. I know,' I said, pushing my hand down into his black trousers. His cock was still hard – felt harder, in fact, though I knew that was probably my imagination – and I gave it a squeeze. Just to say hi.

'Don't do that, Jade. I might come like a teenager.'

I laughed and let him lead me into the kitchen. He checked the chicken in the oven – his lemon chicken, I could tell by the lovely rosemary-citrus smell – and I checked the small window over our kitchen sink. There it was, as expected, a brightly lit rectangle of glass. The laundry room window for our neighbours across the alley.

Wednesday nights they did laundry and fucked during the first dryer load. Wednesday nights we had dinner and fucked while watching them fuck during the first dryer load. It was a win-win situation. A secret situation, but I liked to think we'd created a beneficial symbiosis. Everyone got fucked and Clark and I had a secret thrill, a naughty Wednesday night tradition that kept the spark alive in the bedroom – or the kitchen, actually.

'See, good to go. No need to worry,' he said, smacking my ass and then at the last second cupping his hand to my bottom and giving me a squeeze.

I sighed before I caught myself.

'Like that?' he murmured against the back of my neck.

The sensation had my nipples pebbling inside my bra and my belly aching low and heavy with a need to be with him. To feel him inside me.

I could only nod.

'Tell me.'

'I like it.'

99

'I need proof.' I heard him chuckle and his hands, warm and familiar, slipped below the waistband of my skirt and then down into my panties. His fingers stretched to find my clit and he pressed and swirled over and over again until my fingers curled to the lip of the sink.

'We're supposed to ... wait,' I managed, though my voice had come down to a growl I was so close to coming.

His teeth found my earlobe, my neck, my shoulder. 'Think of this as an appetiser for you, wife.'

I nodded repeatedly like a deranged bobblehead – I sure as hell felt like one at the moment – and pressed my eager body against his seeking hand. When I came, I bit my lower lip to keep my outburst tamed.

I shuddered against the sink, against his fingers and felt my heart pounding in my temples. 'God, Clark.'

'You can thank me later,' he said and moved from me to wash his hands.

Our dinner was delicious but we barely tasted it because our excitement was so high – barely contained.

At six o'clock the oven timer went off and we went through the house like a well-practised heist team, shutting off lights and drawing all blinds but for the kitchen. In that small darkened room, we stripped bare and stood, holding our breath, near the sink to watch them enter.

I found Clark's cock in the near darkness and wrapped my hand around his heated length. I squeezed him so that he made a noise that always made my cunt wet – made it flex. I swept my thumb over the tip of him, feeling the delicious silken drag of his precome across his glans.

'Here they come,' he said, his voice a little rougher than normal. I imagined it was due to me stroking his cock with exaggerated slowness.

And there they were. Our across-the-way neighbours. The Donaldsons or the Davidsons or ... something like that. All we knew was we joked about them being our Wednesday night fuck buddies.

100

'Oh look,' I sighed as Mr Donaldson/Davidson, just a moment after the Mrs started their first load, swept his wife up and deposited her on the now running washing machine. 'He's starting early this week.'

And he was. He'd dropped to his knees, crouching there between her parted legs. She helped him get her yoga pants off by lifting her hips. Clark pressed hard against the back of me and cupped my mound. Just cupped it. Nothing more, nothing less. But that bit of pressure on my sex had my blood racing.

When the Mrs was bare, our neighbour went ahead and kissed the small amount of down on her mound. Then he pried her legs far apart and I watched, holding my breath, as his tongue darted out to taste her. I moaned and Clark echoed me.

'This is new,' I said.

He nodded, saying nothing else. A few more licks and he was burying his face against her pussy, eating her in earnest as Mrs Donaldson/Davidson clutched the edge of the vibrating washer, her head tossed back, eyes shut in pleasure.

I almost jumped when I felt Clark's tongue press to me. He'd dropped to his knees and insinuated himself between me and the cabinet door beneath our sink. He stayed wedged that way, tasting my nether lips, flicking his tongue against my clit as I watched them. Seeing her pleasure enhanced mine and I found myself shoving my pussy against Clark's eager mouth, not remembering to use my manners at all.

'She's coming,' I breathed, my voice nothing more than a puff of air.

Clark nodded eagerly, sucking my pussy with his demanding mouth, his tongue darting every which way so I was always locked in pleasure but could never anticipate his movements. 'Good, give it to me,' he said and pushed a finger into my sopping cunt.

I gave it to him, pleasure firing off in my body like hot

electric jolts. I came with the heel of my hand shoved to my mouth – my fear always being that the people across the way would hear us somehow and then they'd know our dirty little secret.

'They're doing it, they're doing it,' I babbled, gripping the edge of the sink for dear life. As if the world would fly away and I would fall through the floor should I let it go. He had me so worked up my lips were trembling, my face tingling.

'Kiss me,' Clark said, turning me for just a second away from the light of the window and the couple on show there.

I kissed him. Softly at first and then more roughly as he made demands of me with his hands and his words. 'Lick yourself off my lips,' he said, grinning in the stark splash of light from the window across the way. It painted his face with dots of white and I could see his lips wet with my juices.

I did as he asked, licking his lips and kissing him eagerly as he held my wrists tight in his hands, keeping them down by my side so I couldn't touch him.

When his lips were clean of me and I could smell myself on his skin and mine, I begged. 'Please. Let's …'

He nodded, turned me, planted my hands on the edge of the counter and knocked my legs apart, wide enough to accommodate him.

'I've been waiting for this all week, Jade.'

I nodded, shivering a little in the chill as the rain picked up to a driving staccato outside our window. I could still see them, though, in the silver spotlight of their laundry room overheads. The driving rain was nothing more than falling tinsel on the scene. It didn't hinder at all, if anything it made me feel safer from discovery.

As Mr Donaldson/Davidson parted his wife's pretty pout with his fingers and slid the tip of his cock to her entrance, Clark mimicked him. His fingers on my slit and his cock sliding along my opening had me feeling so weak I locked my knees to keep from falling.

As our neighbour slowly drove into his wife, Clark slid into me. His hands rough on my hips as he held me steady to fill me in a short thrust that rocked me forward on the tips of my toes. His mouth came down – hot and wet – on the back of my neck, forcing all the fine hairs on my skin to stand at attention.

'He's fucking her,' I whispered.

'And I'm fucking you,' he said, licking my skin. I knew that no matter what he was doing back there, he was watching them over my shoulder, getting off on the tableau they offered as surely as I was.

I leaned forward a bit, grinding myself back against him. Clark growled, gripping my hips so tight I felt branded by his touch.

Mr Donaldson/Davidson was slamming into the Mrs. His mouth was moving as he held her steady and fucked her hard. I wished I could hear what he was saying. But I imagined it to be filthy and rude and perfect. I whimpered and Clark said, 'Hold on, hold on. I want you to come with me.'

I could tell our neighbour was about to do his trick. He did it every week and it was one of the reasons we liked to watch what we considered our own little porn movie.

He reached around to touch his wife, his fingers rolling vigorously, but not seen in detail by us, in front of her arching body. No doubt he strummed her clitoris expertly as he fucked her. Her head tossed back, her lips parted in a silent cry. I whimpered again, pushing my own fingers to my clit, sliding my wet digits over my plump clit.

Clark grabbed my hair and wound it around his hand to pull my head back, hold me still, to claim my momentary submission. That made me whimper a third time and then he whispered, as the Mrs across the way was clearly, but silent to us, singing out her orgasm, 'Here it comes.'

I held my breath, my fingers still moving, every driving

thrust of Clark's cock into my aching pussy accenting that moment in time. He'd repeatedly slammed my G-spot with each entry and now I was trembling, perched there on the edge of release.

As his wife continued to shudder and shake, Mr Donaldson/Davidson withdrew and he came, in great arching jets, all over her lower back. Painting her skin with the evidence of his pleasure.

I came too, biting my lip so hard I tasted the coppery tang of blood.

'Jesus,' Clark growled, driving into me once, twice, three more times and then coming with a low groan that sounded like he was dying.

It made me laugh and then he was laughing too, both of us ducking low below the window sill so we couldn't be discovered. He kissed me and I kissed him back.

'Happy laundry night, Jade.' He tweaked my nipple and I jumped.

'We don't do laundry until Saturday,' I teased.

'Hey, their laundry night is way more fun than ours.'

This time I pinched his nipple and he jumped. 'Maybe we need to do something about that. Maybe both laundry nights can be fun.'

'I like the way you think,' he said.

So did I.

Private Performance
by Lucy Felthouse

It wasn't at all surprising that Robyn's hormones were in overdrive. She was watching London's most popular male dance troupe, after all. As well as being incredibly talented, they were also super-sexy. They had rabid fans that followed them everywhere, battling for front-row seats, screaming and waving throughout the show, then dashing outside afterwards, hoping to catch the men leaving so they could beg for autographs and photos. They were as obsessive as the fans of any boy band, maybe more so. Robyn got it, totally, but she wasn't quite in that league. Not outwardly, anyway.

She, too, followed the group everywhere she possibly could, spending her hard-earned cash on the best tickets money could buy. For once, she was glad to be a City banker, meaning she could afford it without having to worry about paying her bills and mortgage.

What made her different, though, was her behaviour post-performance. She didn't head backstage or outside, hoping to see the boys. Instead, she dashed straight home and masturbated herself into blissful oblivion over thoughts of a single member of the group. Sean Rudd. She'd lost count of the number of orgasms she'd had while fantasising about him.

Her feelings for him could definitely be counted as obsessive. Ever since she'd first seen the group – after being dragged along unwillingly by some work friends – she'd been hooked on Sean. She wasn't even sure why. He wasn't the best-looking of the guys, though of course he was far from ugly. There was just something about him, and given that she'd never been that close – no closer than the front row, anyway – to him, let alone spoken to him, she couldn't put her finger on it.

The way he moved was undoubtedly a huge turn-on; she'd always had a thing for men that could dance and, in the absence of Justin Timberlake, Sean took the number one fantasy spot. But then, all five of the troupe could dance brilliantly. And they were all good-looking with great bodies. So why Sean?

The thought bugged Robyn on and off throughout the show. She studied each man in turn, then allowed her gaze to remain on her personal favourite. Their perfectly choreographed moves brought them close to the front of the stage. He caught her eye and winked. She was grateful that the spotlights weren't on her, because she felt an intense heat wash over her face, then zip straight down her body and to her groin. It was then that she got it. The reason that – for her, at least – Sean stood out.

It was all in the attitude. He had raw sex appeal. The other guys, although good, looked as though to them it was just a job. They had no massive love for what they were doing and were probably just trying to earn enough money to get them through university. Sean, however, was a bit older than the others. Perhaps he, too, had started dancing to pay for an education but had discovered he liked it so much that he didn't want to leave. Whatever the reason, Robyn was incredibly glad he was there.

She stared unashamedly at him as he moved around the stage, muscles flexing, bum wiggling, and a big grin on his face. He looked damn good, and he also looked like he was having the time of his life. Provocative steps as part of the routine had the crowd screaming – heaven knows what would happen if the boys took any more clothes off – and Sean loved it. Loved the attention, the adoration. He lapped it all up like a cat with a bowl of the finest cream.

The idea of lapping, and cream, sent Robyn's mind into the gutter. Thoughts of Sean spreading her legs and eating her eager pussy filled her mind to the point that everything else faded away. The screaming women, the thumping music, the electric atmosphere. It was all gone, except for him. She continued to watch him bopping around the stage, getting mildly irritated when any of the other guys got in her way. Soon, though, she had the most perfect view – better than she could ever have hoped for.

He was right in front of her. And just when their routine became particularly sexed-up, too. Robyn thought she'd died and gone to heaven, especially when he started thrusting his hips in her direction. She was vaguely aware of the screams of the women around her growing louder, and, if it was even possible, shriller. She resisted the temptation to cover her ears.

Her mouth grew drier by the second as she watched him. She felt like a starving woman at a buffet as she drank in the sight before her eyes; his grinning face, mischievous blue eyes, sweat-slicked dark hair, delicious torso, smooth but for the slim line of hair running from his belly button and down into the waistband of his tiny shorts. Her gaze didn't go any further than his shorts, however; the bulging crotch in front of her face did a damn good job of keeping her attention. That was until, suddenly, his face was in the area she'd been gawping at. He was crouching down and beckoning to her.

She shook her head; there was no way she wanted to be dragged up onto the stage. It just wasn't her style. But then, it wasn't the group's style, either. She'd certainly never seen them do it before, not even for hen parties. He waved at her again, more urgently this time. After grabbing her glass of wine and taking a large gulp for courage, she slid out of her seat and took a couple of steps forward to the edge of the stage. A security guard watched her from two feet away, clearly making sure she wasn't going to go crazy on Sean and jump on him or something. When she was close enough, he put his fingers on her chin and gently turned her head before whispering something into her ear. Then he gave her a little shove back to her seat so he could get on with his job.

By the time Robyn reached her chair, she was about ready to collapse into it. She could hardly believe what he'd said. Looking at the glasses on the table, she wondered if she might have consumed enough wine that she was drunk and therefore imagining the whole thing. She wasn't – she was still on her first glass and only a little over halfway through it.

So he had said what she thought he'd said – hadn't he? Because she thought he'd asked her to come to his dressing room after the show. She shook her head in disbelief and looked back up to where the show continued. The next time her gaze met Sean's, he winked again and gave her a smile that reached from ear to ear, and then a couple of extra hip thrusts. She gasped. So she hadn't imagined it.

Backstage after the show it was, then. To his dressing room, no less.

Shit.

The rest of the routine passed in a blur of gleaming muscles and flashing lights. As the guys left the stage after their encore, Sean was last. He turned to look at Robyn, gestured towards the door that led backstage and gave her a thumbs-up. He was gone before she could react.

Soon afterwards, the lights came up and people started filing out of the room. The avid fans were hurrying to the back door of the building and the rest, presumably, were going home or heading on to a bar or something. That left Robyn, sitting at the front of the room, all by herself. The security guard that had eyeballed her earlier when Sean gave her the message cleared his throat, startling her.

Giving him a wry smile, she downed the rest of her wine and grabbed her stuff, then forced herself to put one foot in front of the other and go in search of Sean. She felt a lot like a giddy teenager going on her first date, or anticipating her first kiss. Possibly both.

Emerging into a dimly-lit corridor, she made her way down it, looking at each door as she passed. The boys weren't exactly A-listers, so their names were written on pieces of A4 paper stuck to the relevant dressing room doors. Glamorous it was not, but Robyn didn't care. All she was bothered about at that particular moment was the fact she was about to meet the man she'd been lusting over for the past few months. She could hardly believe it, and part of her wanted to turn and run, and not stop until she was back at home with the door locked firmly behind her. Of course, if she did that she'd regret it until her dying day, so she found the door with Sean's name on it, and knocked.

'Come in!'

Pausing to smooth her hair and attempt to stop the tremble in her hands, Robyn opened the door and stepped inside. Sean turned from where he was packing things into a small suitcase and smiled at her. He'd changed out of his stagewear and thrown on tracksuit bottoms and a T-shirt. Presumably, he planned to shower at home, wherever that was. She wondered if she was going to find out.

'Hey,' he said, crossing the room towards her. He pushed the door closed then turned to face her. 'I'm glad you came. I didn't know if you would.'

'Y-yes, I'm here.' Talk about stating the bloody obvious. She needed to suck her nerves up before she made a complete and utter fool of herself in front of Sean.

He laughed softly. 'So, are you going to tell me your name, then?'

'Oh! Sorry, I'm Robyn.' She offered him her hand. He took it but then, instead of shaking it, he pressed a kiss to her knuckles. Robyn giggled girlishly.

'Nice to meet you, Robyn. But now, you must excuse my forwardness. The minibus will be leaving in about 20 minutes. I asked you here because I've noticed that you've been at nearly all of our shows in London and, unless I'm quite mistaken, you've been watching me in particular. Josh and Mike are usually the ones who have the ladies' attention but you don't seem to look at them nearly as much as you look at me. And what I want to know is, *why*?'

Robyn opened her mouth, then closed it again. She wasn't quite sure how to word what she wanted to say without sounding like a crazy stalker. But then, she wasn't the one that hung around outside the stage doors after each show. So maybe she wasn't as stalkerish as the other women. Certainly, Sean wouldn't have invited her back here if he thought she was some kind of threat. Figuring she had nothing to lose, except perhaps a bit of pride, she decided to bite the bullet.

'Er, well, it's because I love to watch you. Dancing, I mean. It's so sexy and it makes me really hot. The other guys are good, of course, but you're just in a whole other league.' She shrugged, as if her words were no big deal.

Sean took a step closer to her, until he was right in her personal space. The scent of fresh sweat and cologne invaded Robyn's nostrils and sent a zing of arousal rushing to her groin. 'So,' he said, 'why don't you wait outside like the other women? They throw themselves at us, feel us up when we agree to have photos taken with them and all sorts.'

Robyn shook her head, then blushed when she realised what she'd have to confess if she were to tell him the truth. She decided to go for it – after all, you only live once. She gave him a tight smile, then forced the words out before she lost her nerve. 'I don't wait outside because I always rush home and, um, touch myself while thinking of you.' She dropped her gaze to the floor, not wanting to see his reaction.

'Touch yourself?' He put his fingers beneath her jaw and lifted her head, forcing her to look at him. 'Touch yourself how?'

Robyn's cheeks flamed. As if it hadn't been bad enough telling him in the first place – now he wanted all the sordid details! She felt like a rabbit in the headlights as he stared at her, waiting for an answer. Her lips appeared to be stuck together. She couldn't open them, never mind get any words to come out.

Then, Sean removed the need for her to speak. He kept her head up, then moved his other hand beneath her skirt and touched her pussy through her underwear. 'Like this?' he said, cupping her mound and pressing the heel of his hand to her clit.

She couldn't nod, because he was still holding her chin. So she – barely – managed to whisper, 'Y-yes.' Then she gasped, because Sean started to rub his palm against her.

'Do you do this, too?'

This time she nodded, because he'd moved his hand from her chin and wrapped his arm around her back, pulling her up against him. Their chests pressed together, and she could feel his breath tickling through her hair. Deftly, he pushed the crotch of her rapidly-dampening thong to one side and touched her bare skin. She groaned, and immediately Sean traced his fingers up and down her slit, not dipping between the folds so much as grazing against her clit. Robyn rolled her hips forward, yearning for him to stroke her nub or to slip his fingers inside her.

He teased her for a little longer, until it appeared that he, too, couldn't wait any more. Manoeuvring his hand so his thumb pressed against the sensitive bundle of nerve endings at the apex of her vulva, he pushed a thick finger inside her saturated channel. Their combined moans filled the space around them, and Robyn grabbed Sean's biceps, purely for something to hold on to.

'Good idea,' he said. 'Hold on tight, babe, because I'm going to make you come.'

With that, he pushed a second finger into her and curved

them so their tips pressed against her G-spot. Gasping, she craned her neck to watch what he was doing. Watch those talented digits as they pleasured her, teased her to orgasm. She couldn't see much, of course, mainly the inside of his wrist, the heel of his hand and part of his thumb. But it was enough. When he moved a little, she saw the shine of liquid on his palm. Her juices. That, coupled with the squishing sounds that were coming from her pussy, helped Robyn to picture a very erotic image, one that grew increasingly vivid as she got closer to a climax.

And she was getting very close indeed. Her thighs stiffened and a tremble ran through her body as the delicious pressure grew in her abdomen. Its intensity increased, making her feel like a balloon – air continuing to pump into her, stretching her, until she was ready to pop.

Tingles combined with the pressure, and she dug her nails into Sean's arms as she teetered on the very edge, continuing to observe the busy hand between her legs. Then, with a flick of his wrist and his thumb, she plummeted over the precipice. The trembles grew into shakes, and she arched her back as the most delicious pleasure overtook her body, then let out a scream, not caring who heard her.

Sean removed his hand and wrapped his other arm around her, pulling her into a hug and pressing a kiss to her head as she came down from her climax. He murmured sweet nothings into her hair and stroked her back; very intimate gestures for such a random encounter. But Robyn didn't care. It was nice. She snuggled into his embrace as she came back to herself, and felt the flames of her arousal building up once more. She was just about to disentangle herself from Sean and drop to her knees in order to repay the favour when a knock came at the door.

With a murmured apology, Sean smoothed her skirt down, rendering her decent, and moved over to the door. He opened it a little, enough to speak to whoever was there without revealing who was in the room with him. A rushed conversation took place, then Sean nodded agreement and dismissed the person he'd been talking to.

Turning to Robyn, he said, 'You coming back to mine, then? There's room in the minibus for a little one.'

Robyn grabbed her bag and raced after him. She'd had a taster of the man she'd been watching for months, now she wanted a full-on private performance.

Showtime
by Alex Jordaine

Carol and Peter Moore decided to rent a villa in the Provençal town of Dauge for their summer vacation. Dauge, steeped in antiquity and charm but at the same time very sophisticated, was a particular favourite of theirs. The place had so much going for it, the couple felt, with its ancient stone buildings and cobbled streets; its shaded squares and fishing piers; its excellent restaurants and buzzy clubs and bars.

Carol and Peter were now halfway through the vacation and their days, each one as brilliantly sunny as the last, had settled into a familiar pattern. They would rise mid-morning and go straight outside to the villa's pool that shimmered invitingly in the clear sunlight. They'd swim a few laps together, their nude bodies, warmly brown from the Mediterranean sun, glistening with rivulets of water.

They'd towel off and, still naked, would seat themselves at a table on the lawn, in a spot shaded from the bright sunshine, and take a light, late breakfast of juice, croissants and coffee. They were completely private in the garden as the neighbouring properties were screened from view by the high wall of the villa.

As they sat together eating, the nearby pool sparkled and rippled and solid beds of flowers presented a bright swathe of colour around the well-kept grass. As they sipped their juice and drank their coffee and munched their pastries, Peter would flick through *Le Monde*, his mastery of written French more than serviceable, while Carol would read a bit more of her doorstopper of a novel.

The couple would then go indoors to complete their ablutions, dress in cool, loose clothes, and go off together to do the tourist bit. Strolling side by side, they visited the resort's museums and art galleries, shopped for gifts, and explored the maze of cobblestone streets and squares.

They would, more often than not, end up at the same restaurant, one they especially liked. It was situated on the town's main thoroughfare and was a short distance from their villa, a mere stroll. They'd take a seat at an outdoor table under a substantial awning, thankful for the shade it afforded at that time of day, and give their order to the friendly waiter when he arrived with the menu. The couple usually had one of the restaurant's superb salads, accompanied by bottled water and a glass or two of rosé.

Then, as the town drowsed lazily in its afternoon torpor under the burning Mediterranean sun, the air heavy and sultry, they'd go back to the villa for a nap. After that, they'd go out for another swim and to soak up some late-afternoon rays, the sun still high in the clear blue sky and reflecting off the ripples of the pool.

Nearing sunset, when the sky was starting to glow pink and the air was becoming slightly cooler, the pair would go indoors. They would shower and dress – he casually, she seductively. Then they would go downstairs to have a light meal as they waited for the sun to go down completely. Waited for the cover of darkness.

And when daylight had finally gone for good to be replaced by the thickness of night, by that darkness they had both been waiting for all day, truth be told, Carol would go her separate way. She would venture out into the warm evening air all on her own, to find a good bar, to find some good wine, to find a sexual partner to bring back with her to the villa.

They never stayed till morning, these one-night stands of hers. That was one of the rules the couple had decided upon, as was their insistence on the man agreeing to wear a condom. One of their other rules was that, while Peter never had anything whatsoever to do with these fleeting guests, he did get to watch what they did with his wife.

What fuelled this strange and obsessive surrogate ritual the pair had got into was the fact that Carol was an insatiable exhibitionist and Peter an equally insatiable voyeur. Her compulsion fired his, and vice versa. That was the way things were between the kinky couple and neither of them tried to fight it. Quite the reverse, in fact – they both revelled in it.

It was a clear night and a full moon was shining in a star-filled sky. The air was slightly cooler than it had been during the day and a light breeze was making the living room curtains move slightly against the French windows.

Peter was looking good. His handsome face was tanned a mahogany brown, as was the rest of him. He was dressed in loose-fitting denim cut-offs, a crisp white T-shirt, and espadrilles. Standing at the bar that was set up near the fireplace, he moved to fix himself a Scotch. He unscrewed the bottle cap and poured out a decent measure into his glass, adding some ice.

He sipped his drink, ice cubes rattling, and thought about his wife. About how radiantly beautiful she was with her lustrous black hair, her high cheekbones, her large, dark eyes, and her wide, sensuous lips. And then there was that incredible body of hers: those full, ripe breasts, those jutting nipples, that narrow waist, those smooth, rounded hips, that hairless mons, those long, shapely legs.

Carol was so drop-dead gorgeous it was enough to blow your mind, Peter said to himself excitedly. And what was that luscious wife of his doing right now? She was out on the prowl, was the answer. She was picking up some hunk to have sex with – that he could watch without the guy even knowing he was there.

Or maybe she'd visit a lesbian club this time, bring back a girl. She didn't do that often, it was true, but it was certainly not unknown. Just think of what Carol had got up to with that horny little redhead she'd brought home with her the other week back in London. His brain began to flood with the memory of what she and the flame-haired young woman had done, what he'd seen them do …

Peter had been in his usual position: standing on his side of the one-way mirror he and Carol had had installed in the room next to their bedroom. He was naked and ready, cock in hand. He was semi-hard and stiffened further within his fist as he watched his wife and the other woman pad into the bedroom. Both of them were barefoot but otherwise still dressed – if you could call it that.

As usual, Carol looked stunning, incredibly sexy. She was wearing a semi-transparent black blouse and a very short, tight skirt, in mauve leather. The other woman appeared to be in her early twenties, petite with short red hair and porcelain-perfect skin. She was clad in a body-hugging and almost obscenely short minidress, bottle-green in colour, which displayed to magnificent effect her slim but shapely figure. She had small, high breasts, her nipples stiff and sticking out against the thin fabric of her dress.

Carol suddenly grabbed the redhead in her arms and kissed her full on the lips. She responded by wrapping her arms around Carol and kissing her right back. *Showtime*, Peter said to himself salaciously, squeezing his cock, which was now rock hard, and beginning to pull it up and down slowly. Its veins pulsed beneath his fingertips as he worked his palm over it, pressing it, teasing it. He brought his hand up to the swelling of its head and back down again, continuing to pleasure himself deftly.

His heart beating faster, he gazed intently as Carol momentarily pulled free, only to grab the other woman's head in her hands. She then pressed her mouth against the

117

redhead's again, kissing her even more passionately. She painted the girl's lips with her tongue, then shoved it inside her open mouth, quick and tight. The two women kissed voraciously as Peter began to masturbate more vigorously. He pushed his fist up and down in a regular rhythm, all the while feasting his voyeuristic eyes on the developing action on the other side of the glass.

Carol finally broke the kiss to lick her way up and down the girl's slender neck, her tongue travelling all over her throat. The redhead responded by slowly removing Carol's blouse to reveal her big breasts with their erect nipples. She wasted no time in going to work on those beautiful orbs, fondling them with her soft hands and teasing their swollen nipples with her tongue until they were stone-hard. Carol then unfastened her tiny leather skirt, beneath which she wore no panties, and shimmied out of it. At the same time, the redheaded girl pulled off her own micro-minidress and the flimsy G-string she'd had on under it.

Peter felt a thrill run through his body like an electric current as, continuing to masturbate hard, he pressed his face to the glass and viewed the thrilling scenario unfolding before his eyes. He jacked away at his erection, stroking and pulling, as Carol and the redhead, both now gloriously naked, climbed onto the bed. They kissed some more, the redhead on her back, Carol on top of her, their breasts pushed heatedly together.

Then Carol moved down the bed and fastened her bright lips to the girl's pussy, drinking her thirstily. The redhead bucked and tried to move her sex more rapidly against the regular licking. She jerked her hips forward again and again towards the point of Carol's tongue as the dark-haired woman continued to draw it slickly against the dewy folds of her sex-lips. Carol then turned round and positioned herself so that she and the other girl's thighs were scissored together, their wet pussies rubbing up against each other excitingly.

Peter stood back from the glass a little, his breathing heavy, his eyes bright and feverish with lust. Extremely aroused now, he felt as if all the blood in his body had rushed to his cock. It had become ragingly erect and was throbbing furiously within his pumping fist, its glans glistening with drops of precome. He stroked his swollen shaft even more forcefully, staring intently as Carol and the redhead ground their gleaming-wet slits together, their naked bodies entwined. The other girl trembled in delight, her milky-white thighs quivering, as Carol desperately fucked her with her pussy.

Then it happened. Carol's undulating body suddenly shook with orgasmic tremors, as the hot pussy friction built to boiling point and beyond. At the same time the redhead trembled, losing all control as she too was consumed by erotic ecstasy. That brought Peter to the boil as well and, breathing more heavily than ever and jerking frenziedly at his throbbing erection, he came to a climax so powerful that he coated the glass of the one-way mirror with spurt after spurt of creamy come.

Hell no, Peter said to himself with a shiver of excitement, Carol certainly wasn't averse to a bit of girl-on-girl action from time to time. Nor girl-boy-girl action or boy-girl-boy action, for that matter. Admittedly, it was usually lone guys and the occasional lone girl she brought home for sex, but she wasn't totally into one-on-one by any means. Some of her threesomes had been out of this world.

Peter refreshed his drink at the bar, then sat down in a nearby leather armchair. Taking a sip from his Scotch, he let his mind wander again. He recalled another of Carol's assignations back home in their house in London.

Leslie had been the name of the statuesque beauty with shoulder-length blonde hair, he remembered Carol telling him after the event. And she'd been one half of an exceptionally attractive young married couple that his wife had hooked up with at a singles bar. Alan had been the husband's name, she'd also told him afterwards.

In her experience, Carol had said, you'd sometimes get couples like Alan and Leslie at singles bars: couples on the lookout for someone to prove that two's company and three's ... a threesome.

Peter looked across a space inside his head and started to remember what he'd watched his wife getting up to with Alan and Leslie on the other side of the one-way mirror. The images behind his eyes became more vivid as he pursued the memory further, driving his mind into an almost cinematic recollection of what had occurred.

The three of them had been naked on the bed. Alan, well built and good looking with short, dark brown hair, was lying on his back between the two women, his thick cock engorged and pulsing. He leaned over to kiss his wife but she cupped his face and turned him towards Carol. As Alan kissed Carol's mouth hard, Leslie slipped sinuously down the bed and between his legs. She then took his throbbing shaft inside her mouth and began working her lips and tongue over it greedily.

With his wife's mouth bobbing up and down on his stiff shaft, silvery precome trickling from the corners of her lips, Alan's own lips continued to engage firmly with Carol's. Then Leslie slid her mouth from Alan's cock and slithered back up the bed. He in turn stopped kissing Carol and trailed his mouth down her shapely body. She spread her legs around his wide shoulders as he nuzzled her pussy and began to dart his tongue over her slippery clit – flick-flick-flick. She responded enthusiastically, squirming over his lips and pressing her quivering thighs against his cheeks as he carried on kissing and tonguing her sex energetically.

From his vantage point behind the mirror, Peter, naked and stiffly erect within his own pistoning hand, saw Carol glance at Leslie who was herself gazing at what her husband was doing. Leslie was clearly intensely excited. Arousal shone in her eyes and her cheeks were flushed. As she watched Alan continue to lap insatiably at Carol's wet pussy, his face now covered in her love-juice, Leslie began to pleasure herself with a vengeance.

Her fingers were like ramming rods as she slid them in and out of her vagina, rubbing herself all wet and sticky. She continued to masturbate feverishly until her palm and wrist were soaked. Before long, she tensed and clamped her thighs around her hand as she climaxed ecstatically.

Once Leslie had come down from her orgasmic high and removed her fingers from her sodden pussy, she turned towards Carol and smiled wickedly at her. Then she kissed her softly on the mouth. This gentle contact, combined with Alan's lips and tongue as they continued working tirelessly on her sex, caused Carol to tremble.

In due course, the couple paused, and Alan put on a condom. Then he was above Carol, driving his forceful penis into her sex, his rhythm strong and fast. Over and over, he thrust into her slippery wetness, filling her as his body pinned her to the bed. Leslie was watching them again, and masturbating hard again too, her fingers working violently between her own labia.

Peter was also lost in self-pleasure, as he watched the show. His heart was beating like a drum, his breathing was laboured, and his cock was a stiff, burning pole against his palm, hot from its friction.

All the while, Carol and Alan continued to fuck like crazy, she now rocking her hips up to meet his thrusts. Her body trembled against his as he increased the pace more and more, thrusting in and out in a furious rhythm. Then he climaxed. And so did she. And so did Leslie, shuddering in unrestrained release.

And as that stunning threesome reached its tumultuous crescendo, so too did Peter, the desire that coursed through him having built, by now, to fever pitch. Out-of-control spasms began to shake his body as he coaxed his raging-hard cock to a climax. Squirts of warm semen leaped out of his shaft and spilled in pools on the shiny hardwood floor beneath him.

Peter was still all alone in the villa although he knew that wouldn't be the case for much longer. He would be watching and wanking again very soon; he would be the complete voyeur. At the moment, however, he was listening, and very intently too, from the open door of the unlit bedroom on the first floor.

There was not long to wait now, he was sure of it, and he was right. Peter could feel the excitement shivering through his body as he heard the rattle of a key being worked in the front door, followed by the creak of that door opening and then an emphatic bang as it was shut. *Honey, I'm home!*

His pulse beat faster as he heard the click of Carol's stiletto heels and the echo of male footsteps on the marble floor downstairs. Soon, soon. He heard the drinks cabinet behind the bar being opened. Indeed, you could have heard a pin drop at this time of night. As always, he'd have to make sure to be exceptionally quiet himself.

'Vodka?' he heard Carol say. There was perhaps a nodded assent from her companion, Peter surmised. Vodka had presumably been the man's drink of choice in whichever busy club or bar Carol had picked him up in. He heard the metallic twist of a bottle top and the splash of liquid in a glass followed by the clink of ice cubes.

Now Carol's voice again. 'Enjoy your drink, Pierre,' she said huskily. 'I'm going for a skinny dip.'

'OK,' the man said. The reply sounded deceptively flat. Peter could only imagine what lubricious thoughts must be racing through his French namesake's mind.

Such thoughts were certainly racing through his own head. Peter was naked and already fully aroused, blood pumping into his erection. He felt his cock harden even further as he moved gingerly through the inky blackness

122

towards the bedroom window, which was wide open. He leaned against the wall at its side, taking the weight of his body on his left arm and his stiff cock into his right hand.

He looked down at the pool, illuminated first by its side-lights and then by the main external lights as Carol switched them on. Peter saw a breeze ruffle the still water, and then he only had eyes for his wife. His mouth was dry with excitement as he watched Carol, naked as nature intended, stride towards the pool, pausing only to place a towel and, he knew from experience, a pack of condoms on a sun lounger. He admired anew the seductive sway of her hips and the way her calves tapered to her slender ankles; watched as she walked, barefoot and bare-arsed, to the shallow end. Peter's pulse beat faster still at the sight of her. He could feel it in his cheek, in his nose, in his eyes … in the veins of his rigid, straining cock.

Peter watched Carol sit by the edge of the pool for a moment, watched her step into the rippling water and then begin swimming on her back. He watched as she kicked her feet and let her hands propel her body slowly along the pool to the deep end. He watched her turn again and, lifting her arms, swim back to the shallow end. He looked admiringly at her lovely face and beautiful breasts and shaven mons. She wants me to see everything, he thought. He watched her turn once more before standing up. He looked at the way her hair dropped down like shiny black satin when she did this. He watched as she stepped, graceful as a nymph, out of the pool.

He watched her wring the excess water from her hair and bend down to pick up a towel from one of the sun loungers. He watched her fluff her hair with the towel then use it to dry her body too, rubbing at the back of her neck, under her arms and along her legs.

Peter was looking down at Carol but she, his nymph, his nymphomaniac, was not looking up at him. She would not have been able to see him in that darkened bedroom even if she'd tried. No, she was looking at her companion, this Pierre guy, who had come to join her now in the pool area. He was, Peter noted, tall, dark, well-built and good- looking, just the way his wife liked them. He could also not fail to notice that the man was buck naked and displaying an impressive hard-on – just the way she liked them too. Pierre had evidently taken a leaf out of Carol's book and had shed his clothes before coming outside.

Peter watched as that darkly handsome man took a step towards his wife, watched as he held her in his muscular arms, in a powerful embrace, her full breasts flattened against his chest. She lifted her face to his and Pierre began kissing her on the mouth, holding her even more tightly to him. Peter watched this too. He could only watch, watch as Carol took control now, watch as she got hold of Pierre's right hand and pushed it between her legs, watch as he masturbated her. He watched too as his namesake took one of her engorged nipples first between the thumb and forefinger of his left hand and then into his mouth as he rubbed her harder and harder with his other hand, working it all over her hot pussy.

Peter watched and was further inflamed, pure lust burning behind his eyes, as Carol dragged herself away from Pierre and moved over to the sun lounger. 'I want you to fuck me now,' he heard her say. She then lay back, splaying her legs wantonly wide. The Frenchman slipped a condom on to his cock with practised ease then moved on top of her. He pushed himself inside as she arched her back and wrapped her thighs around him.

While he thrust his shaft rhythmically in and out, Carol held him tightly and looked over his shoulder and … yes, she did look upwards then. She looked up into the dark, right into what she knew would be her husband's line of sight. And he knew that she knew just what he was doing, knew that he was watching, watching it all and pumping his cock frenziedly in his hand as he did so.

Trembling, Peter felt the waves of his sexual excitement rise ever higher at what he was watching and wanking over. He pulled furiously at his erection as he watched his exhibitionist wife being fucked ever more energetically by this stranger while she in turn looked, or appeared to look, straight back at him, her voyeuristic husband.

And that voyeuristic husband was now in a state of the most intense sexual arousal. His tongue flicked lasciviously in his mouth, his heart beat wildly, and his hard cock flexed and throbbed within his pounding fist, ejecting spurts of precome from its tip. Peter felt giddy with desire, light-headed with his own aching, burning need for release. He could feel the determined thrust of his own imminent eruption. He was on the verge of ejaculating, right on the very brink. But don't let that happen yet, he told himself urgently – please, not yet.

He stilled his hand, wanting to hold back his orgasm before it was too late. But then it was too late. He watched Carol climax, heard her animal-like moan carry into the night, joined almost at once by the strangled cry of her companion – and joined almost at once, too, by his own stifled gasps. Peter closed his eyes and convulsions shook his body as warm, liquid seed burst from his shaft.

Peter made his way quietly to bed and, soon after that, he felt Carol slip in beside him. She brought with her an aroma of chlorine and sex.

Pierre had been sent on his way, of course. Like they all were. Carol always made it clear that this was going to be a once-only experience. That was the deal, take it or leave it. Pierre, like all the others before him, had taken it.

'You awake, darling?' Carol asked softly.

'Uh-huh.'

Carol cuddled into him, her body warm. 'How did you enjoy the show tonight?' she asked.

'It was fantastic,' he replied. '*You* were fantastic.'

'How do you feel now?'

'Thoroughly sated,' Peter replied with a yawn.

'Me too – at least for now,' Carol said, letting out a throaty chuckle. 'But tomorrow is another day.'

Escape at *Erotica*
by Philippa Blaise

To be honest, I was feeling a bit miffed. There was nothing wrong with the authors' panel, in fact it was going really well. The chair was doing a splendid job and my fellow writers were as charming and witty as ever. It was just that old comment that always seemed to crop up, about us looking so "normal" and being ordinary women who write very sexy stories. We slip on our pseudonyms and escape the daily grind – husbands, kids and work – by plunging into a different, sexier world.

The thing was, I had a secret, known to only a few of my closest female friends. I longed to act out the sexual fantasies I wrote about and today I planned to do it. Here at *Erotica* I was going to live out my dreams.

Erotica is *the* exhibition for all things erotic. Everything was here from anal plugs to yoni massage. There are trade stands, workshops, displays and thousands of kinky people dressing up to enjoy themselves and each other.

I had taken on the persona of my alter ego, "Bella Javeria", becoming her for this one special day. I was here to have some serious sexy fun, but no one seemed to have noticed! The day was passing pleasantly enough but, sadly, without any passion. Maybe it was my outfit. A little – as in extremely short – black dress and four-inch heels just couldn't compete with the array of leather, latex and lace on display.

Losing concentration, I surveyed the audience – and spotted him immediately. He was slim, fit in every sense of the word, and he was staring at me. Glancing down, I realised my dress had ridden up to expose my suspenders, the tops of my black stockings and a band of white thigh above each one. Instinctively, I moved to pull my hem back into place but instead, remembering why I was here, I wiggled in my chair to give him a flash of my bright red knickers. His smile and the bulge that appeared in his tight black jeans showed that he appreciated the display. He glanced up and our eyes met. He held my gaze and grinned. Things were looking up!

As soon as the session ended, I made a bee line for him. I wasn't going to risk letting him get away. But there was no need to worry – he greeted me like an old friend. He kissed my cheek and hugged me and then, leaving his hands resting on my hips, he said, 'Hello, darling! You look wonderful.'

I stammered, 'Thanks, er …'

'Phil. Call me Phil.'

His voice was rich and deep, and now I was sure we hadn't met before. I would never have forgotten that voice.

'I'm so pleased to meet you at last – I love your work. You've given me so such pleasure I feel I know you intimately already.' I couldn't help but notice a slight emphasis on the "intimately".

'Er … that's good,' I replied weakly.

He grinned. 'You can tell a great deal about a writer from her work, especially an author of erotica. It is true you write your own deepest desires?'

I wasn't sure if this was a statement or a question but I nodded in agreement.

Phil gripped me tighter, his hands sliding down to touch my bottom. He pulled me even closer and said softly, 'I know why you're here, *Bella*.' He emphasised the name, my sex writer's pseudonym, saying it as though it were a magic word, using it like a key. And then, without warning, he kissed me.

After a moment's resistance, I found myself returning the

kiss. I wrapped my arms around his neck, drawing him close. Fortunately, my fellow authors and most of the audience had left the room. The last few stragglers were queuing by the door, waiting to leave.

Phil looked thoughtfully at me. 'So, let's see, what do you like again? Oh yes, illicit love. Sex when you know you shouldn't. Well, that's why you're here, isn't it? Exhibitionism, we're in a great place for that. And mild sub fem – you like that too, don't you? Yes, that will do for a start.' Then, with a hard edge in his voice, he said, 'Take your knickers off.'

I gulped. 'What?'

'Take your knickers off. They'll get in the way.'

I looked around doubtfully; this was a very public room. 'But I can't – not here.'

'Come on, take them off. The next session starts soon – we've got about five minutes before the crowd for that one starts to gather. You'd better do it now before they arrive, unless you *really* want an audience.'

Why, oh why had I worn stockings and put my knickers on before attaching the suspenders? Mercifully, the stragglers soon left and we were alone. I pulled up my dress and began undoing the straps. Phil watched, savouring the glimpses of my thighs. I had intended to finish the task as quickly as possible, aware that someone was likely to come in at any moment, but my Bella persona was in control and she couldn't resist teasing.

She took her time, slowly unclipping the suspenders then easing the knickers down. She deliberately showed my pubes – or, rather, the bare skin where they had once been – as I stepped out of my panties. I had shaved them especially for today. Defiantly, I handed the knickers to Phil. He put them in his breast pocket and arranged the flimsy silk like a handkerchief. Anyone looking closely would see what they were.

'Good,' said Phil. 'Better fasten your stockings again.'

I had forgotten the suspenders. I started to do them up, hitching up my dress to reveal my nakedness ... just as the doors opened and the crowd burst in for the next session. Blushing as scarlet as the knickers in Phil's pocket, I hurriedly finished and pulled the dress down to cover myself. Chuckling, Phil took my hand and led me out to the main hall. 'Time for us to go – it's a dominatrix workshop in here next. Not your scene at all.'

Looking round the great hall bustling with people, I wondered how Phil was planning to ... actually, what exactly *was* he planning to do? This may have been *Erotica* but full nudity and public sex were forbidden and, even as Bella, I was unsure I'd be able to handle doing something like that in front of so many people.

Phil led me through the hall, guiding me by holding one of my bum cheeks, pinching it just enough to make it tingle. Then, frowning as though puzzled, he said, 'I have to make a few arrangements. Where can I leave you? I don't want you wandering off and getting into mischief ... Ah, I know!'

He guided me to one side of the hall where a whole section was devoted to bondage gear. All types of restraints, whipping chairs, stocks and locks, bars and chains were on display. Phil paused, inspecting the equipment. I shuddered. Was he going to put me in one of those things? I didn't fancy it at all – far too uncomfortable and a bit too far beyond "mild sub" for my liking.

With a sudden squeeze of my buttock, Phil moved me on to a display of giant beds, all fitted with wrist and ankle restraints. 'Just the thing,' he said. 'You can test one of these while I make the arrangements.'

Before I could protest, I was laid on a bed and Phil was fitting the loops round my wrists. The restraints had been set up especially for this display. They were loose and had long straps arranged so casual visitors could play at bondage. I could manage this. It only took Phil a few moments to arrange the straps; he must have done this before. When I was neatly tied up, Phil said he would be gone for ten minutes and warned me not to move.

In theory, I was helpless, spread-eagled on the bed in full view of the crowd. Actually, the straps were so long I could move around and my legs weren't spread apart. Just as well with my knickers in Phil's pocket.

I settled back, enjoying the huge bed and the attention I was beginning to receive. People were stopping to watch me. It was pleasant to be looked at, admired and desired. I was getting turned on. Well, OK, I had been turned on already. The excitement of Phil's commanding presence and his hand kneading my bum had begun to arouse me. My nipples were hardening, my clitoris was beginning to tingle and my vagina was getting moist. If I'd had any panties on, they would have been getting damp.

I wanted to touch myself or to be touched. I imagined Phil's hands on my breasts, pinching my nipples, squeezing, moving down my belly, a finger teasing my clit. My thighs and dress were wet now. I reached down to stroke my pussy. Damn! The straps weren't long enough. I couldn't reach.

Remembering where I was, I looked up. Thank goodness the crowd had thinned. Only two people were still watching me, an older couple wearing rubber body suits. I guess I was making Mrs Rubber hot. She had surreptitiously put her hand on Mr Rubber's groin and was giving him a quick, secret stroke.

The temptation was too great to resist. I spread my legs wide, giving them both a good view of my naked and shaved cunt. It had an immediate effect on Mrs – her hand clenched, squeezing Mr's balls. He squealed in pain and tottered off clutching his groin. Mrs Rubber took another look at my pussy before following him.

Phil returned a few moments later. Thank goodness! By now I, or rather my clitoris, was in urgent need of attention. Phil looked very smug. 'All fixed!' he said breezily. 'Now let's get you out of there and find something interesting to do.'

He took me to a stairway leading to the gallery that surrounded and overlooked the main hall. Giving my bottom a slap, he sent me up the stairs first, allowing him to look up my dress. Well, I'd give him a show if he wanted one! Halfway up, I stopped suddenly and bent over as though adjusting my shoe. I thrust my butt out so my dress rode up. I had timed it perfectly. Phil's nose bumped into my naked derrière. However, he wasn't fazed by my blatant display – he blew on my bare bottom! The sharp stream of cold air passed down my bum then over my pussy and clit, inflaming my desire. Phil took my arm and guided me quickly to the top of the stairs.

A barrier of wrought iron topped with a wooden rail surrounded the gallery at just over waist height. I could look over it into the hall but anyone glancing up would only see my upper body. Two narrow marquees had been set up along the barrier on one wing of the gallery. In one, a lecture about London's fetish scene was taking place but Phil led me into the other, which was empty. I looked around in panic. We couldn't do anything here ... could we? The canvas walls were practically transparent and the entrance opened directly onto the balcony.

On the far side of the marquee, one of the joins between the sheets of canvas had been unfastened and Phil pushed me through the opening, into a narrow gap between the marquee and the barrier. It was just wide enough to allow me to stand and look down into the hall. Unless someone came into the marquee, we could not be seen from the gallery. My heart pounding, I wondered what Phil intended to do in this hidden but very public space.

Something that looked like a microphone had been clamped to the balustrade. Phil squeezed through the gap behind me – it was a very tight fit. He pressed me against the rail, manoeuvring me directly in front of the microphone. It had been arranged so it was level with my crotch. Its head was a soft ball the size of my fist and Phil stood behind me, forcing me tight against it. I could feel his cock through his jeans – it was erect and hard against my buttocks. He kissed my neck on the sensitive spot behind my ear, sending a wave of pleasure rippling down my body. His hand cupped one breast and squeezed the soft flesh. He found and pinched the nipple through my dress, sending another wave through me.

Phil's other hand rested on my belly, holding a small box. He pressed a button and the "microphone" hummed and buzzed, throbbing against my groin. It was some kind of vibrator! Phil pressed me down harder, his hips pushing me so my clitoris touched the head of it through my dress. The simulation was intense, such a fierce sensation that I instinctively jerked myself away from it. Then I writhed to move myself back into contact with the lovely torment.

Phil slid his hands down my body and grasped the hem of my dress. He eased the front up, slipping the material out from between the vibrator and my hairless pussy. His fingers moved back, sliding down my thighs and massaged the juice that was seeping from my cunt over my labia. Easing the lips apart, he manoeuvred my vulva directly onto the vibrator.

All this time I could feel his cock, rigid, straining in his jeans and pressing against my bottom. I wanted it inside me. I imagined reaching back, undoing Phil's trousers and guiding him into me. Then I couldn't think at all. My clit was responding to the devastating stimulation. Pulsing with each vibration, the little bud expanded. I felt it growing bigger, filling up like a balloon. The insistent waves of pleasure radiating from my clitoris drove every other thought from my mind. I couldn't feel anything else.

The throbbing pleasure was building quickly, flowing into every part of me, filling my body more and more, the pressure building. Faster and faster, wave upon wave of energy. Searing-hot pleasure flowed from my clit. Every part of my body tingled, expanded, sensitised. The pressure became so intense I thought I would burst. I arched back, rigid with tension. I couldn't breathe. There was a moment of pure ecstasy that seemed to stretch out forever. Then came a shuddering release. My body convulsed with the sheer power of my orgasm. My stomach contracted violently, over and again. My hands clasped the rail in a vicelike grip. I groaned and sank to my knees, barely conscious.

I was still groggy as Phil took me to the nearest bar and he had to hold me upright until I was able to lurch to a seat. He looked shocked; the intensity and speed of my climax had surprised him as much as it had me, and his confidence and control were now replaced by concern. My head cleared quickly but my legs were still wobbly and my clit was throbbing. After a drink I felt better, though. In fact, I felt great – content but still aroused and so alive.

When Phil saw that I had recovered, he said, 'Well, that wasn't *exactly* the effect I thought I'd have on you – do you always do that?'

I was amused by Phil's consternation and touched by how worried he seemed. I do have great orgasms, both from fucking my hubby and from my toys (I wondered where I could get a "microphone" vibrator to add to my collection!) but nothing like the orgasmic tsunami that had just engulfed me. I didn't see any reason to tell Phil, though. I would just let him wonder. I smiled to myself, enjoying the shift in the balance of power.

After a moment, he gathered his wits and asked if I wanted to continue our game.

Oh, I did! What else had he arranged? Playing it cool, I just said I was fine now and what did he fancy next?

The look of relief on his face was so sweet but seeing that I was OK restored some of his cockiness. With his voice taking on an amused, slightly imperious tone, he said, 'Let's see. What else does Bella enjoy? Doesn't she do fem on fem?'

Well, I certainly have written some very sexy girl-girl stories. In fact, I've won awards for them. But in real life, my lesbian experience was limited to chaste schoolgirl crushes and one disastrous experiment at Uni.

Phil, sensing my apprehension, took the lead again. 'Are you fit?' he asked breezily.

I nodded and he took my hand and led me back into the main hall, to a corner where performers from The House of Burlesque were displaying their skills. Two pretty girls in vintage corsets shimmied and twirled.

Phil paused, watching them thoughtfully. Then, smiling, he said, 'No ... these burlesque cuties are far too sweet for a horny little slut like you.' Somehow he made "slut" sound like a delicious compliment.

He led me into the next aisle where an excited crowd of men had gathered. It was a film company's trade stall. Rack upon rack of hardcore porn was on display. The crowd was watching two girls dressed in lacy underwear. They were sitting astride a blow-up couch, rubbing their crotches together through their flimsy panties. Another woman was encouraging them. She jumped on the couch, bouncing the girls around.

Not hardcore porn! My mind rebelled. Enormous dicks and unimaginative, uncomfortable, joyless humping were not my scene at all. I wasn't going to play this time. Phil had screwed up!

I tried to move away but Phil directed my gaze to another girl at the back of the stand, slender and very pretty. She wore a cream-coloured basque and thong, white lace hold-up stockings and white stilettos and *damn*, her skin was so fair and flawless – the "alabaster complexion" I'd thought only existed in fiction. A short platinum-blonde bob framed her sweet face. Her lips were the palest shade of shocking pink.

She looked up, saw Phil and smiled. As she came

towards us, I saw her boobs were uncovered. She had small, pert breasts. Her nipples were tiny, exactly the same shade of pink as her lips. The hard little buds were sticking out, prominently visible against the whiteness of her skin. She looked fragile, pale and beautiful, like an icing sugar fairy. Demure, yet sexy as hell.

She kissed Phil's cheek then turned to me said, 'You must be Bella. I'm thrilled to meet you. I've read all your books, I adore your work. I do hope you'll like mine.'

Her voice shocked me. She had a cultured Edinburgh accent, the kind of posh Scots that oozes respectability and reliability. It was completely at odds with the girl's occupation. Phil introduced her as Serena, internationally acclaimed adult entertainment star. Serena, her voice sending shivers down my spine, linked her arm in mine, and she and Phil led me away.

Our destination was a luxury lingerie stall. Gorgeous confections in silk and lace were tastefully displayed, but I had no time to admire them. The proprietor, a handsome woman wearing some of her own luscious creations, handed Phil two large carrier bags. She gave me an appreciative glance and indicated one of the changing cubicles. Serena bustled me into the small canvas booth, followed by Phil and the bags. This was going to be another tight squeeze! Although it was quite pleasant to be sandwiched between Serena and Phil, I didn't see how this would work. We couldn't move. Then Serena undid a tie on the canvas wall of the cubicle and it folded open, revealing a small space. This was formed by the changing rooms and the back of the stands in the next aisle – our own tiny playground hidden in the middle of the exhibition. It wasn't big enough to lie down in, but there was room for three to stand comfortably.

Phil said, 'We're going to change you. It's time to reveal your true nature … Of course, the magic won't work if you watch.' He pulled a thick velvet blindfold from one of the bags and moved behind me.

Serena told him to wait and she kissed me.

She held my chin, tilting my head slightly, then her mouth brushed mine. The tip of her tongue tentatively found the gap between my lips and probed gently. Sighing, I parted them, allowing her tongue to slide in, seeking my own, touching and teasing it. She tasted honey-sweet. Suddenly, I was kissing her back. My lips pressed tightly against her mouth. My tongue sought hers, twining round and pushing into her. I embraced her slender body, pulling her to me and kissing her harder. Our bodies and mouths locked together … Then, gently, Serena withdrew, smiling but holding us apart now.

I longed for her. My nipples were engorged, sensitive against my clothing, my vagina wet, and my clitoris, already aching, swelled more. I felt the soft brush of fabric on my head and the blindfold covered my eyes. Then two kisses on my neck and Phil was right behind me – the touch of his hard cock against my bottom now familiar.

Serena kissed my mouth again and I heard and felt the zip on my dress being pulled down. The straps were eased off my shoulders and the garment slid down my body to the floor. The kiss went on. Now I was in a dreamlike state, the darkness enhancing my senses. The sounds of rustling cloth and skin brushing skin, the smell of Serena's perfume, of Phil's body, the musky smell from the juices oozing from my pussy, all combined to make me dizzy. My bra was unfastened and slipped off. My breasts were held. Phil's hands cupped them, squeezing gently.

Serena's mouth found my right nipple, her tongue circling and then flicking the sensitive bud. Her lips closed around it, toying with it. Then she sucked hard, pulling it fully into her mouth, pinching and stretching it and teasing it with her tongue. She moved to the other nipple, her mouth working the same magic. As Phil's hands moved down, unfastening my stockings and suspender belt, Serena's wonderful tongue moved to my belly, playing with my navel, tickling. My tits, the nipples standing out stiff and hard, tingled as the air dried Serena's kisses.

My suspender belt was removed and I felt Phil's hands brush my pussy as he rolled down a stocking. My cunt was soaking, the slippery fluid tricking down my thighs, touched again as Phil removed the other stocking. Then he was behind me again, holding me, caressing my breasts and stomach. He pulled me into his body, his jeans-clad shaft rigid and straining against my backside. Cunt throbbing, aching, I yearned to feel him inside me.

I convulsed as something flicked my clit, flicked it again and again. Serena's magic tongue began licking the swollen bud, circling it as she had my nipples, sucking it, throbbing, into her mouth. Phil held my naked, shaking body, toying with my breasts, rubbing my belly and pressing his cock against my bottom. I felt the tension grow again, building swiftly. The concentration on my clit was becoming unbearable, my orgasm approaching too quickly. As though sensing this, Serena moved her attention to my labia. She kissed them, her tongue probing the slit in between, echoing how it had first flicked into my mouth. My cunt lips parted, drawing her tongue in. Thrusting deeply, she began to lick, exploring the velvet walls, probing my G-spot. Teasing at first, then in earnest, she stabbed and sucked hungrily. My climax was building now and the walls of my cunt contracted, gripping her. Phil's hand moved down, stroking and pressing my clit and I came. I cried out, my hips thrusting forward and my cunt clenching as though trying to swallow that lovely tongue. I leaned back panting, floating in the darkness, Phil holding me, as my orgasm slowly ebbed away.

When I could breathe normally and stand unaided, they dressed me. Serena guided me to step into a garment. Phil pulled it up. I felt the caress of soft fabric against my skin as he fastened it. My breasts were not covered. Stockings were rolled up my legs, hold-ups gripping my thighs. I gasped as my pussy was kissed. Then knickers were pulled up, adjusted and smoothed into place. Shoes were put on my feet and Phil's voice said, 'All ready?' The blindfold was removed.

Blinking in the light I saw Serena gazing at me. 'You're beautiful,' she whispered.

I was dressed in a costume very much like hers, a basque, tiny G-string, stockings and stilettos. My breasts showed above the basque. My clothes were pure white, contrasting with my darker skin and hair. Phil and Serena led me through the cubicle. I looked at myself in the mirror – I *was* beautiful. My skin was flushed and glowing and my breasts, larger than Serena's, stood out full and proud, the nipples huge, still engorged and very dark.

Serena kissed me, gently, sweetly, almost shyly. As she left she whispered, 'Thank you.'

I think I was in love with her.

Phil and I were left in the great hall. I felt high as a kite, drunk on sex and excitement. I was a goddess, hot and horny, dressed like a porn queen. I basked in the admiration I was receiving. Here, in this temple of the erotic, I was a star. Everyone passing stared at me, at my naked tits and the tiny cloth, already damp, that covered my pussy. My sexuality was blatant and on display.

I had Phil too, his teasing cockiness replaced by a mixture of adoration and sexual desire. His penis was still hard, clearly outlined and straining against his jeans. I remembered that he hadn't had any release. All the attention had been lavished on me. He had given so much and received nothing. I'd had a shattering mega-orgasm and the one of most sensuous experiences of my life. I should have been sated, but I wasn't. Looking at Phil's cock I suddenly wanted, desperately, to be fucked by him. I felt a wave of panic as I realised it was getting late. The exhibition would close in less than two hours. I would have to leave and go home to my family. It couldn't end without that final consummation.

Phil held my hands. I felt the tension in him, saw lust, hunger and love in his face. His voice thick with emotion, he asked was I satisfied. Did I want anything else?

I knew then he already had something planned, the clever, clever, wonderful man! I looked into his eyes, my own gaze matching his intensity. I said slowly, enunciating each syllable viscously, 'If you don't take me somewhere and lay me down and fuck me, I will kill you!'

The effect was electric. Phil ran, dragging me with him, through the hall. The crowd leaped aside and stared, stunned by the sight of us – Phil with his erection huge and straining his pants, me with my tits bouncing, and both of our faces twisted in a grimace of lust. Up the stairs, around the gallery, breathless, Phil fumbling in his pocket for a swipe card, through a door marked "Staff Only". A short corridor, then through another door marked "First Aid – Private". He pushed me in, threw the bags on the floor and slammed the door shut behind us.

I looked round the room. I saw the bed and didn't look any further. Phil picked me up and threw me on it, tearing off my thong in the same movement. I reached out to undo his jeans but he was already pulling them down and kicking off his shoes. He wasn't wearing pants. His cock sprang free, jutting up, rigid. He paused briefly to put on a condom but there was no foreplay, no caresses or kisses. We were both ready, desperate.

I opened my legs. My pussy was flooded, sopping wet and gaping wide. Phil leaped on the bed between my thighs. With an animal grunt, he thrust into me. His shaft entered me easily, sliding deep into my slippery cunt. I wrapped my legs around him, drawing him in further, thrusting my hips up, grinding my pussy into his groin. There was no finesse, just a fast, desperate coupling, Phil's hands on my arse, gripping tight as he pulled me onto him.

Panting, our hearts pounding, the climax came quickly.

Phil came first, his cock suddenly getting even bigger, his thrusts more frenzied in the seconds before his come gushed out. Moments later, my own orgasm hit – my pussy spasmed, closing round the hard cock inside me, holding it tight as we rode the long, rolling waves of pleasure. We lay together, still joined, till the passion subsided, then dozed for a while, side by side on the narrow bed.

Phil recovered first. He kissed my throat, waking me. He stood and gazed at me. Smiling, he asked if I was satisfied now. I was. But he looked so good standing there naked, his penis beautiful, its purple head glistening. I might have been satisfied already, but I'm such a greedy girl! I stroked it, licked its smooth head, lapping a moist, salty bead from its tip. Then I flicked my tongue down to his balls, tasting my own juices on them.

"What time is it?" I asked.

I had an hour, a whole unhurried hour, a bed and him.

On the train home, dressed in my ordinary clothes – *sans* knickers, which Phil had kept – I dozed and dreamed. I was looking forward to seeing hubby, smiling as I imagined the effect my porn star costume would have on him. I smiled again as I thought of writing up my *Erotica* adventure – who would imagine it had happened for real when I scarcely believed it myself?

Again, my mind drifted to Phil. How could he have known so much about me? Known exactly what I wanted, how I longed to become Bella? Who *was* Phil? Then, as I looked through the carrier bags, full of my *Erotica* goodies, I found that special "microphone" vibrator, and a glossy business card, very similar to my own.

"Philippa Blaise: Author of Erotic Fiction for Women."

Philippa! My fellow writer, my closest internet friend and confidante. Phil was Philippa. I'd had no idea!

Next time I logged on, I would have a few things to say to her … er, *him*!

Coming Attractions
by Landon Dixon

I guess you could say I had my "coming out" coming in.

I'd just turned 18 and gotten a job at this department store when I met Chris. He was a year older than I was, had been at the store a year longer. So, he showed me the ropes. As it turned out, in more ways than one.

I liked the guy right off. He was friendly and fun to be around, and (although I wouldn't have admitted it at the time) good-looking and, OK, damn sexy. He was about medium-height, shorter than me, with a slim, tight body and smooth, tanned skin, a delicately-chiselled face featuring sultry brown eyes and suckable red lips, a dimpled chin. He sort of looked like James Dean to my ... I don't know. Chris O'Donnell?

He always wore just a simple white T-shirt and faded blue jeans and scuffed sneakers. But that shirt and those jeans fitted him like velvet gloves, hugging to the taut curves of his butt cheeks, highlighting the protruding puffiness of his nipples. Our job was to stock the shelves between the store shutting at night and opening the next day, so we worked some strange hours, close together. And I started to get some strange ideas because of him.

I guess I'd always been gay, of course, but I just wouldn't, or wasn't ready to, admit it. Sure as shooting wasn't ready to admit it to my parents, whose house I was still living in. I'd had a couple of awkward encounters with guys at school – wrestling in the locker room and shower after volleyball and lacrosse practice – some quick, innocent grip and gropes. But I was still dating girls at the time I met Chris, trying to work up some sexual enthusiasm for the female of the species that I just wasn't feeling. I loved hanging out with women, but I wasn't loving the idea of hooking up with them, so I hadn't.

My second morning on the job, Chris invited me over to his place to play video games after work. I admired him for having his own place, and his taste in recreational activities. 'Just buzz me,' he said, 'and I'll leave the door open for you – come right on inside.'

I said, 'I'll be there.' And he gave me the address.

Turned out it was a 20-storey apartment building in the funky section of town. I kind of wondered at the time where Chris got the money for rent, since the pay we were getting was barely above minimum wage and the hours well below living wage. I later found out he had lots of friends, many with "benefits" that they bestowed on the handsome hunk.

Anyway, I buzzed his apartment number – 1514 – and got an answering buzz in return. I opened the inner door on the lobby and walked to the elevators. And when I walked down the hallway to his apartment on the 15th floor, sure enough the door was open. Only, there was no Chris standing behind it, or in the living room or the connecting kitchen to greet me. The place seemed to be deserted. Until I walked down the hall and peeked in the cracked-open door of the bathroom. And then I got an eye and crotchful.

Chris was standing in front of the sink gazing into the huge mirror on the wall. The guy had his white T-shirt rolled up almost to his chin, and he was admiring his face and chest in the mirror, striking poses. His chest was as smooth and sunkissed as his arms, pecs two small humps tipped by lighter-brown, puffy nipples. His blondish-brown wavy hair shone under the lights, his eyes, I swear, twinkling as he sucked in his stomach and popped out his chest, tilted his hips. He could model for me anytime. My face and body warmed, something stirring in my balls.

I wasn't sure if I should say something to announce my presence, or just see where the show would go next. I chose to see where the show would go next, when Chris slowly slid his hands up from his narrow hips and onto his chest, circled his forefingers around his nipples. I gulped and glared through the crack, staring in the mirror like he was. The guy swirled his soft, rounded fingertips around and around the pebbly bumps of his wide, darker-brown areolas, and I could clearly see his big nipples stiffen with the twirling sensations.

I held my breath and silently pulled my own tee out of my jeans, pulled it up over my nipples. And when I twirled my areolas like the honey in the mirror, I almost gasped right out loud. My pink pebbles were prominent, my pink nipples hardened stiff as they would go. I hadn't realised just how excited I'd gotten just watching the guy play with his chest.

He slid two slender brown fingers and thumbs along either side of his nipples, gently pinched and rolled, his pouty lips forming an O. I did the same, and was jolted with feeling, electricity arcing from the charged plugs of my nipples and coursing all through my body, making my cock surge. I had to bite my lip to keep from crying out.

We rolled our nipples together, pulled on them, teasing the rubbery protuberances to sing the body electric, as someone once said. My cock swelled up even bigger and harder, just fingering my nips, watching Chris finger his.

Until the mesmerizing mirror reflection suddenly unlatched his fingers from his chest and rolled down his T-shirt and tucked. He took a last look at himself in the mirror and then turned to leave the bathroom. I barely pulled my fingers free and shirt down in time, took off down the hall like a shot. I had to keep my back to the guy for two minutes or so, to allow my cock to fully deflate to normal, undetectable dimensions.

He beat me at every video game we played. I guess my

mind – and my mind's eye – were elsewhere.

Chris invited me over again at the end of the work week – for pizza and beers and a movie. I accepted without hesitation, maybe a little too enthusiastically. I'd become almost infatuated with the guy, watching his every move at work, sort of rubbing up against him or slapping him on the back or patting him on the arm whenever it seemed appropriate. I could hardly control myself. He didn't seem to mind, either. He took it all good-naturedly. But he didn't really respond, neither, except as one friendly co-worker to another. I was woefully unskilled in the art of man-on-man flirtation, having had virtually no experience.

I buzzed his number again, got buzzed inside again. His door was open. I entered. And just like last time, no Chris. To the naked eye, anyway – in his living room, kitchen, or bathroom. But to the naked wide eye: nude Chris in his bedroom.

I'd caught the guy in middle of a self-pleasure session. His bedroom door was half-open, and he was sitting up on his bed, his back propped up against the headboard, his body totally, stunningly nude. My jaw dropped and my jeans almost popped. I hugged the wall alongside the door, staring into his bedroom, at his sleek, smooth, sunbronzed body. I'd gotten half of the erotic picture the time before – the upper-body half – but now I was getting the really good parts, in living, lusting colour.

His lithe legs were spread, and he had his cock in his hand, his balls in his other hand. He was stroking and squeezing, his eyes directed in the opposite direction from me at his laptop up on a dresser. His cock was absolutely towering, smooth-skinned and cut and sculpturously capped, his large balls shaven bare. They and he took my breath away; the way he was swirling his soft hand up and down his length, cupping and fondling with his other sensitive hand, made me choke up with emotion, swell up with sensation. The movie playing on the laptop was a gay skin flick, two naked guys jerking each other off.

My nails dug paint out of the wall, splinters out of the doorframe. But Chris was completely oblivious to me, taken up with the sexy task at ... hands. It was a picture worth a thousand spurts, the room glowing with late-afternoon sunshine, Chris's body burning before my eyes, his cock and balls and the sensual way he was working them making me blaze with passion.

I just had to get in on the act, in my own hidden way. I scrambled my fly open and dug around in my briefs for my dick. It was and it wasn't hard to find; I was poling up and out, pumped with pure pleasure pressure. I gripped my almost fully erect cock and quickly stroked the last couple of inches of arousal into the joystick. Staring at Chris waxing his cock and mauling his balls.

I bit my lip, beating off slow and sure like my hero. But while he was focused on the hardcore actors on-screen, I was focused on the homoerotic star of the show. His chest was pumped, pecs clutched, lean muscles on his arms clenching, slender legs stretching out with cute little curvy soles showing, edible toes twitching. Fuck, but I wanted to tear into his luscious nipples with my teeth and tongue all around his toes and feel up his chest and legs. But most and excitedly of all, I wanted to replace his polishing and pulling hands with mine on his beautiful cock and boisterous balls. And vice versa on my own throbbing prick and boiling nuts.

Precome shone in my slit, my fist flying up and down, other hand tugging on my fuzzy sack. I was ready and willing and more than able to blow right then and there, watching Chris jack and jerk. And I was about to shower his door and carpet with my spunky applause at his one-man, two-hand show. But then he suddenly gave his head a shake and released his tools of delight, jumped off the bed and shut down the scene on his computer. Like he just remembered he had a guest coming over.

I stumbled backwards away from the door, and almost fell on my ass in my haste to tuck and zip. This time it took, like, five minutes of back-to-the-man attitude, before I could get my cock and self safely under control and underinflated again.

I gnawed on the pizza and choked down the beer, watching the movie with one eye and Chris with the other. Until, finally, I had to relieve the "tension" with a visit to the bathroom. I only wished, as I spanked my monkey and sprayed, that I had the guts to act on my raging impulses – *mano a mano.*

Things did finally come to a frothy head on my third visit to Chris's apartment, however. This time it was for dinner and drinks. This time there was no stopping me, given what I stepped into the middle of.

I buzzed. He buzzed back. I went up in the elevator, walked down the hallway, found the door open. Only, when I entered my lust-interest's lair, I didn't have to look far for the guy this time. He was right there in his living room, getting fucked up the ass by another guy.

Chris was down on his hands and knees on the tan carpet, bare bronzed body arched and butt upraised, getting pounded by cock. His head was tilted up and his mouth was hanging open, his eyes closed, fingers clutching carpet, butt cheeks rippling and body rocking to the wicked hardcore homosexual beat.

The other man was about our age, but built bigger and badder. He had tattoos all over his hulking body, a shaved head, rings in his ears and nose and nipples. He was pile-driving his huge cock into Chris's anus, huge hands gripping and smacking my man's ass.

I stood in the doorway and stared like I'd never stared before, shocked to the cock. The scene was right out of one of my wettest wet dreams, only someone else's cock was playing the part of mine pumping Chris's ass. My mouth opened and closed, my eyes bulging.

'Hey, Chris,' the muscle-stud suddenly said. 'We got company.'

He was looking at me gaping at them. Chris opened his eyes and turned his head.

'Oh, geez, sorry about this, Darren. I forgot all about our date.'

I was in a fuzzy state, but I wasn't that stupid. He'd buzzed me in – all three times. He knew I was coming, had been putting on a show for me every time, topped off by him getting topped by the muscle-hunk. It was his form of seduction. I guess I did have to be hit between the eyes and legs to finally see it.

'This is James,' Chris said, nodding back at the big man. 'He lives down the hall. Maybe you'd like to come back in a few –'

'I'm coming now,' I proclaimed proudly. 'Coming in and coming out!'

And I waded out of the closet and into the sexual fray, stripping off my clothes, every stitch, striding up to the two coupled men and presenting my hardened cock to Chris's pretty mouth. He grinned up at me, then glided his lush, red lips over my bloated hood and down my swollen shaft. I pumped my fist with delight, then grabbed on to Chris's soft hair and pumped my hips with determination. I was gay as a fruitcake, and damn glad to be so. Especially with friends like Chris and James to show me the way.

Chris bobbed his head in my hands, sucking on my cock. I went from a crouch down to my knees, pumping into the man's hot, wet, tugging mouth. James went back to fucking Chris's ass, rocking the guy on my cock. I stared at Chris's dick-filled face, at his curved body, at James's rugged torso and face. It all felt so right, so wonderful – getting sucked by a man, watching and feeling that man get fucked by another man. Home sweet homo!

James pulled out of Chris. 'How 'bout you hit his ass for

148

a while?'

He said it to me. I looked down at Chris vaccing my cock to make my body and brain shimmer. He nodded. I pulled my prick out of his mouth and stumbled on my knees around to his ass. His cheeks were brown and bubbled, his pink manhole showing where James had gaped it.

This was it! The final plunge into my new and open sexual life. James lubed my cock for me, then kissed me good luck, with lots of tongue. He moved around to Chris's head, fed his cock into the gorgeous guy's mouth. I gripped my own cock and took a thrust at Chris's pucker. My hood squished against his starfish. I boldly pushed forward, and burst inside the man, plunged into his burning hot anus.

'Yes!' I cried, in, and in deep.

I gripped Chris's boyish hips and rocked back and forth, ploughing in and out of the man's rectum. He was tight and soft and sucking. I was on fire, hammering my newfound sexuality home.

James grasped Chris's ears and fucked his face. I fucked Chris's anus. We pumped in rhythm, hard and fast and heated beyond belief.

It couldn't last long – not my first time – and it didn't. The clasping, velvety friction of my virgin cock in a man's beautiful ass was just too much to resist. I dug my fingernails into Chris's flesh and wildly pumped his chute. Then I spasmed, blew the top of my head and the bottom of my genitals off, my cock exploding and erupting, shooting searing sperm into Chris's trembling ass. It went on and on and on.

It will go on and on and on. For the rest of my "natural" sexual life.

Watch and Learn
by Chloe Richmond

During my second year of university I discovered that a girl I knew, Kelly Seymour, was a voyeur.

She shared a house with a guy called Tom who was friends with Sam, my boyfriend at the time. Sam wasn't a student like us but he was staying with Tom, Kelly and the others for a bit while he sorted out a flat. Anyway, this meant Kelly and I saw each other now and again, friendly without really being friends, if you know what I mean.

We became a bit closer when, one night, she caught me having sex in her living room.

It happened on the sofa. I was lying on top at the time, kissing the guy as he held my arse under the skirt I was still wearing. My knickers were on the floor somewhere, my top and bra discarded among the sofa cushions. When the kissing strayed to my breasts, I sat up to tease him, grinning down at his disappointment but moving slowly back and forth against him. I took his hands from my arse and guided them up to my breasts as compensation, tossed my hair back … and that was when I saw Kelly.

She was standing in the corridor, straight ahead of me. She'd been out with some of her housemates but had come home early and now she was looking directly into the living room. She didn't do or say anything, and any gasp of surprise I might have made was lost on Tom as one of many I'd been making for the past half hour or so.

Oh yeah, it was Tom. Not Sam. Not my boyfriend. Sam was working nights.

Tom tried to sit up, to lick or kiss my breasts again, but I shoved him down so he was still hidden by the armrest and cushion. It was a little more aggressive than I'd intended but he didn't seem to mind. In fact, he seemed to rather enjoy it.

Kelly still hadn't moved. I was in no doubt she could see me as the TV was on, casting its glow on me, and she could hear us because the sound was off.

Because I'd stopped grinding against him, Tom released my breasts and grabbed at my waist to encourage me to move again. So I did, although only slowly while I wondered what to do about the situation.

Kelly leaned against the wall to show me she wasn't going anywhere. She smiled. There was something arrogant in her expression that I didn't like. I didn't quite smile back, but I carried on fucking Tom to show I didn't care that she was there. I thought it might wipe that look off her face, or embarrass her, but she still watched. She watched until I came. It didn't take long: Tom and I had been at it for a while already, and with Kelly there I was even more excited. I came hard, and loud enough that she didn't hear Tom.

She actually gave me a thumbs-up before going upstairs.

'Fuck, that was great!' Tom said. 'Hey, where are you going?'

'I think Kelly just came home.'

'What?'

'I just heard the door.'

'Shit!'

He helped me gather my clothes and I dressed quickly while he used the downstairs loo to flush the condom. He took his clothes with him.

'Quick, before she sees us,' he said, buttoning his shirt as he came out. She'd already seen me, but he didn't know that. And he'd just flushed the toilet, so she'd know someone was home. With any luck she'd think Sam had finished work and called me over.

'Walk me home,' I said, to get him out of the house too.

Halfway down the street, I looked back. Kelly was at her window, watching, but it would be too dark to see who I was with.

'What are you grinning about?' Tom asked.

'I think we got away with it.'

We didn't get away with it.

Kelly came to mine the next day and, instead of hello, said, 'You shagged Tom.'

'Shh!'

'Nobody else is home,' she said. 'I've been watching.'

'Of course you have.'

She smiled at that.

'You'd better come in,' I said, wondering what the hell I was going to say about the incident.

I needn't have worried. Kelly got right to it. 'So, is he any good, then? He must be, I saw your face and heard the way you were –'

'It was Sam. He finished early and called me over.'

It was worth a try.

Kelly only smiled again. Arrogant. Knowing.

'I saw you,' she said. 'Both of you.'

'You only saw–'

'Doggy style first, wasn't it?'

OK, she'd seen us.

'What do you want, Kelly?'

I don't know what I expected her to say, but it wasn't what she came out with. 'I want you to do it again.'

We looked at each other for a moment in silence.

'What?'

'I want to watch you both.'

I've let people watch me quite a few times since then, but at the time, the idea was new to me and, apart from Kelly catching me in the act, I'd never done it before.

'Why?' I asked her.

She shrugged. 'I like to watch.'

That wasn't it. Not all of it, anyway. So I waited.

She huffed and said, 'All right. You're good at it, OK?'

'What?'

'Sam told me. And so did a few others.'

'Who?'

She opened her mouth to tell me but I stopped her.

'It doesn't matter,' I said.

'If you don't do it, I'll tell Sam you did. That you've been fucking his mate.'

This wasn't quite the big deal she'd anticipated – if I'd been happy with Sam, nothing would have happened with Tom in the first place. But I agreed to her demand anyway. 'OK, fine, but I'm not sure Tom will be up for it.'

'Don't tell him,' she said. 'I don't want him to know I'm watching.'

'What are you going to do, stick a camera in his room?'

She shook her head. 'No. I'm going to be right there with you. Watching it live.'

'How? If you don't want him to know?'

The smile cracked into a grin. She had a plan.

The plan was simple.

At the time, I lived with two other girls, whereas Kelly was sharing with four people plus Sam temporarily: it had to happen at mine. Not a problem, as my housemates went home every holiday to see their friends and family.

Tom was only too keen to keep me company while they were away. 'I didn't know you were so kinky,' he said as I tied his wrists to the bedposts.

'There's loads you don't know about me.'

'I dunno about that,' he said. 'Sam brags a lot.'

'There's a lot he doesn't know either.'

'I bet,' Tom said with a chuckle as I leaned over him to check the knots. I teased him with my breasts close to his face. I was wearing my red set: lacy bra, knickers that fastened with side ties, and stockings. Hold-ups that didn't

153

need suspenders. I'd had my red heels on too when I opened the door to him and he'd almost come right there in the street. It was a job to stop him taking me in the hall. That wouldn't do when Kelly was waiting upstairs.

'How's that?' I asked him. 'Not too tight?'

'It's fine,' he said. 'Come on.'

He didn't need to say anything for me to know how eager he was. Stripped naked and tied to my bed, his eagerness was there for anyone to see. I touched it, ran my hand lightly up and down it.

'Do you like my outfit?'

Of course he did.

'Oh yeah,' he said, but that might have just been because of the way I was touching him.

'Take one last good look,' I said, and he did, and then I showed him the blindfold.

'Aww …' he said, disappointed at being denied the sight of me.

'Shh. Be a good boy.'

I fastened it around his eyes and stepped back to admire him. He looked good like that, in the soft sunlight that shone through my curtains, all tan and abs and hard cock with nowhere to go but my bedroom.

'So you're up for this, right? No matter what happens next, it's all OK with you?'

'Yes!' he said.

'Right, then – I'm off to the pub.'

'Hey!'

'Just kidding!' To be sure, I gave him a safe word to say if he wanted me to stop before adding, 'Getting a condom, back in a sec.'

I stepped into the room next door to mine where Kelly was perched on the bed, waiting. Her eyes widened with approval at my lingerie and when I beckoned, she followed me quietly.

She whimpered a little at the sight of Tom and I realised

this wasn't just about the watching. It was about him. She liked him.

'You OK?' Tom asked.

'Definitely,' I said, making a "shush" gesture to Kelly. 'You just look so good, I had to touch myself.'

'Let *me* touch you,' Tom said.

Kelly nodded and signalled for me to go to him.

I approached the bed and stood where one of his tied hands could reach me. He put it to my thigh and I turned slowly so his fingers traced over my behind, then stepped closer so he could feel between my legs. He put his palm to the crotch of my knickers.

'You're so warm here,' he said, moving it as best he could. I ground back and forth to help him, enjoying the pressure of his fingers and the feel of the fabric against my skin. Enjoying how wet it was getting, so quickly. Within moments, my knickers were soaked through. Part of it was knowing someone stood behind me, watching.

'I can't wait to feel this on me,' Tom said. He stopped stroking to pull at one of the side-ties on my knickers but couldn't get it undone from his position. I stepped away from him as he held it, and the pretty bow I'd knotted at my hip loosened and came free.

Kelly was filming us on her phone.

'Hey!' I said.

'What?' said Tom. 'You don't need to wear these.'

Kelly mimicked my "shush" gesture from earlier and continued to watch. And to film.

'If Sam or anyone else finds out …' I said.

Kelly shook her head and crossed her heart, and her face told me that, this time at least, she was sincere.

'He won't,' said Tom, enjoying the illicitness of our affair. If it could be called that, really.

Kelly motioned for me to move forward again so I stepped to Tom's eager hand and turned for him to grab the other tie – hardly necessary now, as the knickers fell away with minimal

155

urging. His fingers were suddenly between my thighs and I sighed as he slipped one inside me.

Returning the favour, I cupped his balls and massaged them very lightly. When Kelly mimed a request, I obeyed by stroking up and down his cock. With Tom's finger inside me I could just about reach by leaning slightly.

'Yeah,' he said. 'Oh yeah. Get on that.'

'OK,' I said. Kelly shook her head and waved me to the head of the bed. I frowned at her. She pointed to her lips.

I leaned down and kissed Tom. It meant releasing his cock and stepping away from his hand. We missed each other's touch immediately but enjoyed the way our lips connected instead, opening and closing them against each other a couple of times before slipping our tongues into each other's mouth. We moaned as we kissed and I rubbed my hand over his chest. I wanted him to rub mine too and it was such torment for both of us that he could not.

I broke away from the kiss and looked at Kelly, my hair hanging over Tom to tickle his face. She smiled and shook her head again. She pointed to her groin and then to her lips and this time I understood what she meant.

I climbed onto the bed and straddled Tom's chest.

'Yeah, that's it,' he said.

I looked behind me at Kelly in the doorway and she moved slowly into the room, her phone held to capture a side view.

'You want to taste me?' I asked Tom.

I glanced at Kelly and she smiled, then nodded, watching me with her own eyes although the phone was still pointed at us.

'Yes,' Tom said.

I moved slowly up his body, letting him feel the moist warmth between my legs on his skin. I knelt above his face, looked down at him, and said, 'You want me?'

'God, yes.'

'Good.'

156

I lowered myself onto him, wet against his mouth, and groaned immediately as his tongue began to work.

I love oral sex and if I can, I love to draw it out for as long as possible. Sometimes I moved with Tom's tongue, and sometimes I pressed down hard, sitting firmly on his face. When it became too much for me, I'd raise myself up and let him lick or kiss my open thighs. Sometimes I looked down to watch him, my hands braced against the wall opposite, and other times I leaned back so I could tease his cock with one hand behind me. Kelly watched and filmed it all, and seeing this turned me on as much as Tom's tongue licking between my legs. The only person not getting to see any of it was Tom.

Kelly pulled at imaginary bra straps and I obeyed. I eased my shoulder straps down first then reached behind to unfasten the back. I turned my body slightly towards her when I pulled the bra down and away from my chest. I dropped it behind me, letting it fall onto Tom so he'd know what I'd done.

Sure enough, he groaned his frustrated approval into me while Kelly nodded hers.

Without her direction, I moved away from Tom's mouth. Immediately he said, 'I want to see them.'

'No.'

'Please? You have such great tits.'

'Yeah?'

'Yeah.'

'Say it again, then.'

'You have great tits. I want to touch them. Suck them.'

I wanted him to touch them too, but Kelly surprised me by getting there first, approaching silently and taking one of my breasts into her hand to squeeze it gently. It shocked a groan from me, not that I'd have tried to stop her had I seen her, and she took advantage by kneading at my other one, all the while avoiding my nipples. Then, just as suddenly, she released me and stepped back again, raising her phone for a close up of my breasts, pointing it first at one then the other, focussing on my erect nipples.

'You want me to touch you,' Tom said. 'I heard you.'

I was still looking at Kelly, in utter amazement. She held up her free hand as if to say sorry, my bad, and gave me that arrogant little smile yet again. But as much as I hated that smile, I wanted the little bitch to grab my tits again because Tom sure as hell couldn't and my nipples ached for someone's touch, someone's tongue.

Kelly fluttered her hand at me – get on with it.

I moved further down Tom's body and bent over him, lowering my chest to his mouth. As soon as he sensed I was close enough he sat up as far as he could and kissed my breasts. His mouth and chin, wet with my arousal, made my breasts slick as he kissed and nuzzled at the soft flesh. My nipples ached with neglect until finally he found one and tongued it. I was still groaning at that when he sucked it in and I gave a drawn-out sigh that was as much relief as exhaled pleasure.

Kelly had come around to one end of the bed to watch. After a minute or so of that, she held a finger up and made a circular motion with it for me to turn around. I sat up, much to Tom's audible regret, and turned around so I was straddling his chest backwards. His cock was pointing right up and I descended upon it with open mouth, easing my pussy back to Tom's mouth as a fair exchange.

We'd only done this once before and he'd come very quickly, so I was going to have to be careful if Kelly wanted to see some sex. I moved on him slowly and pressed myself against him, getting more stimulation from the position than he was. That previous time, he'd clutched my arse to hold me hard against his mouth, nuzzling between my thighs with hungry sounds that echoed my own. Now, with his hands tied, he couldn't grab me but he seemed to like what he was doing well enough anyway.

Kelly came back around to the side to get a good view of

us sixty-nining. She turned the phone sideways to fit the entire bed into the frame. I ignored her, licking the tip of Tom's cock before working my way down his shaft to tongue his balls. His groan was muffled – which struck me as being a bit of a pun.

I pointed to my dressing table and Kelly turned to look, keeping her phone focused on the action. She saw what I wanted and grabbed the condom for me but she didn't bring it over.

'Do you like this?' I said, sucking Tom's cock again before resting my breasts over him. Kelly nodded but I was talking to Tom. I fidgeted into a position that allowed him to speak.

'Yeah,' he said.

I didn't allow him anything else, pushing my pussy back to his face and sucking him into my mouth again. He found my clit briefly with his probing tongue and I moaned around his cock. I brushed my hair to one side so Kelly could see him going in and coming out, and I reached out for the condom, making grabbing gestures. When she didn't hand it over, I eased away so my breasts were dangling over Tom's cock. 'You came really quickly last time – think you can hold on till I fuck you?'

Tom could only make a grunting noise while licking me but I wasn't really seeking an answer from him – I was explaining things to Kelly.

She opened the condom, but still didn't give it to me. I suddenly realised what she had in mind, and felt uneasy. This time the question I asked Tom was genuine. 'You're sure – totally sure, I mean – that you're up for anything?' He grunted a yes, in a tone that urged me to just get on with whatever it was I had in mind.

I nodded at Kelly, telling myself that if she tried to push things much further than this, I'd call a halt. Sighing, I leaned back to allow her more space. It gave Tom access to different areas and I writhed against him, closing my eyes for a moment to enjoy where his tongue was.

When I opened them again, Kelly had put the condom to the tip of Tom's cock. She held it with her fingertips and eased it down over him. When it didn't unroll fully, she pumped at him quickly to get it on. I felt him groan against me and took her hand in mine to stop her, slow her down. With my hand on hers, we guided the condom on, right down to the base. She cupped Tom's balls. She has smaller hands than me but I don't think he noticed.

'Fuck him for me,' she whispered. 'Show me.'

With my thighs clamped over his ears Tom didn't hear, but I still didn't like her speaking. I pushed her away and turned around before she could complain or do anything else, hoping she'd realise Tom would hear her this time if she said anything. But just in case she didn't realise, or didn't care, I positioned myself over his cock, held him in position, and guided him back and forth against me, teasing a moan from him. Then I eased his cock inside me, but only the tip.

'You want to fuck me?'

'God, yes.'

I sat down quick and took all of him in.

We all of us groaned, Tom and me louder than Kelly, thankfully. I sat on him without moving and said, 'How's that, baby?'

'Amazing.'

'Yeah?' I said. 'And this?' Rising up.

'Yeah.'

'And this?' Sinking down.

'Yeah! Oh, yeah, come on. That's it.'

'Like *this*?' I came up quicker, drove down harder.

'Yeah. Fuck me, yeah.'

I faced Kelly for a few thrusts, letting her see me sigh and moan with the pleasure of it, arching my back to push my chest out for her. She filmed me, then panned the phone down to Tom as he pulled against his restraints, wanting to grab me, hold me, draw me to him. When Kelly's phone was on me again, I put my hands into my hair and raised my arms to lift it up and let it drop, rocking back and forth. Kelly loved that. She stepped back to get more of us in frame. Stepped back again. And again. She was close to Tom's end of the bed now, and she didn't know it but another step would put his hand on her leg.

'Kelly!' I hissed.

She stopped. I stopped.

Tom said, 'What?'

'Kelly,' I said again. 'Did she suspect anything?'

I resumed my rocking motion to distract him from the timing of such a question.

Kelly turned to see what had almost happened, saw his tied hand, and, quickly but quietly, moved clear of the bed.

'No,' Tom said. 'Kelly hasn't got a clue.'

She smiled behind her raised phone.

'How do you know?' I said, still moving slowly.

'I just know. Oh, yeah, that's good.'

I didn't like her smile.

Raising myself up from Tom so that almost his entire length slid out of me, I asked, 'What's her story, anyway?'

'Kelly? Nothing.'

I hesitated over him, sensing more. I could tell there was something because not only had her smile gone, but she was looking angry and shaking her head.

'She came on to me once,' Tom said. 'Is that a big deal?'

I sank back onto him to show him it wasn't, to reward him, and he cried out so loudly I thought he might have come already. I sat still but felt no throbbing or bucking beneath me. He was good to go for a while longer. I clenched tight and moved in small circles. He moaned.

Kelly was red-faced but I couldn't tell if it was with anger or embarrassment. I decided I didn't want her angry with me, not with what she had on her phone. And also, thanks to her, I was having fun. She may have been a

161

voyeur, but I was a bit of an exhibitionist, as it turned out, and having her watch me was more of a thrill than even my illicit affair with Tom.

'Why didn't you do anything about it?'

Kelly looked keen for an answer too, but Tom only moaned as I rocked on his lap. So I stopped.

'She's not very experienced,' he said.

Kelly looked like she was about to throw her phone at him. Clearly it was not the answer she'd hoped for.

'I bet you she's eager, though,' I said, resuming my movements. 'I bet she'd love it. And she's so petite. Cute figure. Small, perfect tits.'

Tom groaned but I wasn't moving enough to warrant it. He was responding to the dirty talk.

'Firm. Tiny. Bottom,' I said, matching my words with three hard bounces.

Tom grunted with each one. 'Why are you saying this?'

Kelly seemed just as curious, but at least she'd calmed down now.

I leaned right down, pressing my breasts to his chest, kissing his neck as I looked at her and said, 'Imagine fucking her ...'

'What?'

I braced myself on my elbows and pushed back so he was as deep as possible inside me. He squirmed and I moaned at the way his pelvis pressed up against mine.

'Imagine going into her room when the others are asleep and taking those little tits into your hands ... your mouth.' I put my breasts to his mouth, one and then the other, quickly, keeping the weight of them from him but letting him feel the nipples on his lips, letting him lick them. 'Flipping her over and fucking her.' I clenched his cock into me, withdrew, then pumped back down to punctuate the last few words. 'Hard. From. Behind.'

He groaned with each thrust.

'That nice little bottom pushed up against you,' I said,

slowing down. 'Clutching her tits.' Then, speeding up again, I added, 'Banging. Her. Hard.'

I looked up at Kelly. She was as hot as I was. Flustered and frustrated. After all, it was me getting the sex. She could only watch.

'Like you did me the other night on the sofa,' I said, facing Kelly. 'Doing me doggy style as I clutched the armrests. Before I did this to you.'

I fucked him then with no more talk. I fucked him harder than I had that night on the sofa because all the talk of him and Kelly had turned me on. I could picture them easily, fucking and gasping and grappling in the dark of her room, and in my imagination it was so clear it was like I was the one watching, not her. I thought of that, riding him and riding him, and when I was close I opened my eyes to watch her watching, coming loud and hard like the last time she saw me.

Eventually I slowed, settling still with a sigh.

'Thanks, baby,' I said, panting for breath, chest heaving and sweaty. I leaned down and kissed him.

'You can thank me by untying me. I haven't finished with you yet. I want to fuck you from behind. I want to hold your tits and bang you till you come again.'

I looked at Kelly with a grin, one hand in my wild hair, ready to thank *her* as well, and saw that at some point she'd stripped off her clothes. Kelly was naked.

'Er …' I said.

'What?' said Tom. 'Come on! You put the little housemate fantasy there, let me finish it.'

Kelly beckoned me off him but I refused to move. I still wasn't totally convinced that I should have allowed her to cop a feel of his cock, so I was certain that if I let her take my place without his knowledge, it'd be a form of rape.

Kelly understood.

'Want to do it for real?' she said.

Tom tensed beneath me.

'I'm here, right now,' she said.

'Kelly?'

'Why don't you tell her the real reason why you "didn't do anything about it" when I came on to you that time?'

She straddled his chest in front of me. When he didn't elaborate, she turned and told me, 'He has a girlfriend.'

'What?'

I shouldn't have been hurt, especially as I had a boyfriend. And the truth was, it wouldn't have mattered anyway. But now that I'd learned the truth, the fact that he hadn't told me was what mattered.

I climbed off him, pulled my stockings up, and looked for my knickers.

Kelly shifted herself back so she was near to where I'd been. She directed her phone down at Tom's face. 'Tell her it's true.'

He turned his head to where he could hear me moving, looking for my bra. 'Yeah, OK,' he said. 'But –'

'Shh,' said Kelly. She reached behind to hold his cock before it could wilt during his confession, and moved back still further so his erection pressed against the crack of her arse and stayed hard. 'The thing is,' she said, rising up over him, letting the tip of it play against her as she'd seen me do a moment ago, 'I've just filmed all of that. And if you don't want your girlfriend to ever see it …'

'Kelly,' I said, 'you really don't need to blackmail him. He wants to fuck you.'

'Yeah,' he said. 'Get your –'

Whatever he was going to say was lost to a cry from Kelly as she sank down onto his cock. He cried out too at the sudden force of it. She rode him hard for a few eager bounces then mimicked me in the way she lowered her breasts to his face. He sucked them in as eagerly as she offered them.

I watched. I'd seen porn before, of course, but watching it live was something else. If I hadn't already come so hard,

164

and if I hadn't had a point to prove, I'd have been getting back on that bed. As it was, I only watched. And when Kelly let go of her mobile to take off Tom's blindfold, to sit up and play with her hair, as I'd shown her, I took the phone from the pillow and found the footage she'd filmed.

'Don't,' she said.

'I won't,' said Tom, misunderstanding. 'Not yet. I can hold on.'

I showed Kelly what I was doing. She nodded and forgot about me again to fuck Tom while I sent the film she'd recorded to my own phone. I'd watch it later, maybe learn a few things about myself.

My phone chimed, and I retrieved it from the bedside table. I checked it, message received, and untied Tom's hands while I was there. He sat up immediately with something close to a growl, pulled and squeezed at a gasping Kelly, then pushed her off him. She protested briefly, taking it as a rejection, but all he did was turn her over to do her from behind. She clutched at the bedposts as desperately as he clutched her waist. He pulled her against him as he thrust into her, again, again, again. I'd warmed him up well for this; it wouldn't matter how experienced she was.

I went over to my dressing table and cleared it of make-up and jewellery with a sweep of my arm.

'What are you doing?' Tom said. Maybe he thought I was angry.

Kelly merely looked at me, but her eyes implored me to stay, or thanked me, or something – it was hard to tell with all her open-mouthed noises. Anyway, I wasn't going anywhere. It was my room.

I sat on the dressing table. 'Just getting a better view.'

I raised my phone and filmed every thrust, every cock-hungry contortion of Kelly's face, and I did it smiling.

Skimpy
by Scarlett Blue

'We don't mind what you wear, as long as your pussy is exposed. Totally exposed. Not a slightly see-through skirt, or a long top, or covered with tassels. Nothing at all on the bottom. How would you feel about doing that?'

I have to admit it was the strangest, and undoubtedly the best, conversation I'd ever had with a boss in my life. I got butterflies as she was saying it, but it was as much from excitement as apprehension.

The thought of walking around a party with a tray of drinks, or serving behind the bar completely bottomless was terrifying – in an I-can't-fucking-wait kind of way.

In Australia a "skimpy" is a scantily clad barmaid or waitress, and I'd applied to be one to pay for my post-uni travels there. I'd ended up on the books of a specialist agency and had worked every weekend in a bikini or lingerie, serving red-blooded male clients with their beer and snags, and occasionally treating them to a flash of my breasts if they tipped me well enough. And I'd had a ball – I loved every minute of it.

The tips more than doubled the basic wage and the guys couldn't get enough of my reserved English accent, prim brown bob and pale skin – so different to the Aussie girls with their tall, tanned bodies and sun-bleached hair. I got a kick every time a customer paid me to take my top off, enjoying the warm evening air on my bare breasts but enjoying all the eyes even more. No matter what a man is doing, he'll stop when he sees a topless woman. Being

166

collectively desired by so many men gave me such a rush.

How would I feel about wearing nothing at all on the bottom? I hope I didn't look overly excited when I replied.

'*Great!*'

People who'd known me just a couple of years ago wouldn't believe it if they could see me now. I was fairly quiet and studious when I first went to university. I had a boyfriend back home so I didn't get involved in the crazy sleeping around that went on. I felt a little sad thinking of my high school sweetheart, but I had to follow my heart and travel so we'd made the decision to go our separate ways. I had to admit my sex life as a single was much better, though I still missed him in those little moments alone. But now I *was* following my heart into this naughty little assignment. I didn't actually need the money, really, I had plenty saved up from my more standard skimpy jobs to fund the next few weeks, but I'd developed a taste for showing off and that wasn't about to stop at bikini bottoms.

The manager was still talking. 'That's great – you've been very popular and reliable, we've been really pleased with you. But this is a bit different, a few girls have thought they could handle it but then not liked it when they got there. But we'll send you to a friendly little party on Friday night and see how you get on.'

She handed me the address and timings on a printed sheet. And there were the instructions again. Dress code: waitress's own choice, but pussy completely exposed, nothing at all on the bottom.

Just reading about it was getting my underwear wet. I couldn't wait to rush home and try some half-outfits on.

I ended up standing in front of my bedroom mirror with clothes all over the bed. I eventually decided on a white blouse tied short at the front, black over-the-knee socks and high heels. And nothing else. I stared at the girl in the mirror. She looked hot. *I* looked hot. I couldn't believe I was going to walk round a party like this. I fell back on the bed, my hand going straight between my legs, watching in the mirror as my pussy opened up, my fingers feeling the pool of moisture there. I came in minutes thinking about being a filthy show-off and, better still, getting paid to do it.

When Friday came around I took the outfit from where I'd carefully hung it. I briefly wondered what I should wear to travel there. Jeans or just a coat over the top, or something totally different and change when I got there? It was way too hot to wear a coat or long top so I just put it on with a little tube skirt, and left the panties off. I figured I may as well start as I meant to go on.

As it turned out, I got a little practice in on the way to the job. I was going around in a battered red "ute" – a small pickup truck – which I planned to drive to Sydney after I'd had my fun in Perth. I needed gas so I pulled into a station and had a wicked thought as soon as I came to a halt. Someone was going to get a treat tonight. The attendant, an attractive older guy with a deep tan, started filling up my tank, and I made a big show of getting my purse out of the truck. I leaned over, knowing my buttocks were just peeping out of the tiny little skirt and that he'd be staring at me, not daring to look away in case he missed the chance to see a bit more. I teased him with this for a second, then leaned over a bit further, feeling the rush of air that confirmed my pussy was well and truly out. I heard him draw breath. I allowed him a good look before I "found" my purse, and straightened up again, smoothing down my skirt as if nothing had happened. He was looking at me with pure lust.

I smiled, paid, and then drove away, knowing he'd remember me forever – probably more vividly than he'd recall half the girls he'd actually slept with.

I got to the address given to me by the agent. It was a large bar and I'll admit I started to feel a bit apprehensive as I walked in the door, worried about who I'd meet first and whether they would judge me for being the girl who walks around with her pussy on display all night.

I needn't have been concerned. As soon as I walked in, two guys came up to me – the brother and best friend of the guest of honour, the stag as it turned out, or, as they call them in Aus, the "buck". I saw the best man's eyes dart straight away to my skirt, could almost feel his heart beating faster as he imagined me out of it. I don't know who was more excited by the prospect.

I was paid up front, way more then I'd ever earned in one night before, and assured that I'd make more from tips as the night wore on. I learned that there a bar which would be attended by another bottomless girl from the agency, that she'd make up the drinks orders and I'd be on tray service to the tables. The guys pointed out where the buck would be sitting and said to make sure I gave him plenty of attention. Also, the bar was hired privately so normal rules didn't apply and I could go as wild as I liked. I smiled, not yet sure how wild I *did* like.

The other skimpy was already in the back room that had been set aside for us. A tall brunette from Canberra, she wore a black tube-top over her perky breasts and nothing else. Despite my excitement, and even though I'd tried on my own outfit, there was still something shocking about seeing her dressed like that in the flesh. Her pussy was shaved and I could see *everything*. I hoped she didn't notice me staring as she extended her hand and introduced herself as Anastasia, telling me I could call her Anna.

'Jessica,' I said, shaking her hand.

'Ever done one of these before?'

'Never.'

'You'll be fine. If you get pissed doing tray let me know and I'll swap ya – the bar's easier.'

She seemed totally businesslike about the whole thing, I didn't think it was the right moment to admit that I'd much rather work the room than the bar as I'd have the opportunity to show my pussy to more guys.

Eight o'clock rolled around and we got to work, if you

can call it that. We walked out on to the floor, where the bucks were gathered, rowdy and excitable. They cheered and jostled when they saw us, compliments and lewd comments mixing together. Anastasia was nonplussed by both in equal measure, while I was equally excited by both.

Anastasia made a bee line for the bar and I was suddenly alone in the middle of a group of men, naked from the waist down. I've never felt panic and arousal so strongly at the same time. When you're wantonly exposing yourself in public you've already broken a major social taboo, and this lays the way open for everyone else to break with conventional etiquette too, so the guys never mince their words with strippers and naked waitresses.

'Wow, baby, that *is* a pretty pussy. I'd love to stick my tongue in it, your legs around my neck. What d'ya say?'

'Come here so I can finger-fuck you. I bet you'd love that, wouldn't you?'

'Are you wet? Hey, Dan, she's all wet! Horny bitch, bet you'd love to take us all on!'

I smiled, feeling a bit overwhelmed and faint, actually wanting to just let them grab me and have their way, but simultaneously enjoying the fact that I could be coquettish and professional with no knickers on.

I went to the bar, wiggling my bum as I walked, knowing every eye in the place was on me. Anastasia had lined up a tray of shots and pointed me over to the buck's table. I realised that, as the men were seated, my bare pussy would be right at eye level as I served them.

The guys were all gathered round the buck so I had no trouble guessing which one was him, and I approached him from the side. His friends saw me before he did so when he turned his head, my naked lower body was inches from his face. I put the tray down and handed him a glass. He looked me up and down, lust-struck. The guys cheered and all took a shot, without taking their eyes off me. They tipped me a few bucks, and a few more compliments.

170

I took my time getting back to the bar, smiling at guys as I went, lapping up the attention. I caught sight of myself in one of the bar's mirrors, bottomless in a roomful of men. This wasn't work!

I served another table, a couple of quieter guys sitting apart from the others. 'Why don't you sit with us for a bit, baby girl?' One of them asked.

I looked around, checking everyone had a drink who wanted one – I took my waitressing duties as seriously as the rest of my job! They all seemed satisfied so I sat down, crossing my legs and placing my hands on my knee.

'Aww, that's such a shame, hiding away like that,' the same guy said, pulling a fifty out of his wallet and casually folding it on the table in front of me. 'Why don't you show me a bit more?'

I took the bill, tucked it in my top, then briefly uncrossed my legs. The guys just stared appreciatively, so I leaned back and spread my legs across the chair, giving the two of them a good long look at my pussy, enjoying it as much as they did.

'How about a little dance? Just jump up on the table.'

I climbed up, struggling a bit with my heels and the slippery table top. They stared up at me, transfixed, as I circled my hips and ran my hands up my thighs. I was getting wet so I opened my legs a little way so they could see the effect all this was having on me. I got down on my knees, stretching face down with my uncovered arse and pussy towards them, enjoying the filthy comments and unblinking stares from the two men.

The buck's table was signalling for more drinks so I made my excuses, leaving the duo looking blissed out. I picked up another tray of shots from the bar and made my way over to the buck. I put it down on the table and deliberately dropped the tip tray. I turned and bent over, taking my time picking it up to the cheers of the men.

I glanced at Anastasia, who was clearly bored and

checking her mobile, seemingly unconcerned about her state of undress and my going above and beyond the job description. She was the one missing out, I decided, and I was going to have some real fun.

'OK, guys, who's up for some body shots?'

They all cheered.

I lined up the tequila shots along the side of the table, and hopped up onto it. Money started to fly straight away. I laid a long line of salt down the centre of the table, from one end to about halfway up, and lay down with a leg on either side of it. I placed sliced limes all over myself, on my stomach and the tops of my thighs, then slowly splayed my legs wider. I told the guys to start licking up the salt, with one condition – the buck had to go last.

They had all gathered at the bottom end of the table to get a good look at my spread-open pussy. Then the first guy licked up a bit of the salt, took a shot, and picked a lime off my thigh, lingering slightly, his breath on my skin and the juice dripping down my leg.

Another guy took his turn, then the next, then yet another, the diminishing line of salt bringing each successive one closer to having his face in my pussy. And as it went on, each seemed to take more liberties with the limes, taking his time and licking and sucking my skin as he picked up a juicy slice with his teeth.

Finally, the buck's turn came around. He licked up the last few grains of salt, his hair brushing my swollen and throbbing lips, making me moan involuntarily. I felt him breathe in, inhaling the scent of my juices, struggling against an impulse to bury his face in my wet pussy. He groaned slightly, took the shot, and pressed his lips to my lower stomach as he bit into the last lime. I was sticky with lime juice, drunk on desire, and covered in money. I wanted him to eat my pussy, and so did our audience, who were chanting, 'Lick her cunt! Lick her cunt!'

The buck was in no rush to finish the lime, loitering

around my pussy, but there was a pained reluctance underlying his lust. I guessed he'd made a promise to his fiancé that he'd behave, and didn't want to break it.

The best man eventually pushed him out of the way.

'If you're not going to lick it, then I am!'

The guys were all pushing each other to keep a clear view as he pressed his lips to my clit, gently at first then becoming more and more insistent. I was already so horny from my night of showing off that my orgasm started to build quickly as his tongue traced over my clit and lips. My nipples strained against my bra, the feeling of being naked on the bottom but fully clothed on top strange and somehow dirtier than being completely nude.

'Finger-fuck her!' Someone in the audience yelled out. This caught Anastasia's attention from the bar. She looked over, disinterested – it obviously wasn't the first time she'd seen this kind of debauchery, even if she wasn't up for getting involved herself. This idea excited me more, that this wasn't likely to be a one-off, and I could be doing this every weekend.

I felt a finger slide inside me, then two, finding the sensitive spot deep within, rubbing in circles and thrusting in and out. My hips started to lift off the table, pushing towards him. The guys cheered louder as my arousal was clearly out of control, and I came loud and hard, grinding my pussy into his face and hand. A few more tips landed on and around me.

I lay in a sticky heap on the table, till one of them asked me to get some more shots.

'I don't think she can walk straight yet,' said another guy, and he definitely had a point.

My legs were still very shaky so it was with some difficulty that I teetered on my heels towards the bar. Anastasia had laid out more shots, and other tables were shouting and beckoning me over, yelling that they wanted to do body shots too.

'You look like you're enjoying yourself at least,' Anastasia said with a wink.

'Nothing wrong with mixing a little business with pleasure,' I replied, heading for the next table, and the next gang of men. She shook her head, but she was smiling.

I lost count of how many orgasms I had that night and of how many men ate my pussy and fingered me in front of their friends. Anastasia dressed and packed up quickly, pecking me on the cheek and saying she had a date to get to. At 2 a.m., I knew exactly what she meant by that.

I sat for a few moments, in no hurry to dress – I'd had so much fun going bottomless I didn't want it to end. I counted my money – well over 800 Aussie dollars and that was on top of the basic wage I'd be getting. Honestly, though, I'd have done it all for free, not that I was going to admit that to the guys who'd tipped me so generously!

I was just about to put my skirt back on – reluctantly – when I heard a soft knock at the door. I instinctively made to cover myself but remembered everyone had seen everything already, and answered it just as I was.

The best man was standing there. He looked me up and down again with a lazy smile, the memory of his licking me to orgasm in front of everyone fresh in both our minds. He handed me a business card.

'I've been looking for someone like you to do a few jobs for me. A bit of cooking, gardening, washing my car, and … well, just hanging out at my place. Dressed exactly like that. Good money. What do you say?'

I took the card and tucked it into my skimpy cropped top. I'd definitely be making that call. Nothing wrong with mixing a little business with pleasure.

Your Ultimate Fantasy
by Elizabeth Coldwell

At first, I thought it was the cheapest, laziest present Grant could have given me. I've never measured the strength of his feelings for me in terms of how much money he spends – he's always had plenty of other ways of making me feel valued and special – but it was my birthday, after all. At the very least he could have picked up a bunch of flowers from the all-night petrol station down the road. Instead, when I opened my card, a small, rectangular piece of paper fluttered out. I immediately recognised it as one of the Love Notes from the book in my bedside drawer.

I'd been given the book as a Secret Santa gift at work a couple of years ago. The minds of the blokes in my department never seemed to rise very far above crotch level, so you knew you had a more than even chance of opening your beautifully wrapped parcel to discover a pop-up copy of the *Kama Sutra*, or something edible and penis-shaped. These were a little less tacky, if no more practical. I'd never felt any inclination to make use of them. Designed to look like banknotes, they carried the message "I promise to pay the bearer on demand ..." followed by some kind of romantic or vaguely naughty action, from breakfast in bed to a lapdance. At the back of the book were half a dozen notes deliberately left blank for you to come up with your own suggestion. On the one I was holding now, Grant had written in his usual messy scrawl, 'Your ultimate fantasy.'

I must have failed to disguise my disappointment, because Grant said, 'Sorry, Roz. I really did mean to nip out and get you something before the shops shut, but the main server went down, and by the time we'd fixed it …'

'It's OK,' I said. Sometimes I wanted to tell Grant he didn't need to work such ridiculously long hours, but he'd heard rumours of cutbacks within the company and he seemed determined to do whatever it took to make sure he wasn't affected personally. I tucked the Love Note into my jeans pocket. 'I'm sure I'll be able to make good use of this. Now, let's have dinner.'

Grant came home the following evening with a box of handmade Belgian truffles and a bouquet of roses so large I had to split it between every vase in the house, making me feel guilty about my petulant response to his original present. I knew he cared about me; I just resented the fact that, increasingly, I seemed to come lower down his list of priorities than maintaining the hardware in the IT department he oversaw.

The more I thought about it, though, the more I discovered I liked the idea of being able to ask him to fulfil my ultimate fantasy. It gave me a delicious feeling of control, knowing that at some moment entirely of my choosing I would be able to order him to …

To what? It wasn't as though my mind wasn't packed with fantasies. Some Grant knew all about. We talked about them in bed sometimes, because he enjoyed how excited it made me. His hand would snake between my legs, feeling the wetness there, as I told him how I'd love him to rent a hotel room across town so I could travel to meet him there wearing nothing but high heels and a full-length faux mink coat. Or twist my hair in pigtails and put on knee socks, then drape myself over his knee for a bare-bottom spanking.

We both liked that one so much we'd actually tried it out. Grant relished the role of my stern guardian, forced to chastise me for disobeying him. I squirmed and yelled on his lap as he spanked my arse till it was red and sore, then sighed in bliss as he kissed the hurt away before working his way lower so he could tongue me to a soft, melting orgasm.

Remembering that particular scene brought a glow to my cheeks all over again, but when it came to it, I intended to ask Grant for something a little less predictable. I thought of the fantasies I'd never shared with him. Now we were venturing into edgier territory, desires I wasn't sure I would be entirely comfortable confessing to him.

How would he react, I wondered, if I told him about those visions I had of him lying face down on the bed while I fastened a long, thick dildo into the harness around my waist? There would be a tense, excited silence in the room as I slicked lube along the length of the dildo, before dribbling a generous amount down the crack of Grant's arse. The breath would catch in his throat as my fingers gently probed his tight rosebud, slowly opening him up in preparation for receiving my fake cock. I wanted to feel him writhing beneath me, moving to the rhythm I set, learning how wonderful it felt to be filled to the brim.

Even that was tame in comparison to the fantasies where I brought a lover home. In my mind, this was always some faceless hunk, never a specific person. In truth, I didn't have any friends or work colleagues I found as attractive as Grant; with his intense blue eyes, dirty grin, and world-class arse he was everything I'd ever wanted. So the man who stalked these fantasies was a composite of every pouty underwear model with a sculpted six-pack and a suspiciously generous bulge in his tight white briefs, and he wanted nothing more than to make me his submissive plaything.

Sometimes, Grant would be reduced to a bit part in these fantasies, tied to a chair and unable to do a thing about it as my lover took me in every position I could think of. Grant's cock would be almost impossibly hard, aching for the merest touch and continually frustrated. In other versions of the fantasy, he was given the privilege of licking me clean of my lover's come after I'd been reduced to a sweaty, thoroughly satisfied mess.

The scenario I loved the most, however, the one that never failed to have me fingering myself to orgasm after orgasm as I pictured it, saw both Grant and me being required to suck my lover's cock. He would have us down on our knees in front of him, wrists cuffed behind us so we could only use our lips and tongues to satisfy him, then he would move from mouth to mouth in turn. The kinkiest depths of my imagination pictured this as some kind of contest, each of us using all the tricks we knew to bring him off. Punishment lay in wait for the loser. I had no idea what it said about me that, almost every time, it was Grant's mouth my lover filled with his seed.

Even without what I saw as the sheer impossibility of finding someone to be the third party in this delightfully depraved ménage, I knew this wasn't what I would present to Grant as my ultimate fantasy. When I finally realised what I actually wanted from him, it was something much simpler and yet infinitely more complex.

'You want me to *what*?' Grant asked, the Sunday afternoon I clicked off the TV and presented him with the "ultimate fantasy" Love Note.

'Like I said, I want to watch you pleasure yourself the way you do when I'm not around.' I'd been thinking about this for a few days now, and every time I did I felt my knickers growing sticky with the sheer naughty perfection of it. I knew Grant enjoyed wanking – the dog-eared stash of porn mags he kept tucked away in a box under the bed was more than enough evidence of that – but in all the time we'd been together, I couldn't remember him ever doing it in front of me. Maybe the odd tug or two to get himself fully hard before he sank his cock into me, but never all the way from start to finish.

'And how is this going to work, exactly?' Grant was clearly baffled, and I could understand why. With all the outrageously filthy things I could have asked him to do for me, this must have seemed so mundane in comparison. But it was what I wanted: the chance to see the man I loved enjoying a private moment alone with his right hand. Somehow, I was sure that sharing this fantasy would move our relationship on to a whole new level.

'Well, I'll make myself comfortable in the wardrobe and you … You just do whatever feels good.'

'If you're absolutely sure this is what you want.'

'It is,' I assured him, and with that, I went into the bedroom, leaving him to follow me. By the time he arrived, I'd made myself a cosy hiding place in the wardrobe, the hangers pushed to one side and the door left slightly ajar so I had a good view of the bed, less than a foot away.

Grant looked a little embarrassed as he shucked out of his jeans, throwing them over the back of the chair in the corner like he always did. He rooted under the bed, bringing out one of the magazines I was sure he believed I didn't know about. For a moment, I wondered whether he had any idea about the books I kept in my bedside drawer, the erotic anthologies with spines so bent and broken they automatically fell open at my favourite stories. Then my attention was drawn to the photos Grant had chosen to get him in the mood for what he was about to do.

The magazine was clearly at the amateur end of the market, packed with women posing in suburban bedrooms that weren't so very different from our own. They might have looked plain and ordinary in comparison to the models in the glossy wank mags, but the men in their life were so crazy about them they just had to show them off to other readers, appendix scars, cellulite and all. As I looked more closely, I realised Grant obviously had a type. With her shoulder-length blonde hair and small-breasted frame, the girl in the spread bore more than a passing resemblance to me, though I didn't possess any lingerie as tacky as the cheap-looking red lace bra and panties she wore. The photos showed her with her tits pulled out of the cups of the bra and the crotch of her panties pulled to one side, revealing the vivid pink split of her shaven pussy. There was a little silver barbell through her left nipple and some random Chinese character tattooed just above her hip bone. Her expression was one of undisguised lust and wanting, and unlike that of a professional model, it clearly wasn't faked.

I was still digesting the implications of Grant's choice as he peeled down his boxer shorts. His cock hung between his thighs, head still partly covered by its sleeve of skin, just beginning to rouse from its slumbers. As I watched, he hunted round for something on the bedside table, giving me a tantalizing glimpse of his bare arse beneath the hem of his faded black T-shirt. He picked up my pot of hand cream, unscrewed it and scooped out a generous amount of the contents. Lying down on his side, facing me, he slowly stroked up and down the length of his cock with his cream-covered hand.

I'd always wondered how I managed to go through that hand cream quite as quickly as I did. Now it all made sense. Making a mental note to treat Grant to a decent bottle of lube for his private moments, I was drawn to the way his cock was rising and stiffening. He almost seemed unaware of what was happening, his concentration solely on the anonymous girl in the photo. He turned the page, selecting a shot where her panties had come off and she was spreading the extravagantly frilled lips of her pussy with two long, acrylic fingernails.

What was Grant thinking as he looked at that photo? Was he imagining what it would be like to have her there in reality, splaying her cunt so wantonly for him, or was it me he wanted to see like that, stripped down to nothing and displaying my readiness to be fucked? So many questions, so much I hadn't thought about when I'd asked Grant to masturbate for me. But this was how I would learn about his needs and desires; this was how our relationship grew and strengthened, I was sure of it.

And watching him was having another, equally powerful effect on me. I was getting horny. It was hard to stay detached when the man I loved was so close, so thoroughly wrapped up in the act of giving himself pleasure. Any thoughts he'd had that this was a crazy idea on my part had clearly been forgotten as his hand moved rhythmically along his cock. I'd played with him many times, but I'd never wanked him in quite the way he was doing now, fingers close to the spot where the head met the shaft and moving in a rapid sequence of long and short strokes, like some erotic form of Morse code.

My pussy was heating up nicely, juice trickling into the pyjama bottoms I wore for loafing round the house. Eyes glued on those shuttling fingers, I rubbed myself through the material, pushing the thick, double-stitched seam against my clit and enjoying the thrill of the friction.

Grant had flopped on to his back, heels drawn up close to his arse, T-shirt rucked up almost to his hard little nipples. The magazine was forgotten as he concentrated on bringing himself to his peak. One hand cradled his balls, the other pumped his cock ever faster. What were the images his mind was projecting on to the screen of his tightly closed eyelids, and how closely did they match my own? I pictured myself, decked out in that cheap red lingerie, two fingers pushed up into my pussy as a third danced on my clit. Grant watching me; me watching him. Breathing fast and heavy, tension building as Grant ordered me to remove the fingers from my cunt and thrust one deep into my arse instead. Such a dirty request, but one I'd be only too happy to comply with.

Part of me wanted to step out of the wardrobe and join Grant on the bed, taking his cock in my mouth to finish him off, but that wasn't part of our arrangement. My knees had gone weak, and I had to steady myself against the side of the wardrobe, almost as close to coming as Grant appeared to be.

His face was screwed up, veins standing out tautly in his neck, and in that moment just before his orgasm hit, I thought I'd never seen him look so masculine, so magnificent. 'Roz … Roz …' he grunted, lost in some place that was peculiar to him alone. 'Oh fuck, Roz!'

With that, his cock jerked in his fist and his come shot out, landing on his belly in thick, creamy ropes. I couldn't stay hidden any longer. I stepped out of the wardrobe to join him on the bed, so I could dabble my fingers in his quickly cooling spunk.

'Thank you,' I murmured, planting a long, sensuous kiss on his mouth and feeling closer to him now than I ever had in all the time we'd been together. 'Thank you for living out my fantasy.'

It gave me such a boost, such a reinforcement of the bond between us, to know that at the moment he came, I was all he was thinking about. He put an arm round me, pulling me into an embrace, during the course of which I kicked my pyjama bottoms away.

His fingers sought out my soaking pussy. I shuddered as one brushed lightly against my clit, enjoying a swift, fleeting orgasm that left me hungry for more.

Grant pulled his hand away. 'I'm glad you enjoyed my little performance so much, but what about putting one on for me? Why don't you get out that vibrator of yours, show me just how you manage to go through so many batteries when I'm not around?'

As I reached for my trusty vibe, I thought of the remaining blank Love Notes in the book, and all the fun I could have filling them in. Or maybe I should give a couple to Grant, let him come up with some kinky requests for me. After all, now he knew my ultimate fantasy, all bets were off. And when I went to buy the lube for him, perhaps I'd throw a surprise toy into the basket. A toy that strapped into place around my waist ...

Smiling wickedly, I spread my legs and started to play.

Between Friends
by Roxy Martin

Everyone loves Jen. She's pretty, funny and smart. The only unexpected thing about her is that she's single. We met in the school playground, I was there picking up my daughter, Jen picking up her son. Our children got on well, my Sarah being a little bit of a tomboy and more than happy to play at action heroes with young Ty.

Jen and I fell into an easy routine of coffee on Monday mornings, an exercise class on Wednesdays and a bottle or two of wine on a Friday night, while my Mike went down the local for several pints and a game of darts. Jen and Ty often came home with us after school and stayed for dinner, and Mike never complained. He said it was nice that I had a new friend.

One Friday night, Jen and I were halfway through our second bottle of wine, when a documentary about infidelity came on the television.

'Do you think Mike would ever play away?' Jen asked.

'Why? Are you interested if he did?' I'd replied with a flippant laugh – then stalled as I saw the look in her eye. 'You fancy Mike?'

Jen had the grace to blush. She shrugged her shoulders. 'Well, *you* must. He is your husband, after all.'

'Yes,' I said. Then, hiding behind the rim of my glass, I confessed, 'But I've sometimes wondered what it would be like to see him with another woman.'

'Are you giving me your consent?'

'Well, if I'm going to watch him with anyone, it might as

184

well be you,' I replied.

As we poured a glass each from a third bottle of wine, a plan was hatched. Maybe I should have been concerned by Jen's eagerness, but I put it down to the drink, and it had been my suggestion, so I could hardly back down now. Plus, I had one more confession to make, though not to Jen just yet. I was giving my consent because I fancy her, and had often wondered what it would feel like to kiss her. So far, I'd got no sense that she was into women, so I thought the next best thing would be to get my pleasure watching her with Mike.

Mike always gets home at just after eleven and likes to join us on the sofa for a shot of whisky before going up to bed – I wondered how upset he'd be to walk into the house and find the downstairs floor dark and empty.

'This could go badly wrong,' Jen said, as she stripped off and pulled my black nightie on. I tried not to look at her too much. She patted down her hair. 'Well?'

I smiled and replied, 'Just get into bed and we'll see what happens.' Then I spritzed her with my favourite scent.

'Are you really sure about this?' Jen questioned, chewing her lip.

I nodded, just as we heard Mike coming in downstairs.

'Sally, if you don't want–'

'Shh!' I put a finger to my lips.

I step out of the room and pull the door gently behind me, though not fully shut, then I go into Mike's office, where I wait. It doesn't take long for him to come upstairs. I hear the floorboards creak and I stand with my hand over my heart, trying to hold my breath and be quiet. I wait for Mike to go into our bedroom then pad silently down the landing, careful not to be seen as he steps out of his trousers and pulls his shirt off over his head.

Our bedroom is lit by moonlight. I've never liked the dark since suffering nightmares as a child, so we only have thin nets at the windows. An orange light glows in a plug socket, once a nightlight for our Sarah. Mike steps out of view but I hear him climb into bed. I imagine him pulling the covers over himself and draping an arm over Jen, maybe kissing the back of her head.

The suspense is killing me – and turning me on something rotten. I half-expect Jen or Mike to leap out of the bed. Instead, I hear Mike softly murmur, ''Night, love.'

I swallow, not too loudly I hope, and dare to move to my right. I can see the two shapes in the bed, my husband and my best friend. From under the covers, Jen stirs. She inches back into Mike, like I told her I do when I'm showing him that I want sex. I almost gasp at the thought of her bottom, covered in nothing more than a lace thong and my nightie, pressing against the front of Mike's boxers. It never takes him long. I've told Jen that for sex, my Mike was born ready. I bite my lip.

He could, as they lie under the covers, release his cock, and slide into her hot pussy, and I could be standing here, oblivious. His fingers could be probing her at this very moment, and I'm presuming her pussy is hot, because she must be wanting sex with Mike. Otherwise, wouldn't she have sprung out of the bed by now?

I watch, mesmerized, waiting for something to happen, then I hear movement. Mike is putting his arm around her. His hand, I know from experience, will fall on her breast. When, I am eager to know, will he realise it's not me in our bed? Will he care? What will he do? How will he react?

Jen groans gently. Again, I have told her that this is what I do. A soft moan, the sound of encouragement – is that what I sound like? I hold my breath and wait to see what happens. I shift slightly, wanting a better view. Jen has pulled the covers down slightly. I can make out the shape of her bare shoulder, and Mike leans in to kiss it.

'Sal?' Mike questions, and I know he is a little drunk, but not too drunk. In any case, I've never known drink to affect his potency. If anything, it makes him hornier.

'Hmm?' Jen replies, and shuffles further back into him. Mike pulls the covers back down to their waists, and I see that they are spooning. Surely he must realise that he is pressing against another body and not his wife's?

'Sal?' He questions again.

'If you're going to do it, then just do it, Mike,' Jen replies in a sexy growl, and I sense him faltering. He must know now, and *I* know he'll be pressing hard against her.

Just as I'm wishing they'd throw the damn quilt off completely, so I can see better, Jen, maybe reading my mind, does just that. She kicks it down the bed and positions herself back against Mike.

He has a hand on her hip. He has no excuse now. He has heard it isn't me, he can feel it isn't me. I wonder where his loyalties and his passions lie? Will he turn her away? Push her away? Will he be enraged that she's trying this on with him, that she's offering herself for sex?

He moves, and I fear he is going to get up, that he's caught me out, but Jen whips round to face him. She puts her hand on the side of his face.

'She's in with Sarah, said she'd be there all night,' Jen says, her voice heavy with temptation. We planned that she would say this to him when he realises who he's with, if she feels there's a risk he might run scared.

'And you're in my bed because …?'

She silences him with a kiss, and I feel my quim shudder with delight.

If he is going to turn her away, then he's taking his sweet time about it. She's running her hand through his hair, through the thick, dark curls, down his cheek and across his jaw, and then he's returning the kiss. His hand drops down over her shoulder, follows the contour of her body, over her hips, along her thigh, and then it returns upwards. It comes to a halt on her bottom.

'I'm in your bed because I would really like you to fuck

187

me,' Jen finally replies. 'I have always wanted you to fuck me, ever since I first met you.'

I gasp, silently. We hadn't actually rehearsed this bit – the words that she is saying are all new to me. Has she really wanted him to fuck her since she first met him? I have no idea.

'Jen,' he sighs, and I know that he is lost, that there is no turning back now.

The hand resting on her bottom inches the fabric of my nightie up – now it's touching the bare skin of her cheek. I imagine he's working the lace of her thong to one side, that his fingers will be brushing against her pussy lips, and it turns me on so much that I have to touch myself.

I trail my fingers between my thighs, then slide first one finger and then a second inside. I pinch myself, gently at first, building up the pressure, as I watch Mike grab hold of Jen and roll her onto her front. He hauls her onto her knees, he splays her legs and then he enters her from behind and I have to shove the fingers of my free hand into my mouth to stop the two of them from hearing my pleasure. My only regret, as Mike thrusts into Jen, is the view. I can see his bare arse, can hear the sound of his balls slapping against her, but I can't see her.

It doesn't take long until Mike grunts. Then he sits back and catches his breath. I won't be surprised if he scratches his head in puzzlement next. Maybe he thinks he's dreaming. I wonder if I am? He collapses down onto the bed next to Jen. She has rolled onto her side and he puts his arm around her.

'I can't stay here,' she tells him. 'In case Sally does come back through.'

'Yeah … sure,' is his reply.

He sounds half-asleep already. I watch as Jen gets out of the bed. I think my husband quite a fool to let her slip away so quickly. I wonder if he has satisfied her – she was quiet throughout. I step backwards from the shadows.

'Jen?'

She joins me on the landing. My nightie is flimsy, and I can see her nipples poking hard against the silk. I wonder if she is cold or turned on. I wonder if her flushed face is the afterglow of an orgasm?

I catch hold of her hand and ask her, 'Are you OK?'

She nods. She looks bewildered.

'Jen, can we do this again?' I ask, because I know that tonight wasn't enough.

We have a new plan. Two weeks have passed since my husband had sex with my best friend. Jen tells me that Mike has texted her several times. Asked her if what happened really happened. Told her he was glad that it had, but I was never to find out. She says her replies were just words of reassurance, that she wouldn't be telling me, but she was glad it had happened too.

I ask her to send a message, suggesting they should do it again. He says yes, they have to. That he wants it more than anything.

I have to try hard not to feel a little offended by that – what wife wouldn't? But luckily for Mike, I also want it to happen again, at least as much as he does.

Jen and I choose another Friday night. Mike leaves for the pub, giving me a kiss on the cheek and Jen a lingering look. She and I put Sarah and Ty to bed, then open a bottle of wine. We watch an X-rated DVD to put us in the mood for what we hope will happen later. Now we both want it more than ever.

'Last time, did he make you come?' I finally ask, though I don't look at her.

'Very nearly,' she replies.

'Me too,' I whisper.

It's half-past ten and Jen sends Mike a text to say that I've gone bed, that I'm not feeling very well, and maybe he should come back and take advantage of the situation? In truth, I am feeling perfectly fine. I hide out in the front room, a room that would be the dining room, if we ever got around to eating at the table.

Jen is waiting for him in the living room which opens on to the kitchen. We have pushed an armchair in front of the door to the stairs, mainly in case either child should wake and come wandering down, but also to keep me from appearing, so Jen is going to tell Mike. On hearing this, he tells her she is full of good ideas.

The scene has been set for their illicit act. The main lights are off and the room is softly illuminated by candles – candles scented with opium and amber. Norah Jones sings softly from the stereo.

'Jen?' Mike questions her. 'Is this what you want?'

'More than ever,' she replies.

I don't want to miss a thing, but I have missed that first lunge, for as I sneak in from the front room, my breath caught, they're already kissing. I've told Jen to keep him by the sofa so that I can hide by the second armchair. I think, maybe as I watch Mike kissing Jen, that I could march boldly into the room and he wouldn't notice – at least I *think* he wouldn't. And even if he did, I guess he wouldn't care enough to let it stop him doing what he's doing, because my husband is lost in passion.

His kissing is noisy, as is his breathing. He pulls Jen's jumper off over her head and he unclips her bra. She has gorgeous tits, smaller than mine, but firmer, with darker nipples. She's looking at me, over his shoulder, as Mike leans in to kiss them. She runs her fingers through his hair and winks at me, mouth part-open as she gasps and groans.

I could, if I touched myself, come there and then.

'Hey, tiger, slow down!' she chides him.

'She could walk in on us at any moment,' he replies.

'The doorway is blocked,' Jen returns in a whisper. 'Let's enjoy this, not rush it. We don't know when we'll be able to do it again.'

He pulls back from her, peels his own shirt off, and I look at the cobra tattoo that snakes over his shoulder and down his back. The times I've followed that ink with my tongue, gently kissing and biting him … She turns him, as I have asked her to, so I can see them both in profile.

'You're gorgeous,' he tells her.

I nod in silent agreement. Jen's breasts may be smaller than mine but so is her whole physique. Her body is more toned, her stomach flatter, and as her skirt drops to the floor, I see that her legs are more delicate, that her bottom lifts higher than mine. She is my focus, not Mike, who I can see naked any time I like.

'Ohh, baby …' he groans, as Jen drops to her knees and pulls down his jeans.

I know that Mike will think all his Christmases have come at once, that I'll never be able to get him anything for Christmas ever again that will compare to this.

I'm not a huge fan of oral sex. I mentioned that to Jen and she told me it was all about position and that I must be doing it wrong. Now I watch her take Mike in her mouth, as she gently rubs his length with one hand. I mimic the movement, rubbing myself at the same speed. Mike lasts longer than I do. I squirm in my knickers, pressing my fingers against the nub of my clit as I come to a silent, but shattering orgasm.

'I can't … take … much … more …'

'Shh …' Jen silences his protest, licking the glistening tip of his cock. 'Come all over my tits.' She aims it at her breasts, works him harder for just five or six more rubs and then he grunts and squirts, and I watch, and I feel like I'm going to come again.

She smiles up at him. He drops down onto his knees.

'Look at the mess you're in!' he says.

She draws him in close, wraps her arms around the back of his neck and pushes her breasts against his chest. Then they kiss again, as Mike gently lays her down on the carpet.

He pulls her legs out from under her, pushes her knees up. 'Lick. Me. Out,' she says.

I watch, wait for his reaction. I'm not the only one who's not really into oral. I can count on one hand the amount of times that Mike has gone down on me. I wonder what he'll do? I don't have to wonder for long. He has Jen's knickers off and is lying on the carpet, pulling her legs apart with his hands, nestling his face into her pussy before I can even catch a breath.

From here, I can't really see them that well, so I stand up and peer from the back of the chair. I inch further around, my fingers actually crossing that I don't disturb Mike. I don't want to spoil this moment. The new view is body-tingling fantastic. Mike is using his fingers to hold Jen open. He has told her to arch her back and he is licking her and slurping up her juices like a very thirsty man. I don't know which thought is turning me on more – the desire to be the licker or the licked. All I know is that the sight of my Mike feeding on my best friend's pussy is driving me insane with desire, and this time I slip three fingers inside myself, and I come again as Jen buckles.

'Good?' Mike questions.

Jen's eyes are closed.

My breath is caught.

'Now I'm going to fuck you.'

I gasp, then cover my hand with my mouth.

Mike moves his head, but Jen grabs him and kisses him. He is easily distracted by her, so whatever he thought he heard doesn't bother him for long.

I suck my fingers, salty from my pussy. I imagine it's the flavour of Jen that Mike has just been relishing, but now he's going to experience his cock in her pussy again.

'Stand up,' he tells her. 'Bend over.'

Jen shakes her head. 'No. I want you to do it while

looking at me. Looking me in the eye.'

He runs his hands over her body, down over her hips. 'Is that so?'

'Yep.' She pushes him towards the sofa, pushes him down onto it and then she straddles him.

He folds his arms behind his head, looks every inch the man who is about to receive absolute pleasure. I feel inside my pocket for the vibrator I've stashed there, pull it out and flick the switch to on. Although it's designed to be totally silent, it's pulsating crazily in my hand. When Jen holds Mike's cock in place and slips herself down onto it, I insert my silicone friend.

As Jen starts to increase her rhythm, I thrust my sex toy in and out of my pussy. She leans over Mike, presses down on his shoulders. He unfolds his arms and reaches around her, grasps her bottom. Now Jen is really enjoying herself. It starts with soft whimpers, then longer, more laboured gasps. I know my Mike is a man who can last a long time when he wants to. He is very dependable like that, and I guess that makes me a lucky woman. But it's Jen who is lucky now. She has slowed down, but beneath her he is taking charge. He moves his hands down on to her hips, then pulls her feet towards him. She lies back along his legs, then he withdraws his cock and uses the head of it to tickle and tease her pussy lips.

'Put it back inside me!' Jen groans.

'I like it like this,' Mike replies. 'I can see every twitch, every single movement.'

I groan along with Jen. I have removed my vibrator and use it to tease myself as Mike's teasing her. Then he pushes himself inside her, angling his cock for deep, deep penetration. I shove my vibrator back in as far as it will go, and I come as Jen does. She calls out Mike's name, grabs hold of his legs and cries with pleasure.

I collapse back behind the armchair.

'We'll have to do this again,' Mike says.

'Oh, yes, we will,' I reply silently, my body pulsing in the afterglow of what has been the best sex I have ever had. We most definitely will be doing this again.

The Watcher
by Catelyn Cash

I drift.

It's what I do.

This night, with newly awakened consciousness, I find myself on a darkened street. Parked cars, stone houses with well-kept gardens, pale light from street lamps, a distant, barking dog. I flex slowly, taking in my surroundings, placing myself in time, in space. No real reason. Habit, I suppose. That all-too-human urge to know: where; when; what; why?

Except, of course, I am not human.

A couple walk towards me and I still as their laughing, clinging humanity draws me in. I smell alcohol, perfume, cigarette smoke. A thrill passes through me and I am pulled towards their warmth and solidity. The woman is pretty, curvier than was in fashion when I was last here. I like curves. With no body of my own, lushness, softness, pliancy are magnets to my starved senses, and my excitement soars. To inhabit this woman, to be absorbed into her flesh and live within her for one night. Yesss.

I glance at her companion and slam on the brakes.

I have all night. There is no rush.

Stockily built, his head seems to rest on his shoulders and he carries a faint scent as though he hasn't showered. After so long in the darkness, my need is strong and I almost persist but something holds me back. A Watcher must have some standards. Are cleanliness and a neck too much to ask? I swirl impatiently as they pass and turn my attention to the houses.

The first I come to is not promising. Garden, neat to the point of obsession, filled with tubs and ornaments. Gnomes? I recoil as I recognise the image. I once attended a gnome sex party. You don't want to know what went on there. Really, you don't.

The brass knocker and letterbox are polished to perfection. The curtains tightly closed to keep out the night. They will not keep me out but I have no desire to enter as I already know what I will find. An elderly couple, drinking cocoa and watching TV. While it's always good to catch a rerun of *Inspector Morse*, there are other, more pressing needs to attend to.

I look along the street and anticipation shimmers through me. How many people are in these houses, pleasuring themselves and each other? Soon to be sharing their pleasure with me.

I glide through a few gardens until I feel the energy change. I stop. Young people inhabit this house, vibrant, noisy, full of life. A quick glance around the garden confirms this. A box of empty beer bottles left over from a party. Fag ends tossed in a barren rockery. An old bicycle lock still attached to a drainpipe, bike long gone. I smile. Students? My favourite kind of people. So full of energy.

Wasting no time, I float up to the bedroom window. Curtains pulled together but not closed, so easy enough to see in. A young woman on the bed. She is fully dressed but her hand is inside her jeans, moving rhythmically, and I am glad I didn't follow Shrek and his girlfriend home.

Without being aware, the woman on the bed pulls me towards her and I glide through the window. Her eyes are closed, her face soft, lost in private pleasure as her hand works busily. One foot rests on the floor and her legs are spread but with her jeans on I can see nothing. Shame. A wet pussy is one of my favourite sights. Even as I watch, her heels dig in, her hips rise slightly off the bed and she moans softly as her orgasm hits. Gentle and private though it is, the sexual energy flows into me, strengthening me. I inhale, absorbing everything.

Slowly her hips sink back onto the mattress and her hand slips out of her jeans. I don't even try to resist the lure of that scented skin. Eagerly I float across the room, touch her hand, feeling the vibrant, residual energy, the slick, sexual heat of her body flow into me. I close my eyes, and savour what she unknowingly gives me.

She stills and I freeze. Open my eyes. Hers are open too, scanning the room. She looks not frightened, but faintly puzzled.

She knows I am here?

The thought startles me. So few humans have this awareness. Gently I release her hand and rise from the bed. She sits up, still looking around her and rubs her hand. Has she felt my touch? Interesting.

As I say, few humans ever sense my presence. Maybe you are one of them? Have you ever sat naked in front of a mirror, applying make-up or brushing your hair and suddenly felt yourself being watched? Maybe you have lain on your bed with your lover's head between your legs and looked to the door, skin prickling, convinced you are being spied upon?

If that happens, do you drag the covers over you self-consciously? Or perhaps not?

Tell me, have you ever angled your head towards an imagined audience when your lover's cock is in your mouth, bringing yourself to swift orgasm at the thought of someone watching your performance? Be honest now.

I am that someone.

For millennia, my kind have roamed this earth, feeding on the sexual energy you humans have in such abundance and give away so freely. If only you knew what a resource you are. Sometimes there can be two of us, three, in your bedroom at night, circling, moving, touching when we can, but always, always watching.

You have sensed me. I know you have.

Those times you talk dirty, saying words you would never normally dare to use. Those times you allow your lover liberties you would never usually agree to. When his cock gets to go where it has previously been forbidden. When your fingers probe where they have never before ventured and your reward is your lover's shock, their pleasure and an orgasm to die for.

It is my reward too. A satisfied human ensures a satisfied Watcher.

The girl on the bed has relaxed now that I am no longer touching her. Her head is cocked, listening, and I become aware not only of what she is listening to, but the reason for her self-pleasuring.

The people in the room next door are having sex. Noisy, exuberant, wall-banging sex.

I melt through the wall.

They're on the bed. One man, one woman, gloriously naked. His back is sheened in sweat, his muscles and shoulder blades cleanly defined, arms straining with the effort as he holds himself over her. His buttocks are tight, as his hips piston in and out and he is chanting a mantra, 'God-oh-God-oh-God ...'

I prefer to inhabit women but I do, sometimes, take men. Variety and all that. If this were later in the night, had I already satisfied my initial hunger, I would simply take up a position on the bed beside them and watch, basking in the energy pouring off them. But I am needy. A shot of instant, concentrated ardour will take the edge off.

The girl is beautiful. Her long, dark hair, spread over the pillow, is damp with sweat, her arms are raised above her head and she is gripping on to the headboard – the source of the banging that disturbs their neighbour. Her back is arched, her legs wrapped around her lover's waist, holding him tightly as he pounds into her.

From the look on her face, I have arrived just in time.

Without a second to lose, I slide inside her skin. I have no idea how I do this, I'm just glad I can.

The energy explodes like a firework inside me. Had I a voice I would cry out, I would scream with pleasure. But I have no voice and I am grateful for this. This way the energy stays contained, flowing freely from her to me and back again so fast she doesn't even miss it.

And it is so good. It is unbelievable. My pussy is so wet, but even so he is stretching me, his balls are slapping my backside, his pubic bone grinding against my clit as every savage thrust jerks sharp cries from my throat.

Nearly there, Oh God, so nearly there … all that foreplay paid off … so close … will he last? Please, please, please let him last, I'll kill him if he doesn't wait for me. Yes, yes, omigod yes, I love him so much, he's so good at this, he's the best, his cock is the best, I love him, don't let him come yet, don't, let him come yet …

Her thoughts are uninhibited, unfocused, yet at the same time totally focused. Focused on this man she loves but also on the orgasm she fears may elude her.

I understand that kind of need. I do something I rarely do in the middle of sex; I jump into him.

Fuck! The energy is phenomenal! The power of youth could light up a small town. I am all cock. Nothing but cock. My entire consciousness is focused on nine inches of swollen, pulsing flesh as her cunt grips me like a wet little fist and my balls tighten as I race, I race … who am I racing? I have no idea. I only know that it is a race as old as life itself, a race I am so fucking going to win …

No! I pull myself back, remember her plea that he slow down and I slide reluctantly from his cock and into his mind and hear – 'Fuckohfuckohfuck!'

Hmm. I admire his focus but I need to get them working together on this. His energy is tremendous, though, and, this late in the action, hard even for me to control. In fact, I don't want to control him. I want to finish this. I want to be here when he comes. I want to be here when he shoots his load inside her. I can make his cock even bigger. I can, all I have to do is flex my mind …

I shake myself.

Leaving him, I slip back inside her. Her energy is different, but no less heady. She is nearly there, so very nearly there. Her love surrounds them both and he feels it, I know he does, but he is working on instinct now, only one part of his brain engaged.

What is it the feminists used to say back in the twentieth century? God gave man a brain and a cock and only enough blood to work one at a time?

I know what I have to do. I kiss him and it pulls him back from the brink, at the same time providing us with the connection that was missing. I flex my hips, he rolls his, a minute change of angle, a fraction of a degree, but we are now in the race together, hurtling headlong into ecstasy. Job done, I allow her to take over once more and I simply enjoy the ride. She hasn't even noticed my intrusion. Heat builds within her, spreading upwards from their joined bodies, gathering momentum. She tears her mouth from his and screams his name. Her nails rake his back. She is biting him, sobbing and crying with pleasure.

She convulses around him, rhythmically squeezing his cock, her inner muscles milking his very essence as she pulls him with her into the swirling, timeless vortex of pleasure that ensures the future of your race. His head draws back, the veins in his neck distended as with one last, powerful thrust he comes, firing his energy deep into her – and therefore into me – in sharp, hot jets that are life itself to both your kind and mine. Their climax is fierce, untamed and I absorb it all. Every last drop.

He collapses on top of her and, laughing joyfully, they kiss. There are tears in her eyes. In his too, possibly. 'What just happened?' he asks. 'That was fucking brilliant.'

He's right. It was. Fucking brilliant.

Their sweet nothings get on my nerves. That's the problem with expending too much energy all at once, the recovery time takes longer, even for the young. I am ready for more long before they are.

I move on. Terraces are easy. The houses mostly have the same layout so if I start in one bedroom, normally all I need to do to get into the bedroom of the next house is go through a wall. I do this now but have to go through several more houses before I find anything worth watching.

And there she is. A woman lying on a bed, reading. She's young and pretty enough but it's the book that catches my attention. An erotic novel. Yes, *that* one. I may not be sure where I am, but I do know which year it is now.

She's dressed for bed in a short cotton nightdress – not particularly seductive but if she takes it off, who cares? As I watch, she turns a page, then brushes her hand against her nipple, inadvertently drawing my attention to how good her breasts are. I see both nipples pushing against the cotton fabric. Been reading for a while, then?

I find a seat and settle down for whatever is coming next. Masturbation? A dildo?

The door opens and a man walks in, straight from the shower, towel wrapped round his waist. She doesn't look up, but I do. Nice body.

He glances over at the bed, sees what she is reading and grins. 'How's the book?'

She still doesn't look at him and I notice her hand is now resting casually on her chest, rather than her breast. 'OK. Bits of it, anyway,' she says.

Damned by faint praise but he isn't put off. I wrinkle my non-existent nose as he walks past me. Can I smell beer? Now sitting on the edge of the bed, he strokes her calf. 'They had piles of them at the station – I thought you'd like it. Half the women on the train were reading it on the way home.'

She turns a page, moves her leg away, just a fraction. He doesn't notice. 'Did you put the bins out?' she asks.

'Yes. And loaded the dishwasher.' If he's looking for brownie points, he's out of luck. Do I detect a certain chill in the bedroom?

Oblivious, he walks his fingers up her thigh.

'Did you remember to buy milk?' she asks.

His walking fingers stumble. 'I forgot.'

She looks at him now. 'Thanks. The one thing I ask you to do. Pity I didn't ask you to stop off at the pub with your mates while I put the kids to bed. Somehow you never manage to forget to do that.'

He pats her thigh and mumbles reassuringly, 'I'll get up early and nip out in the morning and get it.'

Even I know that isn't going to happen and I've known him two minutes.

She rolls her eyes. 'Yeah, right. Or I will. And then I'll get the kids up for school and make the lunches.' She slams the book shut and puts out the light, mumbling, 'I may as well. I do everything else around here.'

He nods amiably. 'Thanks, love. Fancy a quickie?'

He continues to sit on the edge of the bed in darkness. 'You can tie me up if you like,' he says hopefully. 'Like in your dirty book.'

'Liam, if I tie you up tonight the rope will be round your neck and I'll drop you over the landing. Go to sleep.'

I slip through the wall to next door.

The bedroom here is empty but I hear voices downstairs and check it out. Not too promising at first sight. Two men, mid-thirties, look as if they are regulars at the gym, one blond, one dark. I like the contrast.

They are standing by the front door. The blond has his jacket on, presumably leaving.

'Thanks, Greg,' he says. 'Sorry I've bent your ear all night. I just needed someone to talk to.'

There is a grimness to the other man's expression that

suggests it has been a long night and the talking has been pretty much one-sided. 'Any time.'

There doesn't seem to be anything for me here, but I linger a little. The blond guy isn't bad-looking. Maybe I'll hitch a lift with him, check out his street?

'It's just ... if I knew why she left me, it would be easier to deal with,' says Blondie, sorrowfully.

If this is a taste of how the rest of the evening has gone, kudos to this Greg guy for putting up with it.

'You gave it your best shot, Steve. Sometimes things just don't work out.'

'Yeah,' Steve says glumly. 'I suppose. I'd give anything to know why she left me, though.'

He holds out his hand. Greg shakes it automatically and looks about to say something but instead he pulls the other man to him and kisses him. Like, *really* kisses him. I'm pretty sure there is tongue involved.

I don't know which of the three of us is most surprised.

They break off and Steve stares at his friend, bug-eyed. 'What the fuck?'

Greg still holds his right hand. He presses his left hand against the front of Steve's jeans and I notice with interest the other man is sporting an impressive erection. 'That's why she left you, Steve.' Greg rubs him through the denim. 'You're gay.'

Even I hold my breath in the silence that follows.

'I'm not!' Steve splutters eventually. 'You've known me since university. You were at my wedding. How can you say that?'

In answer, Greg looks pointedly at his hand, still on Steve's crotch. Steve has neither backed away, nor knocked his hand away. Instead, his own hand is covering Greg's, pressing him against his cock.

Well, well, well! I'm glad I stayed.

Steve looks so shocked I'm tempted to slip inside him to find out what he's thinking. But I'm interested in what Greg is thinking too, so I stay put. Sometimes watching is its own reward.

'How – how did you know?' Steve asks.

Still holding his hand, Greg leads him through to a cosy sitting room. 'The question is, how did you not?'

Steve is looking poleaxed. 'Well, I suppose a couple of times I thought I might be,' he admits. 'I mean, I wondered …' Then he seems to pull himself together. 'Hell, I still don't know!'

Greg smiles. 'Well, why don't we find out?'

'How?'

'Take your clothes off.'

There is silence. Steve's cheeks burn. With excitement or embarrassment? I can easily find out but I'm enjoying watching the drama unfold.

'I really don't think …'

Greg touches his finger to Steve's lips. Just a touch. 'Take them off,' he says softly. 'I want to see you naked. I've fancied you for years.'

'You … you never said anything.'

Greg smiles again and this time I detect some sadness. 'I came close a few times. The night before your wedding, for instance. The first time Karen cheated on you. But I thought if you were in denial and trying to live straight, it wasn't up to me to interfere. Now you have three choices. You can leave. You can put on *Match of the Day* and open another bottle. Or you can strip.'

We both watch Steve's mental wrestling match. And then he strips. It isn't a striptease. He's almost in a daze. But he does it. And he looks pretty damn good naked, let me tell you. His erection is at half-mast, hopeful but hesitant. Like a dog that isn't sure it's allowed on the furniture.

Greg kisses him again. 'Now take my dick out and suck it.'

Steve's cock lurches but he looks terrified. 'What?'

'You heard me. It's a pretty sure-fire way to find out if

you're gay.'

Steve's cock has risen like a flagpole. He looks down at it as though he has never seen it before. 'C-can you take your clothes off first, d'you think? I'm feeling a bit overexposed here.'

Greg shakes his head. 'No. You have to do it without my help.' Wise move. This way, tomorrow, Steve won't be able to tell himself that he wasn't totally into this.

Tentatively, Steve reaches over and begins to undo his friend's belt. I see Greg's jaw clench but he holds himself very still. Next, Steve undoes the stud of his jeans.

'Careful with the zipper or we might be spending the night in casualty. I go commando,' Greg says.

I swear Steve's cock grows another inch. It is now standing against his belly, a barometer of the sexual energy in the room, and I sigh happily. Carefully, he slides down the zipper, his hands shaking as he releases a very impressive cock.

'On your knees,' Greg tells him.

Steve licks his lips but says nervously, 'Can we put the lights out?'

'No. You might change your mind, back out any minute. If I only get a few seconds of this, I want to remember every detail.' He puts his hands on Steve's shoulders and gently but firmly presses him down on to his knees on the carpet. Slowly, Steve sinks until he is eye to eye with Greg's cock.

I move closer. No. I am pulled closer by the energy thrumming between them.

Tentatively, Steve touches the other man. Greg hisses in a single, sharp breath and, emboldened, Steve wraps his fist around Greg's erection. Then he closes his eyes and closes his lips around his very first cock.

Greg shudders and draws his head back, hands resting on Steve's shoulders. 'Just suck it like it's your own,' he urges. 'Suck it like you've always wanted to have your dick sucked.'

Steve seems to like the sound of that. He grabs Greg's hips and takes him deeper, so deep he gags. Quickly, he adjusts and begins to suck eagerly, like a man who has been starved and then suddenly turned loose at a feast.

Greg savours this for a few minutes then reluctantly pulls out and draws Steve to his feet. He kisses him, hard. This time Steve kisses him back. This time there are definitely tongues. 'I think you're gay,' Greg tells him.

Steve grins. 'I want you to come in my mouth.'

Greg laughs. 'And I want to come in your mouth. But first, I need to fuck you. I want to be all the way inside your tight virgin arse. It *is* a virgin arse?'

Steve nods and I see excitement fire in his eyes, but trepidation too. 'Can't we just fool around for a while, give me a chance to get used to this?'

Greg kisses him again, more tenderly this time. 'We can fool around all night. After I fuck you. We need to do this, otherwise whatever else we do, neither of us are going to stop thinking about it.'

His hand is cupping the nape of Steve's neck while the other one strokes his cock. He leans closer and whispers in Steve's ear, 'Please. Let me fuck you?'

Steve's hips are moving and he is sliding his cock through his friend's hand. I don't think he is even aware he is doing it. 'Yes,' he is panting.

'Say it,' Greg demands. 'I want to know that you know exactly what you're agreeing to.'

'Yes. Fuck my arse. I want you to fuck my arse.'

I see the relief on Greg's face and the excitement too. 'On the settee!' he commands and Steve jumps to obey, then hesitates, unsure what is required of him. Eventually, going for the obvious, he turns his back and kneels.

Greg stops him. 'No. Sit down. I want to see your face as I slide my dick inside you for the first time.'

Steve is confused by this. 'Facing each other? Is that even possible?'

Greg grins. 'It's more than possible. Just do as I say and sit down.'

He sits. So do I, utterly gripped.

Greg strips off while we both watch him. I catch him sneaking a look at the window, checking the curtains are closed? Does he know I am here? I doubt it. Men don't pick up on me as often as women do. But then I don't watch men as often as I watch women. Wonder why. Something to think about, but not now. Now I am basking in raw, sexual energy.

'Sit back, pull your legs up and spread them.'

It takes Steve a moment to figure out the instructions and obey. For the first time, he shows some resistance. 'Not very dignified.'

Greg spreads his legs for him and kneels between them. 'Steve, mate, there's nothing dignified about sex. Not it it's done properly. Trust me.'

Hear hear.

Greg reaches under a sofa cushion and pulls out lubricant and condoms.

'You were that sure of me?' Steve is indignant.

'No, but I never gave up hope. Now you relax while I loosen you up.' Greg pours a generous amount of lubricant on to his fingers and immediately applies it to Steve's arsehole. Steve tenses but Greg only laughs. 'Don't worry. Now I've finally got you here, I'm going to make sure you enjoy this.'

Greg's fingers circle gently and Steve's eyes lose focus. His head lolls back on the settee as he gradually gives himself up to this new experience. Greg, it seems is something of an expert. I am tempted to enter Steve and experience this with him but I'm enjoying watching too much to make the jump.

After a few minutes, I see Greg slide a finger inside Steve's arse. The other man stiffens, then relaxes without opening his eyes. Then the whole thing is repeated with

207

another finger. And then once again.

Steve's cock is upright. A thick vein throbs along the underside, and I can feel the energy pulse through it.

I am not the only one looking.

'Ahh... fuck,' says Greg softly and drops his head, nuzzling his friend's balls before taking him into his mouth. I get the impression this isn't how he has planned it but I'm happy he's going with the flow. He sucks eagerly, fingers still working.

Steve comes. Just like that. Greg is caught off guard, as I am, but he mans up and gulps down every drop, his throat moving as he swallows. Then he rocks back on his heels, looking dazed but delighted. 'I've waited a long time for that.'

Steve, shaking, breathes, 'That was fucking awesome!'

'Nah, it was good. This is going to be awesome.' In seconds, Greg is rubbered up and lubed. He grins at Steve. 'You ready?'

The other man nods uncertainly.

'Don't worry,' Greg reassures him. As he speaks, he places the tip of his cock against Steve's arse and presses gently. I'm going to go at your pace, OK? If I go too fast, you tell me. I want this to be perfect.'

Steve nods, still nervous but his eyes glow with excitement as his best friend's cock inches inside him. Greg is true to his word. He goes slow and I can see how much effort it costs him. And then he must have pushed past some barrier because suddenly the resistance is gone and he glides smoothly all the way in.

Steve moans.

Greg trembles with pleasure as his balls hit Steve's arse. He reaches for more lube and takes Steve's cock in his hand. It is already hard again. 'Open your eyes. Watch me fuck you,' he urges.

Steve obeys, and Greg begins to move in and out while pumping his friend's cock. Slowly at first, then he builds up speed. As he draws out, he drags his hand up Steve's shaft. As he slams back in, his hand strokes down, matching the movement. Steve's hands are gripping Greg's shoulders. He is breathing hard, as he watches his friend fuck him. In and out, up and down, Greg's hand moving in time with his cock.

It must feel like he is fucking himself.

Again, I am tempted to share the experience but force myself to hold back. I will chose my moment, ride the rush, maximise the impact.

Greg is losing control. Steve too. The rhythm builds and I can wait no longer. I jump into Steve – no, Greg – no, Steve. I realise I am being buffeted back and forth between them. Greg slams into me and I overflow with pleasure. Steve's moans send heat racing through me and I work my cock even deeper, pump my hand even faster. Steve wraps his legs around me and pulls me to an impossible depth and I am gasping, yelling, coming with a force I have never known before. Then I am Steve again and I too am coming harder, more violently than I have with any woman.

And then I am evicted by the sheer force of their climax, their energy too much even for me. But I don't mind, as I duck and dive between them, writhing and rolling in the swirling, white hot energy that pours from them.

What a rush. What a fucking rush.

I love this planet. I love humans. The scope of your emotions, your limitless imaginations. And those fantastic bodies you take so much for granted.

Steve and Greg rest, entwined, unable to believe their luck at finally finding each other. But as the sweat cools on their bodies, already I am restless. Already I crave more.

Without a backward glance I glide towards the door and out into the night air. There I look up and down the empty street.

All those closed doors. So much going on behind them.

Who knows? Maybe I'll visit your street next?

Cheating Made Easy
by Lynn Lake

We'd invited Jiri and his wife, Ivanka, over for a barbeque. They attended the same church we did, lived just a couple of streets over, and since they were fairly new to the country (as well as the church and the neighbourhood), Roger thought it would be a good idea to get to know them better. He wants to go to Europe at some point in time, so he was interested in learning more about the Czech culture from the couple.

Well, it didn't take him long to see what a loving, open culture it is. Because, while we were in the kitchen preparing the salad and prepping the steaks, Roger suddenly said to me, 'Hey, look, Beatrice. They can't keep their hands off one another.'

I dropped the salad tongs and moved over to where Roger was standing, peered over his shoulder. Sure enough, Jiri and Ivanka were passionately kissing one another in our backyard.

They were seated at the picnic table on the patio right next to our deck, facing one another, their arms wrapped around each other, their mouths locked together. Roger and I could see it all clearly through the tinted, plate-glass picture window that looks out onto the backyard. I gripped my husband's shoulder and followed after him, as he moved out of the kitchen and into our open dining room, closer to the window, to get an even better, more close-up view of the action heating up under the hot summer sun in our backyard.

Jiri and Ivanka are both tall and lean and blond and blue-eyed. In fact, they look more like brother and sister than husband and wife. They have high cheekbones and full lips, long, smooth limbs and taut, mounded bottoms; Ivanka a pair of high, firm-looking breasts. But while they may look like siblings, they sure weren't acting like it, kissing up a storm at the picnic table.

'Those two are hungry – and not just for barbeque,' my husband remarked, his eyes glued to the sexy scene.

I bit my lip, my fingernails biting into Roger's shoulder, watching Jiri slide his hands off Ivanka's back and around onto her breasts. He squeezed her tits, their tongues flashing together. And she dropped a tanned, slender hand down into the man's lap, pumped his obviously hard cock up and down in his jeans.

'Boy oh boy!' Roger breathed, gripping the back of a dining room chair.

Jiri cast a quick glance over his shoulder but he couldn't see us through the tinted glass, with the sun so bright. And I don't know if he thought we couldn't see him, or what, but he pulled the green tank top his wife was wearing out of her jeans and rolled it up over her breasts, exposing the woman's tan, conical boobs. Then he grasped the bared pair, plied the hot flesh, bent his head down and lashed a pointed, caramel nipple with his wet, pink tongue.

'Boy oh boy oh boy!' Roger yelped. 'Maybe we'd better take the food out before all their clothes come off? It isn't that kind of buffet, is it?'

He looked back at me, at my glaring violet eyes which were fastened upon the pair of lovers. Still pinioning his shoulder with one hand, I slid my other one around his waist and onto his crotch, gripped his cock and pumped it like Ivanka was pumping her husband's shaft.

Roger jerked, and gulped. His erection was as hard as iron, forged out to its full length in the front of his pants. I shifted my hand up and down, feeling the throbbing heat, adding to it. My pussy was a wet mess in my white short-

shorts, my nipples pricking into Roger's back with arousal.

Our breathing became heavy and ragged, as we watched Jiri suck one of Ivanka's jutting nipples into his mouth, tug hard on it with his red lips, do the same to her other stiffened nipple. She tilted her head back and we could almost hear her moan, her blonde hair streaming down her arched back, her one hand digging into Jiri's shoulder, the other pumping his jeaned cock.

Jiri sucked, tongued his wife's tits, bit into her nipples. Her boobs shone at the trembling tips with the man's saliva, the flesh reddened where he applied his hands in vigorous groping. I ground my pussy into Roger's heaped buttocks, pumping against him, tugging on his hard-on, pressing against his big, strong, hot body. He gripped the back of the chair with both hands, his knuckles burning white. Then we both groaned, when Ivanka shook her tits free of her husband's hands and mouth and freed his cock from his pants, dipped her blonde head down and took the swelled-up tip of Jiri's enormous dong into her wet, red mouth and sucked on it.

My fingernails dug into my husband's cock, palm pumping harder, my breath rasping in his burning red ear. I thumped my brimming pussy against his butt, rubbing my tits up and down his back in rhythm. He swallowed hard and pulled his hands off the chair and tore his pants open, freeing his cock to my gripping, ripping hand.

I jacked his bare erection, stroking and twisting up from his ginger-dusted balls to the bloated hood of his raging cock, giving him a heated handjob to match the torrid blowjob Ivanka was giving her husband. Because the woman was making no bones about it now, bobbing her head, inhaling Jiri's cock three-quarters of the way down and then sucking back up his gleaming, veiny shaft. He played with her tits with one hand, rubbing her pussy through her tan shorts with the other, as she sucked his cock with an urgent passion.

I guess they were racing against time, thinking Roger and I were going to pop out of the back door at any moment and spoil their early-evening delight. Although I'm not sure they would've stopped even if we had.

But we had no intention of interrupting their sex show. Instead, we were feeding off it. I pulled on Roger's prick, jammed my other hand up under his T-shirt and pulled on one of his rigid nipples. He grunted, pumping his hips to thrust his cock back and forth in my shunting hand, reaching back to plant a palm of his own on my sodden pussy and rub it. Like Jiri was rubbing his wife's pussy.

Our hands moved faster and faster, timed to Ivanka's excited cocksucking, Jiri's heavy petting. Her blonde hair flew, her red lips blazing up and down his cock. He yanked one of her nipples out taut, snapped it back, his hand a blur on her pussy.

'Yes! Yes!' I hissed in my husband's ear, riding his rubbing hand, wildly tugging on his cock.

Jiri jerked. Roger spasmed. Semen spilled out of Ivanka's sucking mouth. Semen shot out of Roger's cock, my wrist burning as I torqued out the hot, sticky ropes. Then Ivanka shuddered, bucked on the picnic table, Jiri's jumping hand shooting her full of ecstasy like he was shooting out his joy into her mouth.

'Oh God, Jiri!' I cried, shivering with my own wild orgasm, Roger's flying fingers and the super-erotic visual stimulation making me come as hard as my hunky husband and the handsome pair of lovers outside.

The food tasted all the better because of what we'd all gone through. We didn't say a word about what we'd witnessed to Jiri and Ivanka, but they must have sensed our satisfied satiation. Because they extended an invitation to us to come over to their house the following evening, where they'd play host – first in their backyard, and then in their bedroom.

I was more than a little hesitant at first. But Roger was more

214

than eager and willing. Especially when Ivanka stripped off her sheer yellow summer dress and stretched out on her back on their bed, naked. I could see the excitement in his big blue eyes, bulging the front of his black pants, as Ivanka spread her long, lithe legs and gripped her ripe, succulent tits. And Jiri shed his clothes and dived in between his wife's legs, started licking her blonde-fuzzed pussy.

Ivanka moaned, then smiled at Roger and me. 'You come share your love with us, too?' she said, looking from Roger to me.

The guy was already stripping off his shirt and shoes, pants and briefs and socks, anxious to experience Jiri and Ivanka's "culture" of open, uninhibited sex. I saw no harm, just much pleasure, as long as we kept to our own partners. And the sight of Jiri lapping at his wife's pussy, his cute bubble-butt stuck up in the air, burned away any other inhibitions I might have.

Roger helped me off with my dress and bra and panties and sandals, helped me lie down next to the lovely Ivanka. She and her husband had a large bed, built for multiple partners. Ivanka grasped my hand, as Roger pushed my legs apart and dove tongue-first into my pussy.

I moaned, my eyelashes and pussy fluttering. It wasn't often that Roger performed oral sex on me but the guy was obviously inspired – by the nude Ivanka so close, by the lewd tongue action Jiri was laying down on her pussy. He was slurping his wife's slit full-length, painting her sex with wide, dragging strokes. Roger replicated, tonguing up my twat. It was quite the performance, all right. I squeezed Ivanka's hand, staring down over my heaving breasts at the two men.

They lapped our pussies, dazzling our senses. Then Jiri popped Ivanka's pink clit up between his fingers and sucked on it. Her fingernails bit into my hand. She thrashed her blonde head back and forth, arching her taut body up into her husband's mouth. Roger pinched my clit between his

215

blunt fingers and blew on the button, then took it between his thick lips and sucked.

I tremored, squealed, my entire body flooding with a wet heat that made me dizzy and desirous. So much so that when Ivanka turned her head my way and kissed me on the cheek, I turned my head and kissed her on the lips. Her mouth was moist and soft and warm. We pressed our lips together, our husbands sucking on our clits. Her tongue darted deep into my mouth and I welcomed it, along with her hand cupping and squeezing one of my breasts.

Our amorous girl-girl adventures impassioned our hunky hubbies still more. Jiri jumped on top of Ivanka, plunged his cock into her mouth and juice-wettened pussy. She moaned into my mouth, then turned her head and took Jiri's tongue in hers, as his cock pumped into her pussy. Roger was quickly on top of me, inside of me, stretching and stuffing my overstimulated pussy with his big cock. The men fucked Ivanka and me, all four of us bouncing together on the bed.

I'd always thought sex was something you did in private – one-on-one. But I had to admit, as I twined my tongue around Roger's, thrilled to the beat of his cock drilling deep into my pussy, and watched Jiri fuck his wife, that there was much to be said about sharing one's passion for each other with others. The situation was incendiary, the sensations incredible; making love next to another couple making love.

Jiri pulled out of his wife and turned her over. Ivanka sprang up on her hands and knees on the bed, thrusting out her butt at her husband. He grinned at me and Roger, and then ploughed his glistening organ into Ivanka's pussy from behind, gripping her hips and fucking her. She grasped the bedspread and urged him on, rocking back and forth.

Roger couldn't follow sexual suit fast enough. In no time at all, he was banging me from behind, cocking me in the doggy position. I gripped Ivanka's clutching hand, kissed her bouncing mouth. The passion was as intense as I'd ever experienced.

The men pumped us harder and faster, smashing into our butt cheeks, pounding into our pussies. I had my eyes closed and my teeth clenched. Then, all of a sudden, the fucking abruptly stopped, leaving me and Ivanka empty and speechless on the wallowing bed ... until I felt a cock re-enter my gaping cunt, and Ivanka twisted her head around and smiled.

'Fuck her, Jiri!' she implored him. 'Fuck our good friend, Beatrice!'

That's when I twisted my own head around, and saw Jiri in behind me, grinning. It was his huge member swelling my tunnel, surging back and forth. And I saw my husband, also grinning, as he inserted his erection into Ivanka's pussy, and drove it home.

I wasn't sure what to think, nor how to react. But there was no time for deep thoughts, nor any course of action other than to hang on, because Jiri was blasting his thighs against my buttocks, pistoning pleasure into my pussy with his thundering cock. It was wicked, wild, amazing. Getting fucked by Ivanka's hung, handsome husband. How could I deny my man the evil pleasure of fucking Jiri's wife?

Ivanka and I entwined our fingers again, holding on to one another, jerking together with the pounding beat of the cocks in our pussies – her husband's cock in my cunt, my husband's cock in her cunt. We kissed, frenched, our men's grunting and groaning sounding over the smack of flesh against flesh. They were racing one another again, driving into us, each wanting to be the first to make the other man's wife come on the end of his cock.

I squeezed my eyes shut, the steamy pressure building and building inside of me, stoked higher and higher by Jiri's pole hammering into me from behind. His fingers dug into my fleshy waist, his wiry thighs thumping against my gyrating buttocks. And then I heard him roar, felt his cock jump inside me, spurt. He thrust wildly, spraying my tunnel with heated juices. It was more than I could endure.

I screamed, shuddered, blazing with my own unleashed utter joy. I quivered violently on the end of Jiri's shooting cock, surging molten with ecstasy. I vaguely heard Ivanka shriek, and Roger bellow, as they shared their own brutal, beautiful orgasms.

Everything was going fine; fantastic, in fact. I didn't mind Roger having sex with Jiri's wife, as long as I was there to share in the erotic experience. But then, one night, Jiri suggested that we all go to a "party" at a friend's house. Apparently, there would be about a dozen other couples there, all willing and wanting to wantonly share.

I was furious at the guy. You see, I'd been having an affair with Jiri for over three months, long before he and Ivanka had got together with Roger and me as a couple. And I sure as hell didn't want him cheating on me with anybody but his wife. That was just taking the concept of "openness" to the point where marriage has no meaning at all any more.

To where forbidden fruit becomes tasteless.

Come Underground
by Demelza Hart

The doors of the end carriage shut with that inevitable, inimitable judder and swish, and the Tube train moves out of the easternmost station on the Central Line, heading west. With a lurch of the carriage, I sway on my heels and sit quickly.

As usual, I haven't managed to escape the office before 10 p.m.; next month's edition is proving temperamental. I settle myself and glance around, taking note of my fellow passengers. Along the carriage, a well-toned man in his early twenties, his jeans and T-shirt splattered with copious amounts of paint and varnish, stares blankly ahead. Opposite me is an African-Caribbean in a designer tracksuit. His eyes are closed and an incessant hip hop beat breaks through his headphones. He moves his head rhythmically, tuned into his own world.

It could be a late-night Tube journey like any other.

Seated next to me, so close I can smell his subtle, spiced aroma, is a man whose dark hair curls loose about him like a pirate, but it's in stark contrast to his clothes – he's wearing white tie and tails. He loosens the bow tie and tugs it off before undoing his top button and exhaling in relief. Beside him rests a violin case. A musician fresh from a concert.

As I shift in my seat, I can already feel that familiar tingle. Because, despite appearances, this is not a Tube journey like any other. A half-sigh floats from my tense body, not so much in exhaustion as anticipation.

When the train reaches the next station, the doors of the

carriage don't open, just like I've been told they won't. On the platform, a confused girl, chewing rapidly, her hair scraped back into a high ponytail, frowns before hustling to the next carriage. I glance to the connecting door at the end; as I expected, the window has been blacked out.

The train starts again. My gaze turns to the remaining occupants of the carriage.

Further along is a guy of about 30, vaguely scanning the *Evening Standard* with his vividly blue eyes. His dark blond hair keeps falling rebelliously in front of his face and his gorgeous upper body is concealed only by a tight Abercrombie & Fitch T-shirt. Two seats away is an older man, mid-forties maybe, but with an elegant distinction which tightens my belly. He scrutinises the *Financial Times* as if his future depends on it. His suit is clearly tailored and his black shoes, so highly polished I could do my eyeliner in them, reflect the bright lights.

Judder and swish. The train continues along the track. Judder and swish. Expectation hangs thick in the air. The hip hop guy with the headphones opens his eyes briefly and meets mine before retreating back to his music.

Again, at the next station, the doors fail to open. It's just the six of us, five men and me, and it will stay this way for the duration of the journey. That's the deal. That's the arrangement. It helps to have friends in high places.

As we continue along, enfolded in the muggy air of a subterranean London summer, I recall how this came to be. It was a party, the same as any other, so I thought, until I found myself in an intense conversation with a man I'd never before met. He judged my needs quickly, seeing how I needed release and sexual thrill to counteract the stress of a busy, professional life. Oh, how right he was. He told me that, with the right word in the right ear, he could arrange an encounter: one that would be discreet, safe, and unforgettable. How could I resist? I told him my fantasies; he told me he had a friend in management at London

Underground. I was sold.

And, a few short weeks and various disclaimers later, here I am.

I recognise all my travelling companions from their photos, sent to me with a brief biography (with certain letters in their names carefully redacted) and recent medical test results: all squeaky clean, as indeed is the carriage I'm now in. It smells ridiculously fresh; the floor almost sparkles.

I was asked to submit a list of dos and don'ts of my own. My dos outdid my don'ts.

My breathing quickens. I want it to start. I want it so much. Judder and swish. The heat between my legs is unbearable. My tight skirt, already short, has ridden up, revealing the lacy tops of my hold-ups, perhaps more – I'm not wearing any knickers. That was part of the deal.

My knee touches the piratical violinist's leg. He doesn't move it away. As the train rumbles along the line, our legs bump erratically together. He moves closer, increasing the contact. I watch, hypnotized. On any other Tube journey I would shift apart and avoid physical contact with a stranger, but not tonight. The ache inside is unbearable. I tear my eyes away only to meet with those of Hip Hop opposite. His gaze then drops and he looks directly at where my skirt has risen even higher up my thighs. He can see right up me, right up to my sex, newly-waxed and growing wetter with each second that passes.

And then Violin Pirate moves the hand which has been on the armrest and brings it to my leg. His fingers slowly slide down around it and flex. I suck in air with delighted shock. He begins to stroke the inside of my thigh, each fingertip imparting a delicious building heat to my hungry skin. I want him higher, up, in me, touching my clit which is so ripe with need it physically hurts, but every stroke ends tantalizingly short.

Hip Hop's gaze is now fixed between my legs, but still

his head bobs to the music.

We reach the next station. The doors don't open and a man on the platform hurries to get into another carriage. We're off again.

My legs open instinctively, wider, welcoming the questing fingers of Violin Pirate. And there they are. Fuck! I nearly come instantly. He grazes my clit before slipping down to the opening of my pussy. Curling his fingers under, he pushes up into me and pumps, maintaining the pressure on my clit. Hip Hop stares, his face unfeasibly impassive.

Instinctively, I grab Violin Pirate's wrist and slip down the seat to ease him further in. His fingers work quickly, stroking and rubbing my inflamed clit with certain skill.

My first come doesn't take long, and I release it with an audible groan. The other men stare, none of them surprised, all of them aware. Only The Suit seems disinterested; his head is still in his paper. Violin Pirate brings up his hand and offers his fingers to my mouth. I suck on them avidly, delighting in the salty succulence of my own pleasure.

When I can refocus I look across to see Hip Hop's cock free, lurching out of his pants. He raises his eyes to mine and waits, knowing what I'll do. As if released from a pistol, I'm on my knees. The stupendous black cock before me bobs in welcome. Forcing myself to pause, I place my hands on Hip Hop's knees and give him a little smile. His gorgeous dark eyes twinkle. The music has stopped and his headphones are now slung around his neck. I have his full attention. I dip my head and take him deep in one go, right to the back of my throat. He hisses out a low 'Fuck!' of pleasure before I rise off the thick, long shaft with slow deliberation. Hip Hop holds my head, guiding it along his rigid flesh. He gives me encouraging sighs and moans as I go about my task. I could suck cock all day, but never thought I'd do it quite like this.

It's all going exactly as I hoped. Out of the corner of my eye I notice T-shirt Hottie approaching. At first he stands to one side and just watches, his arms crossed, a sly smile on his delicious mouth. I smirk up at him before tonguing the end of Hip Hop's cock rapidly, eliciting a guttural, 'Fuck, yeah!'

Painter Man is still seated, but he's staring across and, after undoing his jeans, starts to pump his equally impressive prick fast.

My tongue becomes a blur, sweeping along the seamed undershaft to take Hip Hop's heavy balls in my mouth before swirling back up and delving into the slit. He's very vocal in his appreciation, which causes my cunt to leak ever more desperately. And just as I almost cry out for someone to touch me, it happens. Hands, I'm not sure how many, are running over my arse, slipping over my clit, pulling off my skirt so that I'm fully exposed.

Then long, warm fingers undo my shirt, slide into my bra and toy with a nipple. Second only to sucking cock, I could have my tits toyed with all day. Oh, I am being well and truly toyed with now.

At the next station I glance out on to the platform. A young guy tries the door, but when he looks into the carriage his mouth drops open and his eyes widen. He tries the door ever more desperately and his hand moves instinctively to his crotch. I give him a little wink as the train moves on, leaving him stranded. The thrill of exposure makes me sink down deep onto Hip Hop until my eyes water.

'Hold it, hold it, hold it,' he moans, his hands pushing me on to him. Only when my lungs beg for air do I pull up strongly, right off his cock which drips my saliva, and gasp in heady, exhilarating gulps. 'F-finish it,' he stutters, motioning me back to suck hard on the head. I pump the shaft with my hand and almost instantly he tenses. Come floods my mouth. Bloody hell, it's a lot of come. Luckily for him, I love it; I love the taste and the feel and the slip and slide of man juice gliding down into me.

And instantly there's more.

'Turn around.' I turn my head to see the equally stunning

cock of Painter Man mere inches away. 'Open,' he demands. I gape for him. He comes hard on my tongue and lips, each burst accompanied by a litany of rapturous cursing.

He tastes stronger than Hip Hop but still I gulp him down. I've never had the chance for a direct comparison of spunk before; another first, I realise with a grin.

I'm pulled to my feet and motioned over to stand at the pole in the middle of the carriage. I hold it for dear life as there is now an onslaught of sensation over my body. T-shirt Hottie's fingers are reaching up inside me from behind. I crane my neck and offer him my mouth which he takes hard as his fingers delve deeper.

My shirt has been removed – I missed how and when – and Violin Pirate reaches into my bra cups and places my breasts on top so that they jut out prominently. The nipples, dark and hard and hot, are perfectly positioned for toying with. And Violin Pirate does just that. My right nipple disappears into his mouth. And what a mouth. He manages to suck and flick the nipple at the same time, while T-shirt Hottie continues to enthral my cunt and clit. Oh God, I'm going to come again any second. I groan so loudly it reverberates through the usually silent carriage.

Painter Man sees the other nipple sitting there ignored and applies himself to it, slipping my bra fully off as he does so. He is soon sucking away assiduously, adding his teeth to send little sparks dashing through me. Clearly he thinks it's the least he can do after I guzzled his spunk so merrily. I can think of many other things he can do later.

Hip Hop, meanwhile, is recovering. His magnificent cock is slumped, for the time being, in post-come relaxation, but I doubt it will be long before it's stirred into action again. For now, he's content to sit and watch.

The Suit is still reading the *FT*. His hair is greying at the temples and his sharp cheekbones lend him a fascinating masculine beauty. He is, quite simply, deliciously, decadently do-able, but I can wait. After all, I have more than enough to keep me busy.

Another station. A young couple waits outside the carriage. I meet their eyes and they stare in disbelief. T-shirt Hottie slips down to tongue my clit at just that moment and I come with a wail, looking directly into the eyes of the woman on the platform. The train moves on, leaving them standing, gawping.

'Gorgeous come, hey?' says Painter Man.

'Uh-huh,' I slur, unable to voice more.

'She hasn't been fucked yet,' someone says.

'Turn her around.'

Painter Man does, leaning himself against the pole and moving me so that my back is against him.

T-shirt Hottie is in front of me and, helped by Painter Man, he picks me up so my legs are straddling him. I've only just noticed his cock. Jesus! Whoever picked these guys knew what they were doing. I've never before seen such a shedload – or rather, a carriage load – of such stupendous man flesh. This one is long, not as broad as Hip Hop's or Painter Man's perhaps, but it arcs up towards his belly magnificently and, right now, it has the most succulent little drip dangling from its tip. I'd rather like it in my mouth, but I'm about to get it elsewhere. And why not? My cunt is on fire for cock. It's waited long enough.

So, here I am, on the Tube, held up by someone I've never met before, legs splayed, pussy exposed, awaiting impalement upon the outstanding cock of a total stranger.

'Ready?' grins T-shirt Hottie, rubbing the head along my dripping opening.

'Oh, fucking hell, hurry up.' I'm desperate. I think he can tell.

Painter Man holds me tight round the waist, T-shirt Hottie grips onto my hips and – bam! – he's inside me.

A primeval groan rises into the air, guttural and uncontrolled. I think it must be my primeval groan. But, Christ, does that cock feel good.

I look at him and smile, a vacant, sexed-out smile, but at least I manage it. He pulls out slowly, really slowly, studying my every reaction. Fuck, that is good. Fuck! That is phenomenally good. I knew that curve on his cock would work. It rubs against my G-spot and lights flash behind my eyes.

'Again,' I demand. He does. Nudging it back and forth, he notes my every ragged breath and smile of blissful delirium.

'I can't keep this up forever,' he moans. 'You're too fucking tight. Need to start fucking you fast.'

'Do it, do it, do it,' I chant, lost to the perfect penis.

The others, meanwhile, are just watching. Painter Man is holding me up and I can feel his cock stirring again to nudge my arse, but the others just sit or stand around, occasionally stroking their own pricks, otherwise just staring, moving for a better vantage point. I'm ecstatic, not just because of the rapid rise of what may well be the perfect come, but because this is it. This is what I wanted. This is what I dreamed of.

Sex. In public. On a train. With total strangers. Oh, thank you, God of Cock!

T-shirt Hottie is going at me ferociously now. His cock still catches my G-spot with each thrust and, when I meet his eyes, we're both gone. He comes first, his face creasing into a look of agony, and explodes into me. 'Shit! Coming so fucking much!'

With that I follow him, shaking, grateful for the strong arms of Painter Man who grips me so tight the air is forced from me as my orgasm holds and shakes.

Afterwards, they guide me over to a seat. Little drops of leaking spunk splatter the floor as I go.

'Just take some time,' murmurs Violin Pirate, whose cock I now see for the first time. He's naked from the waist down. Judging on what I'm looking at, I'm not going to want to take that much time. He smiles and kisses me.

I let my head fall back against the seat and lock eyes

226

momentarily with The Suit. He's still bloody reading his paper. OK, not everyone has to take part actively, I know that, but … I really, really want him. His arrogant disdain is turning me on more than anything. I'm gagging to reach into those bespoke trousers and take him out and ride him. He averts his eyes and turns back to the peach pages of his newspaper.

We rumble through some more stations. Liverpool Street – still a long way to go.

'Open.' It's Violin Pirate again. He's kneeling on the floor now, pushing my legs apart, and before I know it, his mouth is attached to my cunt lips. His tongue seeks far up into me and he sucks hard, clearly enjoying the taste of another man's come as much as my own juices. That thrills me even more and I grind onto him.

And in the midst of hot, questing mouth, there's something else. A finger. It's probing up my arse. Another favourite. These guys read their notes very well. And another joins it. I can feel my sphincter stretching to take the two digits. It can handle them; it's had more. Hopefully, it'll have a lot more before this journey is over.

I simply sit back and enjoy the feasting on my body, letting my eyelids flutter shut. When I open them I see cock. It's Painter Man, standing on the seat beside me; he is risen again. It would be rude to ignore him. I open wide. He slides in and immediately starts fucking my mouth. I don't have to do much, he's happy to plough in and out through my plumped-up lips while I concentrate on the delicious feelings fluttering through from my cunt and arse. Violin Pirate's tongue is out and along my clit now, teasing and flicking. It responds yet again; can I really keep on coming like this?

The answer is a resounding yes. God, he has a dream mouth. With sucks and licks and nuzzles and pecks, he brings me to a staggering orgasm within a couple of minutes. I take my lips off the gorgeous specimen in my

227

mouth to moan out my pleasure, but I'm soon back to it. Violin Pirate stands and places my hands around his length. I stroke and pump it while still sucking off Painter Man. It's not long before the cock in my hand empties warm spunk over my fingers. I abandon Painter Man's prick briefly to suck them clean.

And, just as the train continues its progress, I now continue mine.

Hip Hop is sitting with another enormous hard-on. Guiding Painter Man over with me, I move closer to Hip Hop. With barely a pause, I straddle him and sink down onto the thick, long prick. Oh, fucking hell, he's big. I'm stretched like never before. Yes! Love it, love it, love it. I start to fuck him instantly, rising and falling on the massive shaft as it forces its way in and out of my tight, hot pussy. My hand is still gripping Painter Man's cock and, turning my head, I take it back into my mouth. It's a struggle to carry on mouth-fucking him while riding Hip Hop, but, impressing even myself, I manage it.

The train slows and stops again. Cock in mouth and another in cunt, I meet the eyes of another would-be passenger – a bewildered looking man in overalls. He too misses the train; he's a little distracted, understandably.

The ride continues. I grind my clit onto Hip Hop every time I plunge down on him and … here comes another.

As pleasure grips again, Painter Man releases full into my mouth. I gasp in orgasm, and a lot of his spunk escapes to dribble out of the corners of my mouth, but I don't notice. Hip Hop is coming now, his hips bouncing me up and down so hard with the force of his climax that my tits leap rapturously before his eyes. He releases a series of expletives which eventually blur into a moan of inarticulate rapture.

This time, I do have to take a moment to recover. Surely I can't come again? I can't remember a session where I've ever had so many orgasms in quick succession. My body is limp:

wet and dripping and heavy and full. Shit, I may even fall asleep. Perhaps I do. My eyes close for a time. The last part of the line takes a while. I can afford the time.

When I do open my eyes, they're all still there, looking across at me with appreciation and awe. 'Are we there yet?' I blearily murmur, with a smile.

'Not quite,' replies Violin Pirate.

'Can you kneel again?' asks T-shirt Hottie.

My knees are sore, but my lust overrides it. Without hesitation, I slip down between the seats onto my hands and knees, wriggling my arse for more.

T-shirt Hottie is soon behind me. His fingers rub along me again but end at my arse. Oh, yes, please. He spits onto my arsehole and squeezes a finger in. I push back, propelling it as deep as possible. My arse has been feeling a little neglected and loves the attention. He pushes in another. Not enough. I want more and resort to demanding it. 'Oh, Christ, fuck my arse.'

I presume he's preparing to, but, suddenly, words break the expectant silence. 'No. That's mine. Get her up.'

It's a voice I've not heard yet. It's The Suit. I'm raised carefully to my feet and I turn to face him. He is at last folding up the paper, which he then places on the seat beside him.

He looks me straight in the eye. My belly writhes for him.

'Come here,' he states, a smooth, crisp demand.

I walk over as straight as I can in tottering heels. My legs have been turned to jelly over the course of the journey and the train is still lurching along erratically.

'Stand there,' he says again. 'Right in front of me. Legs slightly apart.'

I do as he says. Then, letting his eyes take in the length of me – my clothing has been reduced to heels and hold-ups – he slowly undoes his trousers and takes out his erect cock. Another glory. I must be the luckiest girl on earth.

Holding my eyes in his, he extracts a bottle of lube from his bag beside him and coats his cock in it before starting to stroke, spreading the lube liberally. I practically sob with longing.

'Now,' he states in those well-mannered, deep tones, 'I'm going to fuck you in the arse. You're going to sit with your back to me and take my cock up your arse. Do you understand?'

I nod.

'Good. Turn around.' I do.

'Move back towards me and bend your knees so that you sit on me.'

The others have fallen silent. They simply watch.

I move so that I'm standing just in front of him then start to lower myself towards the tip of his magnificent cock. 'Wait. Slow down,' I try.

'Stop!' he demands. 'There's something missing.'

He confuses me. Then, a stinging pain and a crack through the air. He has slapped my right arse cheek. I wince but try not to recoil from it. Thwack! He does it again. And again on the other side. Ten times he whacks his hand across my rump, five on each side, hard, forceful spanks which resound through the carriage each time. I can't stop a little whimpering, as much from hot pleasure as pain.

'There. Much better,' he declares, a definite note of satisfaction in his voice. Some of the others move round for an appreciative glance. 'Now, down.'

I lower myself again, my arse aflame but wanting so much more.

The head of his cock touches my arsehole. For the first time on the entire journey, I tense. Not because I don't want it, but because I can't quite believe this is happening. The other men, some sitting, some standing, watch me intently.

The Suit's hands are on my hips and he pulls me down. There it is. The stretch. My puckered little hole is stretching to take cock. And it does. The thick, full head moves into me. It never stops stinging: that glorious sting of fullness which I so crave. I sigh out rapturously and he takes the opportunity to pull me further down onto him. I brace myself on the armrests, needing to control this as much as possible. Down again. He's deep now; he's fucking deep. I wonder how much of him I can take.

'Good girl,' he murmurs in my ear and I love it. I love that rich, honeyed voice pouring its appreciation into me. I move down again and feel him almost fully in me. 'More.' I sink further. 'Deeper,' he insists. I do so. 'Very, very good girl.' There's a pause. His hot, ragged breath is on my hair – he's as lost as I am. 'Now, move.'

I start to rise up, the pull-off even more sensational and tight. I rise so that only his head is still in me then lower myself again. He holds me, guiding me, but I grip the armrests hard and the fuck is a perfect symbiosis of bodies and wills. We both want exactly what the other is giving and taking.

Just when I think it's enough, when I want to forget myself in the cock in my arse, I hear him. 'Someone take her clit.'

Forcing my eyes open, I see T-shirt Hottie drop between my legs. And – oh, holy fuck! – he is sucking me so beautifully.

'And her tits.'

Violin Pirate and Hip Hop take a nipple each in their hands, managing to grip on to them while I continue to be fucked in the arse. I stop every so often to revel in the clit-sucking, but T-shirt Hottie is a clever boy, able to keep himself on me even as I move.

I'm gone. I'm not even sure which way is up. The train rumbles on, passing more stations, more amazed, gawping faces at the window. Yes, yes, I want it. I want it all.

Painter Man is the only one not touching me, but he seems happy enough. He sits opposite, his eyes glued on the sight, his hand pumping his cock hard. I meet his eyes briefly and know he's close. So am I.

'Don't come yet,' warns The Suit, as if reading my mind.

I groan. 'I can't stop. I can't.' Still I plunge up and down on him, still my clit is tormented. T-shirt Hottie has at least three fingers up my cunt now. I'm not sure I'll survive my next orgasm. It's building so hard and so fast; my muscles are tensed, my skin's on fire. Please, please.

'Don't you dare fucking come,' The Suit hisses again, dangerous in my ear. I sob. A very real tear is forced from my eyes. The train tears along the track, hurtling its way through the tunnels.

'Wait … wait …'

On and on, cock and mouth and hands and tongue.

'Now!'

He holds me still, his cock as deep in me as it'll go. The fingers on my nipples pinch, the fingers in my cunt flex, and the mouth on my clit sucks.

Release. Am I flying? Am I flying alongside the train? I'm a blur of pleasure. My body freezes and shatters. The climax shakes me from head to foot, longer and harder than anything I can remember.

And then, with a sound of sweet abandon from a man I thought wasn't even interested, The Suit comes. He comes hard, I can tell that. I can practically feel his hot spunk as he explodes copiously into my arse.

I slump forward, and all is quiet.

The journey is nearly over. We're approaching the last station.

Silently, but with a contented communion of sexual completion, we extract ourselves from each other, wipe down as best we can and dress. One by one, in turn, Hip Hop, Violin Pirate, Painter Man and T-shirt Hottie come up and kiss me: soft, pliant grateful kisses I'll never forget. Only The Suit does not. He's reading the *FT* again. I shrug; it's his prerogative. That's part of the deal: no names, no numbers, no future.

We all sit in our original seats. Hip Hop puts his music back on.

The train pulls in and, for the first time since we set off, the doors of our carriage open. With a warm look or a smile for me, the men leave. Only The Suit gets up and goes without a glance. It pains me a little, I admit.

But, my body still heavy and happy after countless orgasms, I smile to myself. A night to remember. I'm reluctant to leave the carriage and stand stock still, fixing the scene into my mind. When at last I turn to head off, I see that The Suit has left the *FT* on his seat.

Drawn to this reminder of him, I go over and pick it up. I'm about to toss the newspaper back onto the seat when I notice words written in an elegant script in the top corner.

'You are perfection. Call me.' And there's a telephone number.

A ripple of delectable happiness curls through me.

Oh, don't worry. I will.

Xcite Books help make loving better
with a wide range of erotic books,
eBooks and dating sites.

www.xcitebooks.com
www.xcitebooks.co.uk

Sign-up to our Facebook page
for special offers and free gifts!